T0314751

Bello:

hidden talent rediscovered

Bello is a digital-only imprint of Pan Macmillan, established to breathe new life into previously published, classic books.

At Bello we believe in the timeless power of the imagination, of a good story, narrative and entertainment, and we want to use digital technology to ensure that many more readers can enjoy these books into the future.

We publish in ebook and print-on-demand formats to bring these wonderful books to new audiences.

www.panmacmillan.co.uk/bello

Richmal Crompton

Richmal Crompton (1890–1969) is best known for her thirty-eight books featuring William Brown, which were published between 1922 and 1970. Born in Lancashire, Crompton won a scholarship to Royal Holloway in London, where she trained as a schoolteacher, graduating in 1914, before turning to writing full-time. Alongside the *William* novels, Crompton wrote forty-one novels for adults, as well as nine collections of short stories.

Richmal Crompton

MARRIAGE OF HERMIONE

First published 1932 by Macmillan

This edition published 2015 by Bello
an imprint of Pan Macmillan
20 New Wharf Road, London N1 9RR
Basingstoke and Oxford
Associated companies throughout the world

www.panmacmillan.co.uk/bello

ISBN 978-1-5098-1018-5 EPUB
ISBN 978-1-5098-1016-1 HB
ISBN 978-1-5098-1017-8 PB

This book is a work of fiction. Names, characters, places, organizations
and incidents are either products of the author's imagination or used fictitiously.
Any resemblance to actual events, places, organizations or persons,
living or dead, is entirely coincidental.

This book remains true to the original in every way. Some aspects may appear
out-of-date to modern-day readers. Bello makes no apology for this, as to retrospectively
change any content would be anachronistic and undermine the authenticity of the original.

A CIP catalogue record for this book is available from the British Library.

Typeset by Ellipsis Digital Limited, Glasgow

Chapter One

A GOLDEN haze foretelling heat lay over the house and garden. Through it the clear song of the birds blended with the sharp sound of hammering and the whistling of one of the men who were putting up the marquee on the lawn.

The man who was whistling stopped for a moment to glance around him and say to his neighbour:

"Lucky in the weather for this 'ere garden party, ain't they?"

"Yes," agreed his neighbour. "Leastways, it ain't exactly a garden party. It's a golden wedding."

A woman wearing a blue cotton dress came out of the house and crossed the lawn with a brisk business-like tread. She was thin and upright, and her straight fair hair was dressed very plainly. Her slenderness and erectness made her look young in the distance, but when she came nearer you saw that she must be at least forty-five. Her eyes were penetrating, her mouth rather severe, and there was a suggestion of authority in her bearing that made the workmen instinctively assume an appearance of activity as she approached. She spoke to the foreman in crisp, clipped tones.

"This must be finished by eleven o'clock. I'm expecting the caterer's men then."

"Oh yes, miss," said the foreman, "that will be all right. We'll have finished it by then."

She threw a keen, unsmiling glance around and went indoors. The men set to work with renewed activity and with something almost guilty in their manner as if the woman in blue had by that one keen glance convicted them of inefficiency and idleness. The man who had been whistling whistled no longer. The very birds seemed to sing on a chastened note.

An old man and woman came out of the house and strolled side by side across the lawn. The old man was stout and, except for a few scanty white hairs, bald. He looked good-tempered, almost mischievous, and the rose in his buttonhole gave him a jaunty air. The old woman must have been very pretty when she was young. Her hair, though silver, was still soft and wavy, her pink-and-white cheeks smooth as a girl's, her blue eyes bright as if with laughter. They walked over to the workmen and said good-morning, then stood watching them in silence, smiling. The feverish activity that had been brought into being by the glance of the other woman died away. The workmen smiled back at the old couple and began again to work slowly, sleepily, as befitted British workmen on a warm summer's morning. The man who had been whistling took up his tune again.

Still smiling, the old couple turned away and sat down on a seat beneath a cedar tree.

The workman stopped whistling and stood for a moment watching them.

"They look jolly enough," he said to his neighbour.

His neighbour, too, ceased work and glanced from the old couple to the gracious Georgian house.

"They've call to be," he said. "Always had as much money as they wanted, I bet, and everythin' goin' smooth. I'd look jolly if I was in their shoes."

A small crowd of children suddenly entered the garden and ran across the lawn to the old couple, shouting: "Many happy returns, granny and gran'pa."

Some of them pulled the old man away with them through a door in a high brick wall to another part of the garden. Others ran to the marquee, besieging the workmen with eager questions.

"I bet I could do that. . . . May I try?"

"Why do you do it that way?"

"What would you do if the lawn wasn't big enough?"

"I'm going to take a tent as big as this with me when I go hunting lions."

"I say, do you know what we're going to have for tea to-day?"

A clock struck ten. The work would easily be finished by eleven. The men relaxed their efforts still further and talked to the children, showing them how the marquee was put up, letting them join in the work.

"We *are* helping, aren't we?"

"I should just think so," the foreman assured them.

But the woman in blue had come out of the house again, and whenever she came near the marquee the men stopped talking to the children and set to work briskly.

The old man had returned, prancing over the lawn, pretending to be a horse, urged on by the children, who had tied strings to his arms for reins. He sat down again by his wife, smiling and wiping his glistening forehead.

A girl entered the garden. Though young and pretty, there was something about her that reminded you both of the woman in blue and of the old woman.

She crossed the lawn to the old woman and, bending down, kissed her tenderly. . . .

Chapter Two

ONE May afternoon in 1882, Hermione Pennistone was walking across the fields from the Hall to Lilac Cottage, a tall handsome young man by her side.

So golden was the sunshine, so snowy-white the hawthorn blossom, so blue the sky, so green the daisy-flecked grass, so alive everything around her with the beauty and madness of spring, that Hermione wanted to pick up the long skirts she had worn so short a time and run across the fields for the sheer joy of running.

Only the consciousness that she was now Grown Up restrained her. Being Grown Up was a sudden and rather bewildering affair, less enjoyable in many ways than she had thought it would be. It had begun a month ago with the dance at the Hall (she had worn a white flounced dress of satin and chiffon decorously low at the front and with sleeves to the elbow) at which young men had bowed politely, said, "May I have the pleasure of this dance?" offered her an arm with thrilling courtliness, and after the dance returned her with another bow to Mother. She had not known what to say to them, but they had not seemed to expect her to say much, and on the whole it had been fun, like acting in a play or a charade. She did not realise at first how completely it meant the end of the old life. For now she was a Young Lady. No longer must she range the countryside, paddling in the river, wandering unaccompanied through the woods, living in a world peopled by her own invention, avoiding contact with the real world around her. Too long already had she been allowed to "run wild", said the gossips of Little Barnwell. Disturbing stories were told of her. Janet Martin said that she had come upon her one afternoon in the woods talking to a tree. *Talking* to a *tree*. Without even a hat on. When Janet had said, "What on earth are you talking to that tree for?" Hermione had not been at all confused. She had laughed and tossed back her untidy golden hair and replied, "Why shouldn't I? It's my friend."

"As if Helen weren't odd enough!" they always added when they told the story.

Helen, Hermione's only sister, was ten years her senior, and so beautiful that everyone had predicted a brilliant match for her. Unfortunately, however, she had developed Ideas. Ideas about Education. Looking at the world around her, she had noticed the difference between the education of the two sexes, and it had filled her with a noble frenzy of indignation. That boys should be taught by scholars and gentlemen, while the education of girls was left to governesses who were themselves more often than not wholly uneducated. . . . It was scandalous, it was preposterous. Her fine eyes would flash and her lovely cheeks flush crimson as she discoursed on the subject. . . . People in general laid the blame on her father. He should not have taught her the classics. Classics, of course, were all right for boys. They were indeed necessary to the Formation of a Gentleman. But for a Young Lady they were unsuitable. They tended to Oddness, and Oddness was the one thing to be avoided. . . .

Helen had flouted public opinion, had refused offers that made the mouths of all the mothers in the neighbourhood water, and had finally joined a friend of similar views in the foundation of a girls' boarding-school in Somerset. Her partner had died four years later, and Helen at twenty-seven was now a headmistress, successful, autocratic, impatient of any sort of opposition. Odd, in fact. . . .

The Rev. Alan Pennistone had not lived to see the results of his misdirected application of the classics, having died when Helen was twenty-one and Hermione eleven. It was generally considered that a merciful Providence had removed him in order to prevent him from teaching the classics to Hermione, and making her thereby as Odd as he had made Helen.

And yet, as Hermione emerged from childhood, the village gossips began to shake their heads over her, too. For there she was, saved by her father's timely death from a classical education, developing Oddness of another sort—roaming the woods hat-less, talking to trees, paddling in the river, long after the correct age for such activities had passed. Mrs. Pennistone was severely censured by the village gossips, though to do her justice she was wholly unaware that Hermione was considered Odd.

Mrs. Pennistone was a placid, ineffectual, easygoing woman who saw everything through a thick, rose-coloured mist. The only thing that had ever broken through that mist was Helen's refusal of Sir David Blakeman, the squire of the next village. She had cried all night after that, though in the morning the rose-coloured mist had closed about her again, and she had said to the doctor's wife, "I'd sooner see my darling in her coffin than offered as a sacrifice to wealth,"—a cryptic sentiment that somehow afforded her much comfort. The roseate mist had always functioned perfectly with regard to Hermione. Mrs. Pennistone, lazily, selfishly sentimental, had refused to allow Hermione to go to Helen's school. "You mustn't take my baby from me, Helen. It would break my heart if you took my baby from me." Helen had yielded readily enough, thinking that, on the whole, the less her mother had to do with her beloved school the better. Most of her pupils were the daughters of enlightened parents, and Mrs. Pennistone could not, with the best will in the world, be described as enlightened. Having secured the company of her "baby", Mrs. Pennistone proceeded to neglect her entirely. Hermione was a pretty child, and in certain moods the mother liked to fondle and play with her, sometimes even to tuck her up in bed and hear her say her prayers. Always, when people came to tea, Hermione had to appear with freshly brushed curls, wearing her best lace-trimmed pinafore ("Isn't my baby adorable? I'm *all* mother, you know") for a minute or two before the serious business of gossip began ("Run away now, pet. Mother's busy").

There was not really room in the tiny cottage for nursery or nurse, and both were dispensed with as soon as Hermione was old enough to go to the Hall for lessons with the Carter girls and their governess, a kindly, ignorant, superstitious woman, whose whole energy was spent in trying to hide her growing deafness from her pupils and employer. Helen, on her rare visits home, felt almost an affection for the Carter governess, so perfect an embodiment was she of the evil that Helen had set herself to fight.

Hermione was on friendly enough terms with her fellow-pupils, but their interests were concentrated on the sporting life of the neighbourhood, and in secret they despised Hermione, as in secret she shrank from their good-natured noisiness and roughness.

She always escaped from the Hall as soon as lessons were over, and then, because there seemed to be no place for her in the little cottage ("Have you come back already, darling? Well, if you stay here you must be *quite* still and not fidget. Mother's busy reading"), she formed the habit of wandering over the countryside. She was never lonely in the fields or woods. She was, in fact, only lonely when with other people. She loved the country with an odd, secret passion, investing the trees and flowers with distinct personalities, making friends of them. She had not—few children have—a conscious love of beauty, only a curious sense of peace and gladness when she was alone in the wood or by the river in the rock-strewn valley. Shamefacedly and in secret she wrote poems—turgid, emotional little poems full of morbid pathos and lofty sentiments. She never showed her poems to anyone, but she would bring them to the wood and read them aloud in a gentle undertone, sitting on her favourite seat, the gnarled and twisted roots of an old oak that protruded above the ground. The softly moving leaves above her always seemed to whisper encouragement and understanding. She loved, too, to perch on a boulder by the river where it fell in a cascade over the rocks, her chin in her hands, listening to its murmur, feeling that it was talking to her and that something in her understood.

Her mother saw this roaming of the countryside through the usual rose-coloured mist.

"My little madcap is out somewhere." . . . "My tomboy is running wild as usual."

The heroines of most of the novels she read were "tomboys",

"madcaps", who "ran wild". It was all quite in the tradition of the best romantic schools, though no epithets could have fitted Hermione less aptly than those of "tomboy" and "madcap".

Then, quite suddenly, Mrs. Pennistone realised that Hermione was growing up. Her eighteenth birthday was approaching, and Mrs. Carter, who was giving a dance to mark the emergence of the middle Carter girl from the schoolroom, suggested that Hermione should be allowed to attend it.

"She'll be eighteen soon now. It will do for her coming-out dance. It's time she stopped running wild, you know."

The whole village had adopted Mrs. Pennistone's phrase, "running wild".

So Mrs. Pennistone, roused from her chosen life of intimate tea parties and gossip and novel-reading, had to contemplate a new existence, that of Chaperon to a Young Lady.

She was a good-natured woman, though an incorrigibly self-indulgent one, and she accepted the change in her life philosophically enough. The rose-coloured mist still served her well.

"I've lost my baby. She's grown up now. Soon, I suppose, I shall lose my little flower."

With a deep sigh but with unacknowledged relief at her heart, Mrs. Pennistone looked forward to the time when her little flower should be snatched from her by a handsome, wealthy young man. She disliked the late hours and the society of the young that the position of chaperon forced upon her, but she was anxious to regain the prestige that she had lost through Helen's Oddness and to Do her Duty by Hermione. With this object in view she was eagerly scanning the horizon for the longed-for Good Match when, as if by a miracle, it suddenly appeared. A fortnight after the Carters' dance, Charles Dereham, a nephew of Mrs. Carter, came to pay a visit to the Hall. He was tall, handsome, and twenty-five, and he attached himself to Hermione with open admiration from the first meeting.

It was he who was walking home with her across the fields from the Carters' archery party.

Chapter Three

HERMIONE looked down severely at the small toes that just peeped from the flounces of her dress, as if bidding them repress their desire to skip and run. She must be very decorous, for an Admirer walked by her side. The Admirer was part of the charade of Being Grown Up in which she was taking part. She felt as she had felt on her tenth birthday when for a treat she had been allowed to dress up in her mother's clothes and sweep about the tiny drawing-room in them. Only now the fun was redoubled, for she took people in. They actually believed that she was grown up. They talked to her deferentially, they opened doors for her, they sprang to their feet when she entered a room, they bowed over her hand, they escorted her home from garden parties. She still had the feeling that she was playing a trick on them, and that they would be very angry when they found out that she was not really grown up at all but only a little girl. . . .

Charles climbed the stile that divided two fields, then held out his hand for hers, looking resolutely away lest he should catch a glimpse of the slender ankles beneath the swaying skirts. As she stepped down demurely from the last rung, she laughed to herself, thinking how often and how recently she had vaulted lightly over that very stile.

The sun was warm, but a delicious breeze played through the grass, stroking it, bending it this way and that. With a quick movement Hermione took off her hat and gave her head a little shake, as if inviting the breeze to leave the grass and come to play with her hair.

"Don't you love days like this?" she said happily.

He smiled without answering.

He was looking down at her, noting the sheen of her wind-blown curls, the sunlit blue of her eyes, the wistful curves of her childish, innocent mouth. She saw the admiration in his gaze, and took it as a tribute to her new frock of pale pink organdie flounced up to the knees, with an enormous sash bow behind that made it impossible ever to lean back comfortably in a chair.

"Do I look nice?" she said, smiling up at him.

"You look beautiful," he replied.

The ardour in his voice quenched her high spirits and brought a sudden chill to her heart. She became aware that she had done an indecorous thing in taking off her hat. She was glad that they had almost reached her mother's cottage.

Mrs. Pennistone was in the garden, engaged in cutting the red and yellow tulips from the circular bed that made such a brave show in the middle of the tiny lawn. She had undertaken this task in order that she might have a point of vantage from which to espy the return of Hermione and Charles. She was sure that Charles would escort the child home, and she wanted to see them before they saw her, so that she might discover if possible how things stood between them. She had begun to suspect that Mrs. Carter wanted Charles for Minnie, and so an element of competition had entered into the situation. She was glad that she had bought the child some really nice clothes.

They came in sight, and a quick spasm of irritation seized her. What on earth had possessed Hermione to take off her hat and get all blown about like that! Then the spasm of irritation passed. The child looked lovelier than ever with her disordered golden curls blowing across her white forehead. She thought with satisfaction of Minnie Carter's hair—straight, coarse, of a nondescript brown.

She opened the cottage gate with a bright, welcoming smile.

"You tomboy!" she said, shaking a reproving finger at Hermione. "Well, have you had a nice time?"

Something in Hermione froze and stiffened at the coyness in her mother's smile. She felt a sudden sensation of panic, a sudden longing for the old days of her mother's easy-going neglect. She realised with a sinking of her heart that this business of growing up was not, after all, just a game, just a bit of play-acting; realised that the old life had passed away for ever, that she had entered a new world, an alien world of unknown values, a world in which she walked blindfold, uncertain of her way.

Both of them were looking at her, waiting for her answer.

"I did very badly," she said. "I didn't score a single bull's-eye. Minnie scored one every time."

Mrs. Pennistone laughed. She did not mind Minnie's scoring bull's-eyes, for Minnie, sure-eyed and skilful archer as she was, had a stocky clumsy figure, while Hermione, however many bull's-eyes she missed, looked like a young Diana when she drew her bow.

They entered the little garden. Hermione still felt frightened and unhappy, like a child who has strayed too adventurously from its home and forgotten the way back.

"Won't you come in, Mr. Dereham?" her mother was saying.

Mr. Dereham bowed with his impressive air of courtliness.

"I should like a word with you, Mrs. Pennistone, if you can spare me the time," he said formally.

Hermione gave a quick sigh of relief as the drawing-room door closed behind them. So near was the childhood in which she had been dismissed as a matter of course whenever her elders wanted to talk together, that she had no suspicion that the conversation could possibly concern herself. She went quickly out of the cottage gate and across the fields to the woods, a glad sense of release at her heart.

In the wood the sun poured down upon the trees, filling their cup-like foliage, spilling over on to the ground beneath, and falling in pools of molten gold on last year's beech leaves.

Hermione greeted her old friends gaily as she passed them, and they returned friendly greetings—even the pine tree, who generally seemed to Hermione to be aloof and superior. A rabbit ran across the path in front of her feet. A robin redbreast, perched on a bramble bush, stared at her with bright friendly eyes as she passed. A thrush's song, urgently sweet, rang out suddenly from the undergrowth where he was building his nest. Hermione walked slowly, dreamily, forgetful of everything but the loveliness around her, making no conscious note even of that. She came to a little clearing in the wood where clusters of primroses and tiny ferns grew in the hollows. The beauty of it seemed to catch her by the throat so that her eyes filled with tears. She felt a surging joy of life, a fierce longing for adventure. There returned to her the memory of the expression on Charles's face as he said, "You look beautiful", and the memory no longer frightened her. The sensual element that lurks always behind Beauty threw off for a moment its disguise. Love . . . the theme of all great stories, all great poems. . . . Through her mind moved a procession of the heroes of her childhood . . . Hector, Galahad, Roland, Richard Cœur de Lion. Love. . . . Sooner or later it came to all the heroes and heroines of the stories and poems she had read.

The church clock struck six, and, rousing herself from her dreams, she set off slowly homeward, not by the fields but by the main road that led past the little church and long, low vicarage nestling together among the trees.

At the vicarage gate she stopped for a moment, looking wistfully at the old house. Her childhood had been spent in it, but her memories of her father were indistinct and elusive. She remembered a kindly genial presence, an atmosphere of gentle understanding, but she could not recall his features. Her father's successor—a stout, pompous man with an artificially hearty manner—came out of the front door, and Hermione hurried on, lest he should see her and want to talk to her. As she went, she was conscious of a longing for her father that she had never known before: She felt that he alone could have helped her in this strange new world in which she found herself, that if he had been alive she would have been less bewildered, less afraid in it.

As she entered the hall of the cottage, Mrs. Pennistone, flushed and smiling, came out of the drawing-room. The interview had been eminently satisfactory. Charles Dereham was not a wealthy man, but he had "prospects". It was, perhaps, regrettable that he was in trade, but, as those same prospects depended on his being in trade, it was less regrettable than it might have been. Moreover, it was an old-established, highly respectable trade—the making of gentlemen's hats—and had been founded by Charles's great-grandfather. The fact that before taking to trade the Derehams had been small country squires went still further to remove the stigma. Charles was the only son. There was no doubt at all in Mrs. Pennistone's mind that this marriage at any rate had been made in heaven, made in a merciful heaven intent on compensation for the disgrace of Helen's Oddness.

"Well, my tomboy," she said fondly, smoothing the fair, disordered head, but not too resolutely because there was no denying that the tumbled curls looked adorable above the flounced formal dress. "I just want to put those tulips in water, darling. Will you go into the drawing-room and talk to Mr. Dereham for a moment?"

Dreamily, abstractedly, Hermione entered the drawing-room. The sight and sounds of the sun-flecked wood were still about her. The song of the birds was clearer to her than this young man's voice. . . . Then suddenly the words that he was saying cut sharply into her consciousness.

"Miss Hermione, I have your mother's permission to ask you to become my wife."

Her heart beat suffocatingly, and she began to tremble. . . . Having uttered his proposal, the young man discarded ceremony, and set about pleading his cause with passionate ardour.

"I love you, Miss Hermione. I adore you. I can't live without you . . . I can't go on living if you won't marry me . . . I'm not worthy of you . . . I'm not fit to touch you . . . but I adore you. I love the ground you walk on, the air you breathe. I'll make you happy. I swear I'll make you happy. I'll give up the rest of my life to making you happy . . . I'll have no other thought but you from now till the moment I die. You'll never regret it. I love you so . . . I love you . . ."

His passion swept her up with it, carried her along on strong, resistless waves. She forgot her first instinctive recoil. He was not Charles Dereham, a good-looking but very ordinary young man of 1882. He was all the heroes of all her girlhood romances. He was Hector, Galahad, Roland, Richard Cœur de Lion. . . .

"My sweet, my beautiful, my little love . . ."

His arms were round her, his lips pressed against hers. And abruptly the dream was shattered. This was no hero of romance, no dream lover. The harsh contact of his cheek, the rough pressure of his arms, the whole alarming suggestion of virility that he carried with him, filled her with a blind, unreasoning panic. . . . But before she could repulse him the door opened, and her mother came in.

"My little flower!" said Mrs. Pennistone rapturously.

They were one on each side of her—her mother pouring out breathless congratulations, Charles protestations of undying devotion. Terror and bewilderment held her in the grip of a paralysis.

"But, mother—" she cried in passionate protest, then burst suddenly and unexpectedly into tears.

She was desperately ashamed of her childishness, but could not stop crying. She wanted to cry on her mother's breast, but whenever she turned to it her mother seemed to have vanished and only Charles was there. She sobbed luxuriously upon Charles's shoulder. Gone was his passion, his urgency, his masculine domination. He was tender and gentle, so that he seemed to her to have become the father for whom her lonely childhood had so often longed.

"It's all my fault," he was saying penitently. "I was too sudden. I ought to have prepared her. . . ."

Hermione raised her head from his shoulder and dried her eyes. Mrs. Pennistone made a sign to Charles, and he went quietly away. They heard the sound of the cottage door closing, then the unlatching and latching of the little garden gate.

"My flower," murmured Mrs. Pennistone again. "I know you'll be very happy."

"But, mother—" burst out Hermione again wildly, "*I* don't want to marry him. I don't *want* to."

"My darling, my darling," said the mother, "of course you feel like that now. All girls do. All nice girls, I mean. Love comes with marriage. To a nice girl, I mean."

"But I don't know him," sobbed Hermione. "I only met him a few weeks ago."

"But mother knows him, pet. Mother knows that he'll make her little flower happy. . . . Listen, my darling. . . . You must trust mother. You know mother wants you to be happy, don't you?"

"Y-yes."

"Well. . . . Listen, darling. I know what's best for you. I know that he's a good man and will make you happy. That's all that matters, isn't it? Listen to mother, pet. You like him better than any other man you know, don't you?"

Silently Hermione considered the other men she knew—Dickie Carter, an uncouth if well-meaning young man who made infantile puns and whose interests centred wholly in the stables; the vicar, who hardly counted as a man at all; Roderick Martin, a hypochondriac ascetic who wore silk shirts and velvet jackets over a double chest protector; Gilbert Masters, who had projecting teeth and a receding chin and whose chief pleasure was reciting in public.

"Yes," she answered truthfully.

Mrs. Pennistone heaved a sigh of relief.

"That's all that matters then, darling, isn't it?"

Hermione seemed not quite sure of this, and Mrs. Pennistone continued hastily, "I didn't love your father before I married him, pet, but I liked him more than any other man I knew, and I respected him, and I trusted my parents to know what was best for me. I loved him passionately after we were married, and I was perfectly happy with him always. You want a home of your own and children, don't you?"

Hermione considered this question, too, in silence. Yes, she certainly wanted a home of her own and children. But—not this terrifying urgency of possession, this sudden violent shattering of the only life she knew.

"Y-yes."

"Darling, I know that this is what your father would want you to do."

It seemed an answer to her prayer for guidance. This was what her father would want her to do. . . . And, of course, things could never be now as if it had not happened. She could not return to the old life. Her thoughts went to Charles and to the moment when his rough cheek had pressed against hers. She felt again the stifling, insistent, terrifying virility of him, and again panic seized her.

"But I don't want to marry," she cried.

"You baby!" laughed her mother. "How can you have a home of your own and children if you don't marry?"

"That's different . . ." said Hermione.

Of course it was different . . . a nice little home, babies, a kindly, understanding husband whose socks one darned and who went out to work every day. . . . That picture was familiar. It had always been in her mind as the picture of her ultimate fate. But not so soon . . . and not this thing that stifled and oppressed, this sudden challenging thing that took away one's breath and filled one with terror.

"Nonsense!" laughed her mother again. "And no one's asking you to marry him to-morrow, you little silly. Being engaged and being married are two very different things. I was engaged for three years. Of course, no one will force you to marry him if you really find you don't love him. You want to make mother happy, don't you, darling? You'll let me tell him that it's 'yes'?"

Hermione gave a childish little gesture of resignation. She could be engaged for three years, and then—well, no one would force her to marry him if she found she didn't love him. Mother had promised that. Sensitive and dreamy, she had always shunned conflict. The docility that she had assumed as an armour against the world had become instinctive and habitual. Mother would be pleased, and Charles would be pleased. Mother said that father would have wanted it. . . . She was tired and bewildered. Her heart was torn by a riot of conflicting emotions. She tried not to think of that moment when Charles had held her in his arms. Unsuspected instincts, buried deep down in her, had stirred at his embrace, so that, though she shrank in terror from the thought of its happening again, yet somehow she wanted it to happen again.

"Now come to bed, my darling. You're tired out."

"I shan't sleep, mother."

But Hermione was the only one of the three who did sleep.

Across the fields in the best guest-room of the Hall, Charles Dereham lay awake, tormented by longing for her. In the little cottage bedroom Mrs. Pennistone lay awake, her heart singing a paean of triumph. Hermione was engaged to a Good Match at Seventeen. The disgrace of Helen's Oddness was wiped out. . . .

Chapter Four

HERMIONE now moved in an atmosphere of congratulation and approval. From being an insignificant unit of the little community she had suddenly become its most important member. She was an Engaged Girl. To be an Engaged Girl was an end, a destiny in itself. And yet it led on to another greater, more glamorous destiny, that of a Bride.

Hermione had seen other girls blaze into this sudden glory, become the petted darlings of the countryside, had seen them enter fleetingly the still more blinding glory of the Bride's estate, and then—the drop scene fell abruptly, the glamour fled. They became ordinary married women whose housekeeping was freely criticised, still more ordinary mothers whose children were generally considered to be very badly brought up.

Hermione was sensitive, impressionable, and responsive. Never before had she met with this radiant kindness, this warm unqualified approval. All these people could not be wrong about her. She must indeed have done something wonderful. They were proud of her, too, as if somehow her triumph reflected credit on themselves. Even mothers who had hoped that their own daughters would attract Charles Dereham shared generously in the rejoicing. Little Barnwell was a small village with few social distractions. Such things as engagements, marriages, births, and deaths happened seldom, but when they happened the inhabitants seized on them as the starving seize upon food. Engagements were always made the excuse for a burst of local gaiety. The Young Couple was asked everywhere. There were tennis parties, croquet parties, archery parties, picnics in the wood and on the river. To Hermione it was as if she had been carried off her feet and were flying through the air deliciously, exultantly, as one flies in a dream. Part of her wanted to stop and find out where she was going, but the other part wanted only to fly deliciously through the air like this. . . . Charles was with her, of course, but not too obtrusively. He was there as the Devout Lover, grateful, humble, supremely aware of his own un-worthiness. He fetched and carried for her, he was always in the background, protective, adoring. Hermione found it novel and pleasant to be protected and adored. She found it pleasant, too, to be envied by other girls. For the first time in her life she became conscious of her personal attractions, and the consciousness gave her an intoxicating sense of power. There was no repetition of the rough embrace that had frightened her so. She and Charles were always the centre of a crowd or alone with her mother. Now that they were engaged, Mrs. Pennistone had suddenly become a stickler for etiquette. Charles kissed his sweetheart goodnight on the cheek as a brother might have kissed her, always in her mother's presence. Mrs. Pennistone was very affectionate with Charles, almost coy indeed, but she never left him alone with Hermione. It was less Charles's passion she distrusted than Hermione's lack of it.

It was now definitely settled that Hermione was to be married at the end of July—a week before her eighteenth birthday. She never knew quite how this came to be arranged. There was suddenly a yet wilder burst of excitement and enthusiasm, a fresh outbreak of parties and picnics, and on every hand animated discussion of bridesmaids and fashions and materials. Like another flood, it swept her away with it, so that, by the time she realised what was happening, it was too late to protest. The end of July . . . a month ahead . . . three weeks ahead . . . a fortnight ahead. It couldn't be as near as that. The days couldn't have flashed by so quickly. She felt now like a rider whose horse has bolted. She tugged at the reins in desperate panic to stay its headlong course. . . . Only a week . . . it couldn't be only a week . . . it *mustn't* be only a week. . . . Seven days. . . . Six days. . . .

She began to awake in the morning with a strange feeling of depression that deepened to panic as the mists of sleep vanished and her faculties became clear. Was she really going to marry this stranger? Who was Charles? A handsome face . . . that meant nothing. Adoring looks, a caressing voice . . . those meant nothing either. Those belonged to the Devout Lover, not to the real man. She knew nothing of the real man. And she was going to marry him. . . . The lingering horror of a nightmare crept over her, and she prayed to awake from it and find herself as she had been a year ago—happy, care-free, still a child, running over the fields to the Hall for lessons after breakfast, escaping after lessons to the woods or the river. Then the day's round of gaiety began, and all her fear and depression melted in the sunshine of the love and admiration that surrounded her on all sides. Again she was a queen among her courtiers, a queen who could do no wrong. But, as the wedding grew nearer, the cold breathless feeling of terror that every morning greeted her awakening lasted longer each day. It did not leave her for a moment on the day when she went to visit Charles's family.

Charles's mother had died when he was a child, and his only sister was several years his senior.

"You'll like her," Charles had said, "and she'll adore you. Maud's the best sister a man ever had. I know you two will be friends."

She had tried hard to like both his father and his sister. His father was a stiff, pompous old man, and Maud a handsome woman who obviously wished to be thought much younger than she was. Hermione disliked her at once, and, though Maud was affectionate and confidential (telling Hermione the full story of several love-affairs and hinting at many more), she felt that her dislike was returned. She was aware, too, of a critical atmosphere to which she was not nowadays accustomed. Here she was not the Bride-to-be, the Girl who had Got Engaged at Seventeen. Here she was the Girl who had Caught Charles. It was obvious that they thought her much too young for him. She suspected that they took for granted that she had schemed and planned his conquest. She felt ill at ease with them and could think of nothing to say, though she knew that her silence gave the impression of sulkiness ("A spoilt little beauty," she could hear them thinking. "Poor Charles!"). Even Charles seemed dimly aware that things had not gone well.

"Of course," he apologised afterwards, "I suppose it will take them some time to get used to the idea. . . ."

Only Mrs. Pennistone, viewing the affair through the usual roseate mists, was completely satisfied.

"Charming people," she said to Hermione when they were back in their little drawing-room. "Delightful. And they *quite* fell in love with my darling. . . . What were you and Maud talking about, my pet?" She shook her finger mischievously. "About a certain young man, I suspect. . . ."

"I'm tired, mother," said Hermione jerkily. "I'm going to bed."

She went upstairs to her bedroom and there, locking the door, flung herself on to the bed and sobbed hysterically, pressing her face into the pillow to stifle her sobs.

Mrs. Pennistone came upstairs and tried the door. The sound of muffled sobbing reached her.

"An engaged girl's nerves . . ." she said, sighing and smiling to herself.

"Good night, my little flower," she called affectionately, and passed on to her own bedroom.

Half an hour later Hermione raised her swollen face from the pillow. Tiny pointed knives seemed to be shooting through her head. She tried to think why she had been crying, but all she could think of was the agony of the little stabbing knives. She undressed and lay quite still for a few moments, then the pain left her and she went to sleep.

Mrs. Pennistone and Charles had found and furnished the house in which the young couple was to live. Ivy Lodge was a fair-sized Georgian house overlooking the village green of Abbotford, four miles from Fernham, the country town where the Dereham business was carried on, rather less than four miles from Mettleham, where Charles's father and sister lived. It was Mrs. Pennistone's idea that Hermione should have little part in the choosing of house and furniture. "We don't want her to be tired out before the wedding," said Mrs. Pennistone, but that was not her real reason, though, to do her justice, she honestly-believed it was. Her real reason was that she still did not feel quite sure of Hermione, and that she avoided anything that might make this marriage on which she had set her heart seem real and imminent to the child.

Slowly, inexorably, the days crept on. A feverish unrest possessed Hermione. She dreaded an unoccupied minute, but there were few of them, for Mrs. Pennistone, exalted by her triumph, was planning a wedding on a magnificent scale. There were to be eight bridesmaids including the Carter girls, Janet Martin, and Maud Dereham. Everyone was to be invited, not only from Little Barnwell but from all the villages around. The church was to be decorated. There was to be a full choir and an anthem with a solo. A stream of presents was arriving at the little cottage. Hermione sat at the walnut desk in the drawing-room, laboriously writing letters of thanks in her childish handwriting, the tip of her pink tongue protruding between her lips, her fingers ink-stained to their middle joints.

People were beginning to say that she looked pale and tired, but Mrs. Pennistone smiled the foolish smile that was meant to be wise and said :

"Such a trying time for a girl, an engagement, you know ... and she's in wonderful spirits. I'm the one who's heartbroken. I'm losing my baby. I simply daren't think how I'm going to get on without her."

Helen was to come home the day before the wedding. Sometimes Hermione looked forward to Helen's coming, sometimes she dreaded it. But when Helen came, her arrival made strangely little difference, so infinitely withdrawn was she from the lives of her mother and sister. She had regretted having to leave her school even for two days. Her appearance made no concession to the festivity of the occasion. The fair hair, its waves repressed by ruthless brushing, was drawn into a many-coiled bun at the back of the shapely head. The blue eyes were kind but stern, the beautiful mouth austere. Her dress was of wine-coloured silk, quite plain except for a touch of lace at throat and wrist.

She inspected Hermione's trousseau with grave detachment.

"It's very pretty," she said; "I hope you'll be very happy, my dear."

But she spoke as one speaks of something that cannot concern one, and there was a far-away look in her eyes as she turned over the piles of white cambric underclothing with her slender hands.

"This time to-morrow I shall have lost my baby," said Mrs. Pennistone, patting an embroidered petticoat with absent-minded tenderness.

Helen threw Hermione a grave, detached smile. She had ceased to be interested in Hermione on the day on which their mother had refused to allow her to join her school. She was thinking: "This time to-morrow I shall be back at St. Hilda's . . ."

After supper she sat at the little walnut desk correcting some examination papers that she had brought with her. Mrs. Pennistone, in her armchair by the fire, was putting the final stitches into a dressing-jacket that was part of the trousseau. There was a smile on her lips—complacent, triumphant. Hermione sat on the other side of the hearth, her head bent over her needlework. Her heart was beating with odd hammer-like strokes. It couldn't be to-morrow. It *couldn't* be. . . . She mustn't let herself believe it was to-morrow. She'd scream if she let herself believe it was to-morrow.

Going away with Charles . . . leaving Little Barnwell and the woods and fields she loved . . . living in a house alone with Charles for all the rest of her life, till she was an old woman, till she died. She remembered the moment when Charles had seized her roughly in his arms, pressing his lips against hers, and fingers of ice seemed to close around her heart. "I can't, I can't . . ." she cried desperately to herself.

"You're looking pale, darling," said her mother, "and you've got a tiring day to-morrow. You'd better go to bed."

She rose obediently and put away her work. Mrs. Pennistone, expansively maternal, held out her arms.

"The last time my baby will say good-night to me," she said in a voice that quivered with rich emotion.

"I hope not, mother," said Helen quietly from her seat at the walnut desk.

Mrs. Pennistone threw her an indignant glance. It was just like Helen, of course, to spoil her best moment. And it had spoilt it, for Hermione had managed somehow to escape the close embrace that her mother had intended. She had kissed her, but had evaded the outstretched arms.

"Good night, Helen."

Helen raised her head from the desk and pressed a cool, passionless kiss upon the burning cheek.

Hermione went slowly upstairs, took off her dress, undid her hair, and sat on the edge of her bed in her white bodice and petticoat, her hair falling about her shoulders.

Under the window was her box, already packed with the clothes she would need for the honeymoon. In the wardrobe hung the wedding dress of white embroidered satin. Upon the chest of drawers stood Helen's gift—Gibbons' *Decline and Fall of the Roman Empire*, bound in morocco leather. She sat on the bed, tense and rigid, staring unseeingly in front of her. The pupils of her blue eyes were dilated, her breath was coming and going in quick, dry gasps. Then her frame relaxed, the staring look left her eyes, and she drew a deep, quivering breath. It was as if all these weeks she had been dragged along by some irresistible force that had suddenly ceased to drag her, as if all these weeks she had been deafened by some nerve-racking din that had now died away, leaving peace and stillness. She was calm and composed. And she saw her way clearly. She could not possibly marry Charles. She did not know him, she did not love him. She did not even understand why she had looked upon this marriage as something irrevocable. It was not irrevocable. She must break off the engagement to-night. Tomorrow it would be too late. . . . A strange sense of peace and certainty upheld her. For the first time for weeks she felt sure of herself. Helen would help her. Helen would support her against their mother. She heard the sound of the opening and shutting of the drawing-room door, then the gentle rustle of Helen's dress on the stairs.

She opened her bedroom door.

"Helen . . . please, I want you," she whispered softly.

Helen entered the room and stood just inside the door, looking at her gravely.

"Aren't you in bed yet, my dear?"

"No . . . Helen, I don't want to be married tomorrow. I don't love Charles. I don't think I should mind if I never saw him again. I don't love him. I just—like him ordinarily. Just as I'd like anyone. That's not how you ought to feel, is it?"

"No . . ."

"It's not too late, is it?" The words tumbled out in a breathless stream. "We aren't married yet. It's not too late till you're actually married, is it? . . . Please, Helen, help me. Tell mother. Explain to mother. I *can't* marry him if I don't love him, can I?"

"Of course not."

The door burst open, and Mrs. Pennistone entered tempestuously. She had heard Hermione's summons to Helen, and its urgency had sent a sudden chill through her body. All along she had been afraid of something like this. . . . There was an incalculable streak in the child despite her docility. Her gaze went from Helen, who stood just inside the doorway, to Hermione, who sat on the bed. Hermione looked very lovely, her eyes sparkling, her cheeks flushed, her golden curls tumbled about her white arms, the mounds of her small immature breasts, milk-white, blue-veined, just showing above the cambric bodice.

"What's the matter?" asked Mrs. Pennistone sharply.

Helen spoke in her cool detached voice.

"This marriage must be stopped, mother."

A heavy flush spread in patches over Mrs. Pennistone's face and neck.

"Why?" she said harshly.

"I don't love him, mother," burst out Hermione. "I can't marry him . . . I never knew it was going to be so soon, and when I did know . . . I didn't—I didn't realise, somehow. I can't marry him, mother. I can't, I can't."

Mrs. Pennistone controlled herself with an effort.

"It's too late to put off the wedding," she said shortly. "You're hysterical and overwrought. Get into bed and go to sleep. You'll feel quite different in the morning."

"But, mother—" began Helen.

Mrs. Pennistone cut her short with an imperious gesture.

"Do you think I'm going to take any notice of a child's hysterical nonsense? You ought to be ashamed of encouraging her. Get into bed, Hermione."

A little high-pitched laugh escaped Hermione. The sense of security and peace was slipping from her.

"You can't make me marry him if I don't want to, mother," she said unsteadily. "You promised that I needn't marry him if I didn't love him. You *promised*!"

Mrs. Pennistone turned her angry eyes again from one daughter to the other—from Helen, standing cool and graceful by the door, to Hermione, sitting on the edge of the bed, with flushed cheeks and tumbled curls, her childish lips set stubbornly. The roseate mists that generally obscured Mrs. Pennistone's vision were ruthlessly dispelled. For weeks past she had been publicly lamenting that she was to "lose her baby", but at the suggestion that she was, after all, not to lose her, such rage possessed her that for the first time in her life she felt an impulse to strike the child. Helen's air of dispassionate aloofness increased her anger. The red patches on her face and neck burned more deeply.

"That *you* should encourage her in this folly!" she burst out. "As if you hadn't disgraced me enough already!"

"What have I ever done to disgrace you, mother?" said Helen calmly.

But Mrs. Pennistone had turned back to her other daughter.

"Listen to me, Hermione," she said hoarsely. "No one can make you marry this man against your will, but if you stop this marriage now, on the very eve of it, you'll be disgraced for ever. For ever. No one will forget it. No other man will ever want to marry you. A girl who's once got the reputation of being a jilt never has another chance. People will remember this against you for the rest of your life. Men will be warned against you wherever you go. You can't stay here after this. Life would be impossible for both of us if you stayed here. People will talk of nothing else here for years. And wherever you go you'll be pointed at as the girl who jilted a man for no reason at all on the eve of the wedding."

She paused for breath. Helen stepped forward and stood by her sister.

"There's no need for Hermione to stay here," she said in her cold, gentle voice. "She can come with me. You've tried to drive her into this marriage, and you've failed. You're doing the only right thing, Hermione. What does it matter how near to the wedding this engagement is broken off, as long as it's broken off in time? What does it matter if no other man does want to marry you? Marriage isn't the only career for a woman. You can come to St. Hilda's with me to-morrow. . . . You'll have to work hard, of course, but you'll be happier working and teaching there than idling your time away here."

Hermione looked up fearfully. The flush had faded from her cheeks. They were as white as the cambric bodice that outlined her soft young breasts.

"But, Helen," she protested, "how can I teach? I don't know anything."

"I quite realise that," said Helen. "Your education's been a ridiculous farce. But you're still young enough to learn. You can help Matron with the care of the younger children at first. Meantime, in the evenings and on holidays, I'll teach you myself and try to make up the deficiencies of your so-called education. You had better not come back here for the school holidays. We'll take rooms somewhere, and I'll give up all my time to teaching you, so that before long you'll be able to take a position on the staff as a regular mistress. You've done a very foolish thing, Hermione—not in breaking off this engagement but in ever agreeing to it—but there's no reason why, after all, you shouldn't have a happy and useful career."

Gone was Helen's air of remoteness. Her eyes glowed with an almost fanatical light.

Mrs. Pennistone had recovered her self-control.

"I almost think that that would be the best," she said, "if Hermione persists in this wicked course. I don't see how I could have her here after this. Mind you, I'll not have it said that I turned her out. You can stay here if you want to, Hermione, but you can't expect me to take any more interest in you or do anything more for you. You'll have disgraced me completely as well as yourself. I shall never hold up my head again after this."

Silently Hermione surveyed the alternatives. . . . Helping Matron look after the younger children . . . holidays spent in rooms with Helen, having lessons from Helen . . . Helen never cross, never unkind, but always immeasurably withdrawn. She remembered the schooled patience, the—always kindly—severity that had terrified her so whenever Helen had given her lessons in her childhood. Later she would be a mistress at St. Hilda's under Helen's exacting rule. . . . A happy, useful career. No one, of course, would ever want to marry her now. She turned to the other alternative. Living here with mother. Resentment and hatred always between them. Mother cold and angry and hostile. . . ceaseless reproaches ("You'll have disgraced me . . . I shall never hold up my head again").

Then her thoughts turned to the fate from which she was fleeing. She saw Charles's face, tender, adoring, heard his voice lowered in passionate protestation of devotion ("I love you so, my darling. All I want in the world is to make you happy. . . . I'll be so good to you, I'll take such care of you. I'd give my soul for your happiness").

Her form relaxed, and a little defiant smile played at the corners of her set lips.

"I'm sorry I made such a fuss," she said. "It's all right. I'll marry Charles."

Chapter Five

If her engagement had been a flood carrying her tumultuously along with it, her honeymoon was a whirlpool, a cataract.

Innocence was, in Mrs. Pennistone's opinion, synonymous with ignorance, and she considered that she had done her duty as a careful mother in handing Hermione over to her husband wholly unaware of the functions of sex. No nice girl, considered Mrs. Pennistone, "knew anything". Hermione, absorbed by her world of dreams, had felt little interest or curiosity in the matter. She had long known that the child grew in the womb of the mother, but it had never occurred to her to wonder what process, if any, preceded that growth. One was married, and then in about a year babies began to come. That was all there was to it. . . .

Her honeymoon might have been a nightmare that would have coloured all her married life, had Charles Dereham been a different type of man. He was passionate, thoughtless, and not very reliable, but he was also essentially kind-hearted and intolerant of any form of cruelty. The urgency of his love-making ceased as soon as he discovered her fear and bewilderment, and once more he seemed to her to become the father she had always missed. He reassured and consoled her, soothing her to sleep as if she had been a child. After that her shrinking left her, and the whirlpool swept her up with it.

Beneath her dreaminess her nature was deeply passionate. The discovery surprised and faintly shocked her, as if some tame domestic animal belonging to her had changed suddenly into a wild beast before her eyes. She could hardly believe that she had once imagined she did not love Charles. The passion he had roused in her possessed her so utterly that she seemed to have no thought or will or consciousness apart from it.

They spent the honeymoon at an inn in a Cornish fishing village. Looking back on it in after life, Hermione could never remember anything of it except Charles. It was as if, literally bewitched, she had during those four weeks seen nothing but his face, heard nothing but his voice, felt nothing but the thrilling, agonising ecstasy of his passion.

"I nearly didn't marry you. I was so frightened the night before."

"You darling, you sweet baby! Why were you frightened?"

"I thought I didn't love you. I *didn't* love you. . . . Then it came quite suddenly. What if it goes quite suddenly? . . ."

He pressed hot kisses on her lips.

"Don't say that, my love, my sweet. . . ."

She held his face between her hands.

"It does go, you know. People do stop loving each other."

"We shan't . . . I couldn't live without you. I couldn't breathe without you. I'll kill myself if you ever stop loving me."

"Darling, darling. . . . Helen said I could go and teach in her school if I didn't want to marry you."

"Teach in a school! You!" His voice rang with triumphant contempt. "Oh, my beautiful one, to think that of all the men in the world I'm the one to have you. . . . You're so lovely that sometimes I feel I can hardly bear it."

"Darling, darling, don't talk like that . . . I'm so ordinary."

"My sweet, my beautiful . . ."

"Will you love me when I'm old and ugly?"

"You'll never be old to me, and you couldn't be ugly."

She drew his head to her and pressed her soft warm lips upon his.

Then quite suddenly and unexpectedly, as it seemed, the dream came to an end.

Maud and Mrs. Pennistone were at Ivy Lodge to receive them on their return from the honeymoon. Hermione felt tired by the journey, and the presence of Maud and her mother in her new home irritated and depressed her. She had forgotten that there were other people in the world besides Charles and herself. Maud talked to Charles about friends of whom Hermione knew nothing, and he listened with interest, asking questions, making comments, saying, "Yes, it's an age since I saw them. One must pick up the threads of ordinary life again now, I suppose."

A stab of pain shot through Hermione's heart when she heard him say that. It was as if their marriage and honeymoon were in his eyes merely an interlude instead of the beginning of a new life. Moreover, she suspected that Maud, ostensibly leaving her to her mother with delicate tact, was in reality deliberately isolating her from Charles. There was a faint tinge of pity in her manner to him ("Poor old Charles! We shall miss you at home. . . . I can run over, you know, whenever you want me"), an unbearably patronising tone in her voice when she spoke to Hermione ("Now I suppose your troubles will all begin, my child. Not done much housekeeping, have you?").

Her mother's arch triumph, her veiled demand for intimate confidences, was worse still. Hermione grew more and more unhappy as the evening wore on. She was relieved when at last the time came for Charles to take them down to the station. She sat alone in the strange new drawing-room with its elaborately draped mantelpiece, its forest of ferns supported by ornamental fern stands, its innumerable occasional tables covered by fringed table-cloths and a heterogeneous collection of wedding presents, fighting the depression and apprehension that lay so heavy on her spirit. The brass clock in the glass case that had been a wedding present from Charles's father's employees seemed to tick mournfully and forebodingly in the silence.

At last she heard Charles's key in the lock, and his cheerful whistling as he hung up his hat and coat in the hall. He came into the room and took up his favourite position on the hearthrug.

"Good old Maud!" he said. "It was nice to see her again."

Then he looked down at her, and, suddenly noticing the wan unhappiness of her smile, dropped on to his knees by her chair.

"What is it, my sweet? Are you tired?"

She clung to him, hiding her face on his shoulder.

"Charles . . . I wish we hadn't had to come home."

"Darling, we couldn't spend all the rest of our lives in a Cornish inn."

"Do you love me, Charles? Really love me? Do you love me as much as you did on our honeymoon?"

"My little sweet, we've only been back from our honeymoon a few hours."

"I know, but—it all seems different, somehow. Oh, Charles, you must go on loving me. I couldn't live if you didn't."

He showered kisses on her eyes and lips and the tender hollow beneath her white rounded chin.

"My darling, my little love. . . ."

Suddenly everything was all right again.

But the honeymoon had definitely come to an end, and a new and puzzling life had begun.

At night Charles was still the perfect lover, passionate, adoring. During the day he was a somewhat exacting husband, fond of his comforts and apt to be impatient when the cooking was imperfect or the meals were late. Hermione dreaded his impatience, and wept bitterly in secret when he found fault with her housekeeping. It always surprised him to discover that he had made her unhappy. "But, sweetheart, I only said that it wasn't cooked enough. It wasn't, darling. It was practically raw. I've explained so often how I like it. . . . Yes, but surely you can see that she does it right. But, my darling, I wasn't cross. I merely said it was uneatable. It *was* uneatable. I can't see what there was in that to make you unhappy. You know I'd die rather than make you unhappy. You mustn't get upset over such little things, beloved. It's just that I hate underdone meat. Speak to her about it again and make sure she understands."

Sometimes he praised Maud's housekeeping, and then a wave of fury swept over her so that it was all she could do not to blaze out at him. She controlled herself, however, showing him neither her anger nor, if she could help it, her frequent unhappiness. She was painfully anxious to please him, to be always just what he wanted her to be. He formed her whole world. His approval was the only thing she wanted of life. Once she had noticed a sentence in a Greek translation that Helen had been correcting: "A woman comes to rules and usages she never learnt at home and needs the gift of divination to know how she may please her husband". She often remembered it now. ... She struggled gallantly with the problems of housekeeping. She had had no training or experience, she was naturally impractical, and she was desperately afraid of the cook, a large Irishwoman with a surly temper and a fine skill in covert insolence. An aroma of personal uncleanliness that hung about the woman, moreover, worried her so much that the thought of it kept her awake at night. At last she confided the trouble in Charles. He laughed rather impatiently, and said:

"Tell her to have a bath, then. See that she has it."

"Oh, Charles," she gasped. "I daren't."

He couldn't understand.

"But, good Lord, my dear, you're the mistress of the house, and she's one of your servants."

She felt that her fear of the woman irritated and displeased him. It detracted from his dignity in his own eyes that his wife should be afraid of her servants.

He was curiously imperceptive, seldom noticing when she was tired or depressed. When he did notice he was full of solicitude, waiting on her tenderly, pouring out the old impassioned protestations of devotion. One night, seeing blue shadows beneath her eyes and her lips set in lines of weariness, he carried her up to bed in his arms and undressed her as if she were a child and he her nurse. The situation in the kitchen, however, was growing worse. The cook was now definitely the victor in the never very equal struggle between them. She had discovered Hermione's lack of housekeeping knowledge, and she used it mercilessly, challenging or ignoring her every order. She was, when she troubled to exert herself, an excellent cook, but she cherished a secret bitterness against the "gentry", and fiercely resented Hermione's youth.

The housemaid was a morose, anaemic girl who had spent her life in basements and was a ready convert to Cook's attitude. Hermione dared no longer confide in Charles. Charles was impatient of domestic detail and had a vague idea that every woman was born with a complete knowledge of housekeeping. He had a maddening habit of saying, "Well, my dear, if you're in any difficulty you'd better consult Maud. She's a splendid housekeeper."

Hermione was afraid—poignantly, unceasingly afraid—of losing his love. She endured torments on the evenings when he came home from work tired and distrait. It was as if she had completely lost her own personality. She wanted to be nothing but the woman Charles loved. She tried to conceal from him everything in her that might not please him. His wife must be a good housekeeper—as a matter of course and because she was his wife—so she pretended to be a good housekeeper, hiding her mistakes from him, never confiding in him her failures or worries. This new life that had opened in such a glow of rapture was turning out to be a sort of tight-rope walking ordeal. Each day she walked along the rope, carrying her precarious happiness fearfully in her hands, terrified of making a false step. She became nervous and overwrought. It seemed to her too sensitive mind that the slightest mistake might turn Charles's love to indifference. A dozen times a day she thought that it had actually happened. His frown came so quickly after his smile, his love-making could change so abruptly to impatience.

The cook and housemaid were now her declared enemies. This warfare and their continued triumph in it gave a new zest and romance to their lives and seemed to them in some way to compensate for the tyranny they had so often had to endure from other mistresses.

One night Charles awoke and found her lying by him, her frowning blue eyes fixed on the window where the moonlight showed through the slats of the Venetian blind.

"Are you awake, sweet?" he whispered.

"Yes."

"What are you thinking about?"

"Cook."

He laughed.

"Why on earth Cook?"

She turned to him suddenly, and her words poured out in a tearful, childish stream. "Charles, I don't know anything about housekeeping. I've never learned about it. I'm always making mistakes, and they don't even try to help. They laugh at me when I go into the kitchen to give orders, and they don't care if I see that they're laughing at me. They don't even pretend not to. And they're so rude to me. I can't go on with it, Charles. I oughtn't to have married you. I'm miserable."

He was all tenderness. He gathered her into his arms, kissing her hair and eyes and lips.

"My darling, my little sweet, why didn't you tell me before?"

"I did, Charles. . . . Not lately, but—at the beginning I tried to. Only it annoyed you, so I didn't talk about it again."

"Annoyed me?"

Like most men of quickly changing moods, he was always surprised and incredulous when confronted with an attitude that he had assumed in a different state of mind.

"Sweetheart, I could never be annoyed with you. Never . . . I worship you, every bit of you."

"Charles, I feel I'd rather die than go into the kitchen again."

"I wish you'd told me you were worried, my pet. I wish I'd seen . . . I'd do anything in the whole world for you, my darling. You know that. Look here, suppose we have Maud over to give you a hand till you've got into things."

"No, no, *no*!"

"Your mother, then?"

Hermione relaxed in his arms. Her mother, for all her silliness, was a very capable housekeeper. She had a cheerful, authoritative manner with maids. They were always respectful and contented in her service. For the first time in her life Hermione felt a longing for her mother.

"Oh yes, Charles, please."

Mrs. Pennistone arrived two days later. She was brisk, business-like, and a little less silly than usual. She was aware that she should have given Hermione at least some elementary training in housekeeping before handing her over to her husband, but Hermione's engagement had been a ticklish affair, an affair that she had tried to invest with glamour rather than the humdrum atmosphere of household duties.

A new bond formed itself between mother and daughter. Hermione was anxious to learn everything there was to learn. She cooked all day long in her eagerness to get a dish just right—pouring a reckless stream of badly or mediocrely cooked food upon the official poor of the neighbourhood. She made copious notes of household routine. She studied Mrs. Beeton with frowning intentness. She "did out" each room herself, sweeping the carpet, polishing the furniture. She scrubbed floors on her hands and knees. She cleaned the "silver"—a formidable array of useless and ornate wedding presents of which Charles was very proud. She made jam and baked bread.

"Yes," said Mrs. Pennistone at last, "I think my flower's going to be a wonderful little housewife."

Hermione clung to her mother's presence. She was part of the old, easy-going life of childhood that had existed before this strange, torturing thing had come to her. Her presence gave Hermione a sense of security, made her feel less as if she were walking on a tight-rope. . . . But she was beginning to irritate Charles.

"When's she going?" he said restlessly to Hermione as he stood before the looking-glass in their bedroom in his shirt-sleeves, brushing his hair.

Hermione stiffened, and for the first time looked at him with something of hostility in her blue eyes.

"I hope not for some time. I like having her."

"Oh, all right," he muttered peevishly.

Mrs. Pennistone, on her side, too, was feeling irritation. Though she had taken little enough interest in Hermione when she lived at home, though she had in fact spared no effort to get her married as soon as possible to the first eligible suitor who appeared on the scene, it caused her an unexpected pang of exasperation to watch this comparative stranger exercising authority over her child. It even dispelled momentarily the roseate mist through which she was accustomed to look on Charles as the Perfect Husband for her Little Flower.

"You spoil him, my dear," she said. "No woman should wait on a man as you wait on Charles."

Hermione's blue eyes became icy. "I love waiting on him," she said curtly, "he's so good to me. . . ."

So that all three of them felt a certain relief when Mrs. Pennistone set off to the station in the old-fashioned village cab.

She had left the house in ship-shape order. She had engaged two new maids—a motherly, good-tempered cook, and a pleasant, trim young housemaid. The machinery of the house now ran on oiled wheels. Hermione's brief intensive training had given her a new sense of assurance. Having performed each detail of housework herself, she felt that she knew how it should be performed. The old air of childish shrinking with servants and tradesmen had left her. There was a new element of authority in her manner. On one occasion she even spoke sharply to the butcher for sending tough meat. And, though her love for Charles was as deep as ever, it was losing its first impassioned vehemence. She could think of him calmly now, without that sudden suffocating beating of her heart. The *tempo* of life had slowed down to normal, and the old habits, the old affections, began to reassert themselves.

It was autumn. . . . The hedges were gay with hips and haws and traveller's-joy. In the woods the undergrowth of bramble flamed crimson, and the bracken was touched with gold. To roam through the woods again was like meeting a beloved friend after a long parting. She felt as if there were something in her to which this timeless loveliness was food and drink, something, that would have starved to death without it.

Charles was silent when she told him of her "walks", so that soon, fearing his disapproval, she ceased to mention them. But he began to question her each evening as to how she had spent the day, and whenever she had been in the woods his disapproval became evident. Young matrons, his manner gave her to understand, did not roam the woods aimlessly and unattended. One evening he said:

"Look here, darling, I don't like your wandering over the

countryside like this. Can't you honestly find anything better to do with your time?"

She looked at him warily, the pupils of her blue eyes dilated as if with sudden fear.

"But, Charles," she said breathlessly, "I do the shopping and housekeeping in the morning. I only go for walks in the afternoon." She searched desperately for a reason that would appeal to him. "I need fresh air and exercise, you know."

"Yes, I know, but I don't like your going alone. Couldn't you get someone to go for walks with you? There's Mrs. Kendall or Mrs. Bannister."

She was silent for a moment. To go through the woods with Mrs. Kendall or Mrs. Bannister would be like defiling a sanctuary.

"Oh no," she said. "I couldn't. I—" She pulled herself up sharply, aware that he would never understand what those solitary "walks" meant to her. "I don't think they like going for walks."

"Well, I hate to think of your mooning about by yourself, darling. It's not healthy."

She knew that it would be impossible to make him look at it in any other way.

She continued her wanderings in the woods for a few days. The miracles of form and colour still brought to her the familiar rapture, but the rapture was now dulled and spoilt by the knowledge of Charles's disapproval. She was acutely and in every nerve sensitive to the atmosphere of those with whom she lived. She shrank from causing them pain or disappointment. An intolerable sense of compunction weighed upon her whenever she had been into the woods, and gradually she ceased to go there.

She withdrew instead into her world of books, bringing out the volumes of poetry that had belonged to her father, reading again the Tennyson, Wordsworth, and—most frequently—Keats and Shelley that stirred in her the same unreasoning rapture as the world of nature.

But Charles, it turned out, disapproved of this, too.

"I wish you wouldn't read stuff like this, sweetheart," he said, taking up the volume of Keats she was reading and glancing uncomprehendingly at the open page. "It's not healthy. . . . Look here, if you want to read, I'll get Maud to lend you something. She has plenty of wholesome, straightforward, interesting novels. But this"—he turned over another page—"it's morbid."

He did not, as a matter of fact, like to see her reading at all. In the evening, when he had come home from work, he liked her to sit opposite him on the other side of the fireplace sewing, while he occasionally read aloud items of news from his newspaper. The only books he cared to read were books of foreign travel. Facts had a curious fascination for him. The scenery and history of foreign countries interested him not at all, but the number of their population, the statistics of their diseases, the figures of their exports and imports, the very length of their rivers and height of their mountains, enthralled him.

She gave up reading poetry, not from blind obedience to his wishes, but because the knowledge of his disapproval spoilt her pleasure in it.

Chapter Six

ABBOTFORD was a small village clustered round a village green and dominated by a seventeenth-century manor, whose owner, Sir Lionel Amhurst, divided his time between London and Aix-les-Bains. In the shadow of the manor stood the squat Norman church and its low, creeper-covered vicarage. The vicar was a man of about fifty, who had chosen the life of a clergyman rather because of the opportunity for study that it afforded than because of any evangelistic zeal. He officiated with exquisite detachment in church on Sunday, greeted courteously such of his parishioners as he met in the village, and spent his time in the study of the classics. Abbotford generally was proud than otherwise of his aloofness. "Him's not one of they busybodies, praise be," was the verdict of the Amhurst Arms. Occasionally he coached pupils for Classical scholarships or entrance to the universities, and such pupils were generally annexed by Maud Dereham, who liked to have a young man in tow, and who kept a watchful eye on the doings of all the villages within range of Mettleham.

In the absence of a lady of the manor, Mrs. Kendall and Mrs. Bannister had constituted themselves leaders of the village society. Mrs. Kendall was the daughter of a bishop and the widow of an army officer, and considered herself socially superior to everyone else in the neighbourhood. Mrs. Bannister, her satellite, a pretty, stupid, uneducated woman, the wife of the village doctor, was impressed by Mrs. Kendall's social pretensions and proud of her patronage.

In winter the relaxations of the feminine part of the village took the form of tea-parties, and, since the resources of the neighbourhood were limited, the same guests were inevitably invited, the parties varying from each other only in being held at different houses.

Charles liked Hermione to attend these parties. It worried him that she should refuse invitations without an—to him—adequate reason.

"Sweetheart, you ought to *want* to go out among people. It's good for you. Maud's always going out to tea with the people round us, and you know how bright and jolly and healthy-minded she keeps."

Hermione controlled the wave of anger that his praise of his sister always brought to her, and began to try to explain to him.

"But, Charles, I'm not interested in the things they talk about—servants and the tradesmen and clothes and that sort of thing. And they gossip so hatefully about anyone who isn't there. I—I'm frightened of them, somehow, all the time. I know it's silly. I can't explain."

Charles gave her an anxious, uncomprehending look. Servants, tradesmen, clothes, gossip . . . it was right and natural that women should want to talk about these things at their tea-parties.

"I don't understand, darling," he said. "There's a morbid strain in you, and I think you ought to fight against it. You were left too much to yourself when you were a child. Mrs. Kendall and Mrs. Bannister are very nice women, and I'd like you to be friendly with them."

So, because she loved him and because of the essential yieldingness of her nature, she began to take her regular part in the round of tea-parties, trying to conquer her shyness and shrinking, but facing each one as an ordeal. She was aware that the other matrons sensed an alien element in her, and criticised her unmercifully when she was not there, but that did not trouble her. She could not have explained exactly what did trouble her. She only knew that something in the atmosphere of these gatherings, given over entirely as they were to tittle-tattle and ill-natured gossip, stifled and oppressed her with a feeling of almost physical discomfort. She had, however, given up the struggle to return to her old life.

Her days had now settled down into a regular routine. In the morning she did her shopping and supervised the housework; in the afternoon she sewed, mended, and generally went out to tea; in the evening she sat with Charles, working at a pair of Berlin wool slippers and listening to his indistinct and rather grating voice as he read aloud items from his newspaper or his books of foreign travel. She still loved him, but deep down beneath her love there was growing a feeling of resentment, as if in some way he had cheated her. He knew and cared nothing for her real self. She was to be there in the background of his life, waiting in his home for him to return to her—pretty, pleasant, companionable, and, above all, conventional. His ideal of a woman reminded her of another sentence from a Greek translation that she had once seen on Helen's desk: "That woman's glory is greatest who is least talked of among men for good or ill". She was to have no interests beyond the keeping and embellishment of his home, but she was to enter whole-heartedly into all such of his interests as he cared to admit her to. He did not know her, and he did not want to know her. She was, indeed, not expected to have any individuality. She was simply to be his wife, the perfect wife of his imagination.

For some months he came home every evening after his work, aflame to be with her again. His pride in her and in their home, his joy at the sight of her sitting opposite him, her golden head bent over her needlework, touched her despite herself, disarming the resentment that she was secretly cherishing beneath her love. After a few months, however, he began to look up his old friends, meeting them in town for dinner after his work. She was so innocent that the first time he came home expansive and talkative, the slow deliberation of his voice loosened to a quick fluency, she felt only pleasure in his unusual cheerfulness. But the next time he returned from a meeting with his friends, besides the expansiveness and loosened speech, there was about him a fatuous silliness that, together with a strong perfume of spirits, finally undeceived her. There came a night when she had to help him upstairs. He was so obviously ashamed the next day that she could not bring herself to humiliate him further by referring to the matter. He did not go out in the evening for several weeks after that. Then he began to go out again—once a week on an average—coming back, never actually intoxicated, never after that first time even tipsy, but always garrulous and a little foolish. Inoffensive enough though he always was at these times, she hated and feared the foolish chattering stranger who took her husband's place. Lying in bed by his side, trying to control her trembling, she thought: "I hate him. I loathe him. I can't go on living with him. I'll never love him again. . . ." Yet, when the next day came and the real Charles returned, humble, adoring, penitent (though as yet neither of them had ever mentioned his lapses), her love went out to him afresh and she forgot the stranger who had taken his place.

Occasionally they dined with Charles's father and sister at Mettleham Hall. The old man had been a tyrant to his son, though indulgent enough to his daughter, and it was strange to see Charles in this house become a tongue-tied schoolboy—respectful, nervous, never speaking to his father unless addressed, always afraid of arousing one of his outbursts of temper. Hermione disliked the old man, and it made her furious to see Charles snubbed or ignored by him. She was especially tender to Charles after a visit to Mettleham Hall. Charles, however, had a stubborn sense of family loyalty and would never allow her to depreciate his father. He would often come home from work, tired and exasperated by his father's unreasonableness, and grumble to Hermione without restraint till she began to agree with him, when he would become offended and rally to the old man's defence.

But it was Maud over whom their relations became most strained.

Maud was handsome in a highly coloured fashion (she looked her best on horseback), and had for many years been employing every endeavour to find a husband. According to the general opinion, indeed, her failure was due to her having tried too obviously and too hard. She now concentrated on eligible youths of weak calibre who were at first flattered by her notice, then frightened by her possessiveness, and who finally, after desperate efforts, succeeded in escaping from her. Her breezy, friendly manner made her popular enough at social gatherings, but her "affairs" caused much secret amusement among her friends and acquaintances. Charles, of course, did not see Maud as the rest of the world saw her. To Charles she was the elder sister who had stood between him and his father's unkindness in their childhood, and he gave to her the love and loyalty that he would have given to his mother if she had lived. He was proud of her looks and her popularity. He accepted un-questioningly her picture of herself as a woman, courted by an unending stream of suitors, who yet preferred to remain single. That, in some inexplicable way, helped to lift her in his eyes above every other woman he had known, even Hermione. He had taken for granted that an immediate and lasting friendship would spring up between his wife and his sister, but, despite his obtuseness, he could not help becoming increasingly aware as time went on that this had not happened. He was sure that Maud was willing. It was Hermione who refused Maud's overtures and offers of assistance in her new duties. He felt a secret resentment against Hermione for this. It seemed to him to denote some serious deficiency in her, making her less worthy of the place he had given her. She had never admitted her dislike of Maud, but he was aware of it, and the atmosphere became strained whenever either of them mentioned her name.

He came boldly to grips with the subject one evening.

"I say, Hermione," he said suddenly, "I wish you and old Maud got on better."

"I've never quarrelled with Maud," she said shortly.

"I know, but"—he laughed self-consciously—"she was so wonderful to me when I was a kid. She's been such a decent pal to me always, and—well, somehow, I'd hoped that you two would be better friends than you are."

A half-abashed pleading in his voice and expression touched her poignantly. She was always generous of sympathy, easily moved to pity or compunction.

"I'm sorry, Charles," she said. "I'll try. . . . What can I do?"

"I think she'd like to come and stay here for a bit, but I don't want you to ask her if you really don't want her."

"Of course I'll ask her . . . I'll write to-night."

So Maud, breezy and handsome, arrived the next week. Hermione strove to make her welcome, but she soon became aware that Maud had taken possession of both the house and Charles, and it was Hermione who felt herself the stranger, kindly tolerated by Maud. Maud, especially in Charles's presence, was always very affectionate to Hermione, treating her with condescending playfulness as if she were a pet animal, attractive enough, but unworthy of serious consideration—a treatment nicely calculated to impress Charles favourably and to infuriate Hermione.

The antipathy between the two women was, of course, inevitable. Hermione honestly faced the fact that she was jealous of Maud, jealous of her knowledge of Charles, of her power of managing him, of the childhood's memories that united them, and, above all, of Charles's loving pride in her.

Maud, on her side, though she seemed casual enough on the surface, was by nature deeply possessive. She had poured out upon her young brother all the maternal love of which she was capable, and she would have hated any woman who took him from her. But it went deeper even than that. . . . She was good-looking and popular, and she had taken for granted always that she would marry young. Sometimes now she found it impossible to believe she had reached and passed thirty without having received a single proposal.

And she could not forgive Hermione her easy acquisition of a husband. She hated the youth and loveliness of her. It afforded her an obscure satisfaction to look on her as a scheming little minx who could only bring disgrace on Charles. It was the hint of pity in Maud's manner to Charles that angered Hermione more than anything. She ransacked his clothes to find something that wanted mending, said "Poor old Charles!" with a sigh as she began to darn the pair of socks that she discovered. Always, when the three of them sat together in the evenings, she deliberately led the conversation into channels where Hermione could not follow it—discussing old friends whom Hermione had never met, introducing cryptic jokes of nursery or schoolroom days. Charles told Maud that Hermione enjoyed a "good tramp" and asked her to go with her as he did not like her going alone. Hermione felt that it would be ungracious—almost impossible—to refuse, and so there was nothing to do but to steel herself to endure it. Maud, "tramping" through the woods with quick, business-like strides ("I like to keep up a good five miles an hour"), slashing at the tender undergrowth with her stick, talking in her harsh, strident voice, blind and deaf to the beauty around her ("They ought to be thinned, you know. And all that ivy taken down. Timber choked up like this will never fetch a good price") . . . Hermione felt that the wood was spoilt for ever, felt that always when she came here again she would see Maud slashing at the undergrowth, hear her loud dominating voice above the sound of the brook and song of the birds ("That was a jay, wasn't it? I wish I'd got a gun with me"). Worse even than this to Hermione was Maud's attempt to discuss intimate sexual matters with her. . . .

By the end of the visit Hermione's self-control was worn so near the breaking point that she had to clench her teeth to hide the shudder of revulsion that Maud's farewell kiss sent through her. She stood tense and quivering in the hall till the sound of the cab had died away in the distance. Then she went slowly back to the drawing-room. She had expected that sudden peace would flood her soul as soon as Maud's jarring presence was removed. But it didn't. Maud's presence seemed still to possess the house. Perhaps it would always be there now . . .

Charles came back, pleased and happy. He had been deceived by the surface friendliness between the two women, and took for granted that the friendship he had hoped for was now firmly cemented. He could talk of nothing but Maud—her good nature, her good looks, her charm, her friendliness. "I knew you'd like old Maud once you got to know her."

Hermione endured it through dinner, holding herself in an iron grip of self-control, saying to herself: "Don't listen to him . . . don't listen to him . . . think of something else." But she could not think of anything else.

They went into the drawing-room, and there he continued his praises of Maud. Suddenly he was silent for a moment, then said affectionately:

"You know, darling, Maud and I were having a little talk about you last night . . ."

A gust of anger seized her.

"How *dare* you discuss me with your sister?"

He looked at her, open-mouthed with amazement.

Her eyes were blazing, her face white with passion. This was a stranger, a woman he had never seen before.

"I've no idea what you mean," he said. There was cold disapproval in his tone. Whatever the cause, such a lack of restraint was unbecoming in his wife.

"Then you ought to have," she blazed. "You bring your sister here to insult me. You talk about me to her behind my back . . . I hate your sister, I tell you, hate her, *hate* her. If she comes here again I'll run away."

His anger, too, was rising, but he tried to restrain it, to keep the note of cold, impersonal disapproval in his voice.

"Please control yourself, Hermione. . . . All Maud said was——"

But she was beyond her control or his. The gathered resentments of months had broken their dam.

"I won't control myself. If you mention Maud's name again I'll go straight out of the house and never come back. I *hate* her, I tell you. She's deceitful and vulgar and fast and——"

He was suddenly in a towering rage.

"Be quiet. I won't allow you to speak of my sister like that. You're a spoilt, ungrateful child. I go out of my way to be kind to your mother and make her stay pleasant, and you treat my sister like this——"

"How dare you mention my mother in the same breath as your sister?"

"Maud's been a better mother to me than your mother's been to you. Your mother's an idiotic old fool, and everyone knows it."

Hermione had never felt much affection for her mother, but this insult broke down the last vestige of her self-control.

"I hate you," she sobbed. "I loathe you. I wish I'd never met you. I've been miserable ever since I married you. I wish I'd gone with Helen. . . . You've never loved me . . . you've never loved anyone but yourself. . . . I *hate* you. . . ."

She plunged abruptly from the room, ran upstairs, and slammed the door of her bedroom. Then she sank on to her bed, her body trembling, her teeth chattering. Beneath her anger was an odd, surging exultation. There had been an almost sensual relief in giving rein at last to her long-curbed resentment; a fierce joy in telling him that she hated him and wished she had never married him. The scene had severed the final bond between them. Her anger had killed her love, and with the loss of her love came a wild, glad sense of freedom. She was free . . . no longer need she shrink from his displeasure, no longer try to make herself other than she was. She was free . . . free . . . free. She could be herself, go her own way, live her own life. . . . She was conscious of a strange sense of lightness, as if a thousand heavy weights had dropped from her spirit. She got into bed and lay there, staring at the square of moonlit window behind the dressing-table.

She heard Charles enter his dressing-room and shut the door. In their short married life they had never yet slept apart, and the bed in his dressing-room was not made up. He came into the bedroom and got into bed in silence, lying ostentatiously aloof from her on the extreme edge of it. She felt his anger and was glad of it, for it inflamed her own again to fever pitch. She slept fitfully, and whenever she woke remembered their quarrel, first with depression, then with that thrilling sense of exultation. He rose unusually early the next morning, and she lay motionless with closed eyes, pretending to be asleep. When he had gone into the bathroom, she sat up in bed and looked about her. Immediately a wave of deadly nausea swept over her. She lay down and closed her eyes again. . . . She had never felt so ill in all her life before. She was dying, of course. Charles would be sorry, perhaps, when she died. . . .

Charles returned from the bathroom. With half-opened eyes she watched him through the looking-glass of the wardrobe as he stood at the dressing-table in his shirt-sleeves, brushing his hair. His mouth was set in tense angry lines. He turned to the wardrobe to get his coat. Though he would not look at her, he could not resist stealing a glance at her reflection in the mirror. Immediately the anger vanished from his face, and a look of dismayed concern flashed into it. He came to the bedside.

"What is it, Hermione? Are you ill?"

She tried to speak, but the nausea still held her so that she dared not move even her lips. The drawn pallor of her face frightened him.

"Darling . . . I'll get the doctor quickly."

He ran himself for Dr. Bannister, sending up the housemaid to bathe her brow with eau-de-Cologne.

The doctor examined her, and then went downstairs with Charles. She felt better now. The nausea had passed as suddenly as it had come. She sat up in bed as Charles entered.

"I'm much better now," she said.

He closed the door.

"You know what's the matter with you, don't you?"

"No."

"You're going to have a baby."

She stared at him.

"A baby?"

She was filled with a sudden shrinking horror at the news. For a moment it seemed to her as if the growth within her were something alien, malignant. . . . He saw the terror in her eyes and put his arms about her, stroking back the hair from her forehead, kissing her tenderly.

"Don't be frightened . . . darling, don't be frightened."

Her anger with him had passed as completely as if it had never been. She clung to him for comfort, feeling that there in his arms nothing could harm her.

"Charles . . . Oh, Charles . . ."

"My sweet. . . my little love . . ."

Chapter Seven

THE birth of the baby turned Hermione's fear and shrinking into a passion of love that seemed to absorb her every other interest and emotion. She regained health quickly and looked after the child herself, scarcely allowing anyone else to touch him. Charles was ingenuously, almost fatuously proud of his fatherhood. They had their son christened John, and Hermione was pregnant again before he was weaned. She bore six more children—Monica, Alan, Vere, James, Gillian, Nigel—with intervals of eighteen months or so between each.

She had now settled down perforce to the busy routine of a housewife and mother. The care of home and children filled her days, drugging her with weariness and a warm, happy content.

During the months of John's coming she had had continual need of Charles's tenderness, but at each successive birth he seemed to recede farther into the background. Her love for her children was a sustaining passion. She poured out upon them all the rich treasure of her devotion, filling her heart with them so completely that there was no room left in it for anything or anyone else.

Charles, of course, was necessary to her in that he provided their home and took upon his shoulders the ultimate responsibility of the young family, but otherwise he seemed not only unnecessary but rather a nuisance. She disliked the week-ends when he was at home all day, and felt secretly glad when they came to an end. He got in her way and upset the children's routine and demanded attention from her when she had none to spare for him. Subconsciously she often realised that he was hurt and angry at some impatience in her tone or manner ("He's sulking again," she put it to herself); she was dimly aware that she could easily have charmed him out of his ill-humour, but she had not the time or the energy. It didn't seem worth while. He was a child, but rather a tiresome child . . . someone else's child. She was always scrupulous to accord him the position of figurehead in the little household, to invest him with the semi-divine authority that belonged to the Victorian father and husband ("We must ask father when he comes in." "We'll see what father says"), but he could not help knowing that he had no real place in it.

When, as happened now more and more often, he spent the evening away from home, she accepted his excuses for his absence without interest or curiosity, and even with something of relief. It allowed her to cut out children's clothes in the nursery with Nurse, or tidy drawers and cupboards upstairs. When Charles was at home, she always felt it her duty to make a pretence of sitting with him downstairs, even though she went out of the room a dozen times on household tasks, and though her mind was so busy with affairs of nursery and kitchen that she did not listen to anything he said.

Charles was not introspective or articulate, but he was aware of a growing sense of grievance. He felt himself now definitely outside the warm bright circle of her love, and he became jealous of the interests that separated her from him. He was proud of his sturdy, healthy brood, but he was not what is known as "good with children". He did not understand them and was pompous and dictatorial with them. He disliked their invading the living-rooms of the house, and when he was at home they were kept strictly to the nursery. They looked upon him as an ogre, but he did not resent that. He considered, indeed, that it was as it should be. He had looked upon his father as an ogre. . . . He would, of course, have been fonder of his children if he had not been—half unconsciously—aware that they had diverted from him the rich stream of Hermione's tenderness.

Old Mr. Dereham was growing more and more unreasonable .and autocratic. Charles had worked hard at the business and knew that he should by now have been made a partner, but his father continued to keep him a salaried subordinate, allowing him no voice in the policy of the firm, flying into a rage if he made any suggestions. When, after an unusually trying day, he came home from work, tired and depressed, and attempted to confide in Hermione, she no longer blazed out in anger against the old man. Instead, she would interrupt him almost before he had begun with "One minute, Charles, I forgot to ask Nurse to rub Jimmie's chest," or "I must just speak to Cook about the children's breakfast." When she returned she had so obviously forgotten what he had been telling her that he would relapse into a sullen silence, refusing to sue as a suppliant for what should have been his by rights. He contented himself at such time by exhibitions of bad temper, grumbling incessantly at Hermione, the children, and the household arrangements.

Even Maud, though she was always friendly and cheerful when they met, seemed now to have failed him. In those months of perfect happiness—that second honeymoon—before John's birth, Charles had wanted no one but his wife, and, seeing that Hermione shrank from Maud's visits and Maud's endless discussion of her "condition", had forbidden Maud to visit her till after her confinement. Maud apparently took this in good part, but she had a long memory and could wait indefinitely to punish anyone whom she considered to have slighted her.

Charles had given up drinking when he knew that Hermione was to have a child, but, as the other children' came and Hermione gradually withdrew herself from him, he began again to indulge in recurrent bouts of intoxication, partly in order to drown his vague sense of disappointment, and partly—as a child is deliberately naughty in order to attract attention to itself—in order to force Hermione to feel some emotion towards him, were it only disgust. His lapses, however, did not seem to trouble her, and certainly it never occurred to her that her indifference was in any way responsible for them. She dealt with them mechanically, abstractedly, as if even then she could not spare him the whole of her attention, helping him to bed as if he were one of her children, but without the radiant tenderness that she always showed to her children. As time went on his vague sense of grievance settled into a definite conviction that he was justified in seeking affection elsewhere.

Hermione's absorption in her family was no empty pose. They could not afford a nursery maid, and Hermione, besides doing the housekeeping, shared the work of the nursery with Nurse, taking charge generally of the elder children while Nurse looked after the toddlers.

She now enjoyed an occasional respite from her many household duties and began to take part in the social life of the neighbourhood, animatedly discussing maids and children and tradesmen and village gossip over the tea-table with other young matrons, quite forgetting that a few years ago she had looked upon such affairs with horror and shrinking.

The chief subject of gossip was a Mrs. Payne, who had lately moved into Greystones, a medium-sized house on the Fernham road. There was much difference of opinion on the subject of her looks; some people considered her beautiful and others actually ugly. She was dark-skinned and sallow, with large dark liquid eyes, soft brown hair, and vividly red lips. A faint line of down marked the upper lip. Mrs. Kendall, who was, of course, an authority on such matters, declared that she had a "touch of the tar brush". There was an air of mystery about her, and no amount of skilful probing on the part of the other ladies of the village could elicit from her any information as to her private history or concerns. It was generally agreed that she dressed more fashionably than a lady living alone in the country had any need to dress, and only the most charitable maintained—and that half-heartedly—that the vivid colour of her lips was natural. The fact that a woman reddened her lips was looked upon in those days as being of itself strong evidence of immorality.

Hermione, though she enjoyed an occasional tea-party, had not much time for visiting her neighbours. The custom of the time dictated that a child's first lessons should be learnt from its mother, and she had duly taught John and Monica and Alan and Vere to read and write. Alan was quick enough, but so dreamy and absent-minded that he could not keep his attention on anything for more than a few moments, and so sensitive and highly-strung that Hermione could never bring herself to punish him. Vere, too, was quick to learn, but she was "difficult", easily offended and stubborn, hardly less sensitive than Alan, and reserved in a strange, unchildlike, almost secretive way. When she had been naughty and was sorry for it she would try to show her penitence by small unobtrusive services, but nothing would ever induce her to utter the conventional nursery apology, "I'm sorry I've been a naughty girl". Punishment only made her more stubborn and obstinate, and she possessed a strength of enduring, unyielding obstinacy that was amazing in so young a child. To join issues with her was to court sure defeat. The others were normal enough—John, a solemn, solid little boy, loving and lovable; Monica, passionate, impulsive, but easily managed; Jimmie, sweet-tempered and mischievous; and Gillian, the perfection of healthy, dimpled babyhood.

Hermione taught them till Nigel was born, and then reluctantly gave up the lessons and engaged a governess. Nigel was frail and sickly—the only weakling in her healthy flock—and needed all her care. She turned the one remaining spare bedroom into a schoolroom, and there installed a middle-aged, kindly, efficient maiden lady called Miss Lattimer, who came in from Fernham every morning on an enormous tricycle to teach John, Monica, Alan, and Vere.

Vere was not yet supposed to be her pupil, but she insisted on coming to the lessons, resisting all attempts to make her join the younger ones with Nurse. Hermione and Nurse yielded, neither of them having the time to battle with a four-year-old incarnation of stubbornness, and Vere was admitted to the schoolroom, to the indignation of the elder three, who showed her very plainly that she was not welcome. Miss Lattimer had a kind, authoritative manner with the children and taught them well, but Hermione could never reconcile herself to her presence in the house. She always seemed an interloper, not like Nurse—large, placid, imperturbable—part of the natural machinery of the household. She irritated Hermione, too, by trying to explain her children to her, holding forth on their dispositions and temperaments, as if she, who had carried them in her body, knew nothing of them. As a matter of fact, Hermione's air of youth made her seem to the elder woman pathetically childish and she conscientiously tried to give her whatever help she could. Hermione always refused her offers of assistance on Nurse's "afternoon out". Hermione looked forward to that afternoon all week. She loved to have her children around her, climbing over her like puppies, pulling at her skirts, talking to her in shrill excited voices ("Listen to *me*, Mummy. . .") all at the same time; loved the feeling of warm little arms clasped around her neck, and the familiar tea-time smell of the nursery—a mingled smell of toast and dripping, of damp gaiters drying on the fireguard, of healthy, perspiring little bodies, of well-washed and powdered babyhood. After tea they played with the babies—Monica giving Jimmie rides on her back, John building brick castles for Gillian to knock down.

Sitting amongst them like this, with Nigel in her arms, Hermione was conscious of a serenity that bordered on rapture.

At the sound of Charles's key in the lock she would feel as if an alien presence had entered the house, but he never came up to the nursery to her.

When six o'clock came the elder ones would help her put the babies to bed (John was a skilful nurse and could bath Gillian, his special charge, unaided). Then followed the elder ones' hour when she would read to them—Vere, and sometimes Alan as well, on her knee, John and Monica sitting on the floor, their heads leaning against her. Before they went to bed she let them take down her hair, each drawing out a hairpin in turn till the whole mass of it fell in silky golden curls down her back and over her shoulders. Then they would hold up the golden mesh and let it fall slowly in shining single curls, pressing their hot little cheeks against its silky coolness. She felt their love—the fervent, whole-hearted, uncritical adoration of childhood—as if it were some radiant mist enclosing her, shutting out the rest of the world.

She did not go down till she had kissed each one good-night in bed. Then she changed her dress and slowly, reluctantly, went down to Charles's irritable complaints or sullen silence.

Monica had a party on her eighth birthday, and all the other children in the neighbourhood were invited. Alan, however, had had toothache the day before, and Hermione asked Charles to take him to the dentist.

"Give him lunch in town afterwards," she said, "then bring him straight back. I want to have them all ready in time."

She began to feel rather anxious when the guests arrived and still Charles and Alan had not returned, but she consoled herself by thinking that perhaps they had had to wait a long time for the appointment. She wore a new dress of mauve silk with the tight bodice and enormous sleeves that were then fashionable. The lace collar was held together by a large gold brooch, and the train swept the ground with a gentle rustle as she walked. Her shining hair was drawn into a "bun" at the back of her head, but golden tendrils escaped from the coils and lay on her forehead and in the nape of her neck. Monica and Vere wore white muslin frocks with wide coloured sashes. Their hair—Monica's dark, Vere's fair—was cut in fringes on their foreheads and lay in ringlets—Monica's natural, Vere's the result of curl-papers—over their shoulders. Gillian, too, wore a white muslin dress with blue sash and shoulder ribbons, but her hair was still a mop of short golden curls. She was just learning to walk, and she staggered about importantly on tiny blue satin shoes, sitting down suddenly and unexpectedly at intervals to her own great amusement. John and Jimmie wore their velvet suits. John hovered near Gillian protectively, always ready at hand to pick her up when she fell down. It was one of Nigel's better days, and he watched the party from Nurse's arms with a wan little smile. They had crackers at tea-time and eight candles on the birthday cake, and the party was a great success, but at each moment Hermione's heart grew heavier. Something must have happened, or Charles and Alan would have been back by now. Countless possibilities suggested themselves. Alan had been run over, and Charles, busy fetching doctors and specialists, had had no time to send for her. Or Charles had been run over, and Alan had fled in terror and was lost. . . . Or both of them had been run over. . . .

She hid her uneasiness from the children, telling them that the dentist had had to put their appointment later, and none of them suspected that anything was wrong. The end of the party came. Mothers and nurses arrived to wrap their charges in shawls and cloaks and take them home.

Still outwardly cheerful, Hermione shoo'd her own excited brood to bed. Then she turned to face the sick torment of her anxiety. She must do something at once. She could not sit idle at home tortured by this agony of suspense. She would go to the village police station. . . . She opened the front door, and—saw Charles and Alan coming slowly through the darkness up the path from the gate.

"Charles!" she whispered, her hand at her heart.

They came near. Charles held the child's hand.

"What's the matter?" he said.

"I've been expecting you since three o'clock."

"I'm sorry. . . ."

"Where have you been?"

"I met Grimly after lunch, and we went to his rooms, then somehow time got on and we thought we might as well dine at the club."

She still stood at the front door, facing him with dilated eyes.

"It was Mon's birthday party. . . ."

"I'm sorry . . . I forgot."

"How *could* you drag Alan about like that?"

"He's had quite a good time; haven't you, old boy? Honestly, he's all right, Hermione. Grimly let him have his chessmen to play with. We gave him a good tea, and he was in the porter's room at the club while we had dinner. There were some puppies there. . . . You've had quite a good time, haven't you, old boy?"

Both of them looked at Alan. Alan had indeed thoroughly enjoyed the day. It had been wonderful going about with father and his friends as if he were grown up. He had been thrilled by Mr. Grimly's chessmen and had adored the puppies in the porter's room. Like his father, he had completely forgotten that it was Monica's birthday party. But he was over-tired and overwrought; it had begun to rain and he was uncomfortably wet; he had never before seen his mother like this, her eyes blazing angrily in a white face. It terrified him. . . . He burst suddenly into desolate sobs. Hermione snatched him up with a passionately maternal gesture. Looking at Charles through the darkness, she saw that he was not quite sober. Her eyes blazed at him yet more angrily.

"You *sot*!" she said between her teeth, then turned on her heel and, still holding the child in her arms, crossed the hall to the staircase. He stared after her, suddenly sobered. He had seen her angry before, but he had never before heard that note of savage contempt in her voice. He stood at the open door watching her as she went upstairs. Her dress fell in graceful folds from her slender waist, and swayed about her feet. The gaslight from the half-landing lit up her bent head, showing the little curling tendrils that shone like spun gold against her white neck.

He turned abruptly from the door and set off in the direction of Greystones.

Chapter Eight

MAUD sat in front of her dressing-table, while Sarah, the head housemaid of Mettleham Hall, brushed out her long black hair. Maud's toilet was severely masculine, and she had no need of a personal attendant, but she had in her neglected girlhood conceived a liking for the sort of scandal that circulates most freely in the servants' hall, and Sarah, who fulfilled unofficially the functions of a confidential maid, could be trusted to tell her everything she heard, could even be trusted to do a little discreet detective work herself when occasion demanded. Many a dress of Maud's had been handed on, practically unworn, to Sarah in return for such services.

Sarah was a tall, thin, middle-aged woman with a long, pale face, an unduly projecting nose, and a habit of moving noiselessly as if on oiled castors.

"Seen much of Mrs. Payne's maid lately, Sarah?" said Maud.

Her eyes were closed, and she spoke in a deliberately casual tone of voice as if she were making idle conversation to pass the time, but Sarah was fully aware that Mrs. Payne's *ménage* had had an irresistible fascination for Maud ever since the widow had come to Abbotford. Sarah had been deputed—by an apparently casual hint, of which, however, she fully understood the trend—to find out all she could about the household from the sources open to her. In anticipation of the hint, Sarah had already made overtures to Mrs. Payne's domestic staff. Her personal maid she had found as communicative as a blank wall, and had turned her attention to the housemaid, a young girl whose parents lived in the village.

"Yes, miss, I saw her yesterday. We had quite a long chat about one thing and another. If you'll excuse me mentioning it, miss, she was saying how handsome you were. She said that she admired you particularly in your red hat. She'd seen you in it in the village."

Maud considered this reply in silence for a moment. There was evidently information to be had, but it must be paid for. She was aware, of course, that it was Sarah, not Mrs. Payne's maid, who coveted the red hat. It was practically new, but her father made her a generous allowance. She yawned indolently.

"Oh, that old thing. I've quite finished with it. I was just wondering what to do with it. You can give it to her if you think she'd like it."

"Thank you, miss."

The preliminaries were over. Maud still sat relaxed in her chair, her eyes shut, lost apparently in her dreams. The only sound that broke the silence was the sound of the brush moving rhythmically through the thick black hair. At last Maud seemed to rouse herself and yawned again without opening her eyes.

"What were you saying, Sarah?" she said absently. "Oh yes . . . you were speaking about Mrs. Payne's maid. Well, I suppose she finds service as dull as the rest of you find it?"

"No, miss," said Sarah slowly, "she doesn't find it dull exactly. She was asking my advice, as a matter of fact."

"What about?"

"Well, if you don't mind, miss, I'd like to ask your advice about it. I didn't quite know what to say to the girl, and I thought p'raps you'd be good enough to let me tell you what she told me and advise me what I ought to say to her."

Maud was quite aware that the girl had not asked Sarah's advice, but Sarah was well versed in the rules of the game they were playing. Maud must never seem to be asking for the information for which she paid so generously.

"I don't suppose I can help you at all," said Maud, "but you can tell me if you like."

"Well"—the brush still moved slowly, rhythmically through the long hair—"it was whether she was justified in keeping on in service in a house where there's immorality going on."

Maud considered her nails absently.

"That's a big question, Sarah," she said at last, "and it depends a good deal on what exactly she means by immorality."

"Yes, of course, miss."

There was an odd sparkle in Sarah's ferret-like eyes. She had a momentous piece of news to communicate, but she was aware that she must go carefully. Told in the wrong way, it might prejudice her chances of the red hat.

"You see, miss, she realises that it's not a servant's business what her mistress chooses to do, but"—she was silent for a moment, then spoke slowly and meaningly—"when it comes to a gentleman with a wife and family in the same village and a father and sister living less than four miles away . . ."

Maud drew in her breath sharply. The description could only apply to one person. She threw a keen glance at the woman's face in the mirror. It was blank, expressionless. So it was Charles. . . .

"Is the girl—sure of her facts?" she asked casually.

"Yes, miss. You see, miss, she felt that it was her duty to find out exactly what was going on for the sake of her conscience. So—not to put too fine a point on it—she looked through the keyhole, miss."

"I see." Maud's voice was still elaborately careless, but there was a high colour in her cheeks. "Well, I really think the girl will have to settle the matter with her own conscience. I don't think that anyone else can advise her."

"Yes, miss. I'll tell her that."

"I don't think I shall need you any more, Sarah, thank you. . . . You can take the red hat to the girl any time you like."

"Thank you, miss."

The woman moved towards the door with her noiseless, sidling walk. There was a look of relief on her pale face. It had been a ticklish business, but she'd managed it all right. She'd wondered once whether it would be better to say Mr. Charles's name straight out, but she was glad now she hadn't done that. Miss Maud had a queer temper, and it might have vexed her.

Maud sat staring unseeingly in front of her. The colour still blazed in her cheeks. It was Hermione, not Charles, to whom her thoughts had turned with a strange exultation as soon as the woman had told her news. So this was what her romantic girl marriage had come to. . . . She'd caught Charles with her doll-like prettiness, but she hadn't been able to hold him. She wondered if Hermione knew. Probably not. She was entirely absorbed in the care of her young family. The wife was, in any case, the last person to know a thing of that sort. . . . She tried to imagine the expression on Hermione's face when she heard what Maud had just heard—and she knew suddenly that her triumph would be incomplete unless she saw it.

She put on her riding-habit and went down the stairs and past the library door. There was a little recess just outside the library door formed by the outward sweep of the staircase, and in her childhood Maud had often stood there, cowering and trembling, her head buried in her hands, when Charles was being horsewhipped by his father for some childish misdemeanour. Twice her father had horsewhipped her, once for championing Charles too openly, once because he had discovered that she had disobeyed him. Well, those days were over. Her father was outwardly as blustering and tyrannical as ever, but his faculties were beginning to fail him, and he was dependent on her now for many little services and comforts. His manner when alone with her was conciliatory, almost abject. She had the whip hand of him now. And Charles . . . Charles had deliberately broken the old alliance between them, preferring to her a doll-like chit who gave herself intolerable airs and had refused all her proffers of friendship. She superintended the saddling of her mare Nan, patting and caressing her affectionately, running a keen eye over her gleaming coat.

Maud was very particular about the care of her dogs and horses. The stablemen stood in awe of her. She had been known to dismiss a groom for what was little more than innocent teasing of her animals. Probably the love she gave them was stronger than the love she gave to any human being.

It was a bright morning, crisp and sunny, but with the tang of frost in the air. Maud rode along the country road, fully aware of the handsome figure she made in her well-fitting riding-habit. The young man who had been a pupil at Mr. Swallow's, and who had accompanied her on her rides every day for the last few weeks, had gone home. Some new people called Cornwall had come to Hollow Deep, a house on the road between Mettleham and Abbotford. She had seen one of the sons—a slight girlish-looking youth. She must call on them. . . . Maud, who was herself growing more and more masculine in dress and manner as the years went on, was beginning definitely to prefer effeminate men. Passing Greystones, she slowed Nan's pace and threw a covert glance at the upstairs windows. At one she caught a momentary glance of Mrs. Payne's face—an odd intriguing face with its warm olive sallowness, lustrous eyes, and bright red lips. So that was the room. . . . She saw Charles opening the front door and going up the stairs to that bedroom on the first floor overlooking the garden. With the prying housemaid she peered through the keyhole. . . . Maud's hearty, wholesome-seeming exterior concealed an insatiable curiosity, a secret feverish interest, in all matters of sex.

Reaching Ivy Lodge, she hitched Nan to the gate-post and walked up to the green painted door, rapping on it sharply with the handle of her riding-crop. Hermione herself came to open it, holding Nigel in her arms. She looked tired and pale, but there was still about her that air of untouched youth that Maud resented so bitterly. That she should look like this after bearing seven children. . . .

"Oh, Maud. . . . Come in, will you?" Holding Nigel to her shoulder, she patted his back mechanically as she spoke. He was teething, and had been fretful and in pain for several days. She had been up with him most of the night, and this morning he still could not sleep, but cried desolately whenever she put him down. He seemed to find definite comfort in nozzling his hot little face into her soft, cool neck, whimpering softly every now and then, but not crying outright as he did when she put him down. Her arms were numb with holding him. Once she had managed to soothe him to sleep, but he had awakened with a sharp little cry of pain before she had been able to settle him in his cot. The others at his age had been plump and rosy, but Nigel never seemed to put on weight or get any colour in his wax-like cheeks. He was the only one of the seven whom Hermione had not been able to nurse. She could not find a food to suit him. He seemed to suffer constantly, and there was a suggestion of patient endurance in his subdued whimpering and small, pale face that wrung Hermione's heart.

"Well, how's the infant?" said Maud breezily.

At sight of Maud, Nigel had begun to cry again. Hermione rocked him to and fro soothingly in her aching arms.

"There, there, my sweet, my precious. . . . He's teething, poor little chap. Come into the morning-room, Maud. I've been trying to do some mending, but Baby won't let me put him down."

Maud followed Hermione into the shabby little morning-room. The whole of Ivy Lodge, except the drawing-room, where the children were not allowed, was beginning to look shabby—the carpets worn threadbare by little feet, the surface of the furniture dulled by sticky fingers, scratched and battered in childish romps and fights. Toys lay about the floor of the morning-room. The table was covered with newspaper, and on the newspaper were open boxes of paint, pots of dirty paint water, and several tradesmen's catalogues with half-painted illustrations. The broad window seat was strewn with scraps and scrap-books. Hermione's sewing was outspread on the springless horsehair sofa.

"I'm afraid it's very untidy," apologised Hermione. "The children were here after breakfast. There wasn't room for them in the nursery, and the schoolroom was ready for Miss Lattimer. I said they could leave their things about because they'll be here again this afternoon."

"Let me hold Baby for you a minute," said Maud kindly.

"No, thanks, I think he may drop off in a minute. He's having such a bad time. It seems a shame that a mite like this should have to suffer so much. And he's so good."

Maud glanced at the little face that was half-hidden by the shawl.

"He looks pretty peaky . . ."

A sharp stab of anxiety shot through Hermione's heart.

"He doesn't get on as I'd like," she admitted, "but I'm hoping that once this teething's over . . ."

"I shouldn't worry about him," said Maud in her deep friendly voice.

Hermione looked at the handsome, highly coloured face beneath the hard bowler hat, and wondered why it was that she found it so difficult to respond to Maud's kindness. The old jealousy had long since passed, and yet, despite Maud's unvarying pleasantness, Hermione always felt this unconquerable revulsion from her.

"I try not to . . ." she said.

Maud fastened her handsome dark eyes on Hermione's face and said slowly, but quite casually: "I shouldn't worry over this affair of Charles's either."

Hermione stopped rocking the child and sat very still. Then she said in a small, level voice:

"What affair of Charles's?"

Maud looked at her for some moments in silence before replying:

"This affair of his with Mrs. Payne . . ."

To Hermione it was as if everything around her had turned black. There was a dull roaring in her ears, and her heart was beating wildly. She tightened her hold upon the child, afraid for a moment that she was going to drop him. Then through the black mist came Maud's eyes watching her with an odd gloating triumph in their depth. Hermione lowered the child on to her knee, so that Maud should not see the trembling of her arms, and spoke steadily through white lips:

"I don't know where you heard that rumour, Maud, but you can tell the next person who repeats it to you that it's quite untrue."

Maud rose and took up her riding-crop.

"Oh, well," she said easily, "rumours get about, don't they? In any case I shouldn't worry. Goodbye. I hope the infant gets better."

She went down to the gate, mounted Nan, and cantered off down the road. Her departure was, she knew, an undignified retreat. But, on the whole, she had scored. She went over the interview in imagination, and her lips curved into a scornful smile. Hermione had given herself away completely. The only possible way of dealing with the situation would have been to pretend to know all about the affair and to laugh it off as an infatuation. Childish and ridiculous to say: "You can tell the next person who repeats it to you that it's quite untrue." And she had seen Hermione's face for one moment, at any rate, stripped of its youth. Maud felt, on that account alone, well repaid for her journey.

Hermione sat where Maud had left her, holding the whimpering child on her knee. She was trembling so much that she dared not try to rise to her feet.

For all her ten years of married life she was still extraordinarily unsophisticated and inexperienced. She had realised, of course, that she and Charles had grown apart from each other, but the possibility of his unfaithfulness had never occurred to her. Now her eyes were suddenly opened. Looking back, a hundred little signs told her that Maud's story was true.

So absorbed had she been in the happy nursery life of her home that she had not only lost her love for Charles but had begun to feel him something of an encumbrance. Now quite suddenly she realised that he was the rock on which her happy nursery life was built. Though neither she nor their children felt any conscious need of him, yet he represented something without which the normal life that engrossed her could not continue. She imagined herself deserted by him, and it was like the shifting of the solid earth beneath her feet. And in her emotion was a deeper, more primitive, element. She did not herself analyse the passion that shook her. She was aware only of a blind rage, an unreasoning instinct to fight for the possession of him. He belonged to her. No one should steal him from her. . . .

He had begun to come home after midnight, and she seldom saw him now except at breakfast, but, two days after Maud had spoken to her, he came into the morning-room, where she sat making a party frock of spotted muslin for Vere, and stood on the hearthrug, frowning at the floor. She saw at once that he had something momentous to say to her.

"Hermione," he said slowly, without raising his eyes from the ground, "I want you to know—I'm in love with someone else."

She was staring in front of her.

"I know," she whispered.

"Who told you?"

Even then she could not hurt him by telling him that his sister had brought her the news.

"I heard . . ."

"I want you to divorce me."

She made no answer, only stared in front of her, her face white and expressionless.

He went on as if with an effort.

"If you agree, you'll just have to file the suit, and I won't defend it. The lawyer will see to everything, of course."

She sat forward on the sofa, her hands gripping its edge. Her sewing had slipped to the floor.

"Will you divorce me?" he said.

She answered in a voice that was far away and monotonous, as if she were repeating a lesson:

"No. . . . I can't keep you if you want to leave me, but I won't divorce you."

There was a silence, then he went abruptly from the room.

Neither of them had looked at the other during the interview.

Two definite impressions were left with Hermione—one that something in him had been relieved by her refusal, the other that her rival was determined to secure him at all costs.

Chapter Nine

THEN began the fight. Hermione felt no love for him, no actual hatred of the other woman. She fought as blindly, as instinctively, as she would have fought for her own life, if death were threatening her. Neither of them ever referred to that short interview in the morning-room. Hermione behaved as if it had never taken place, and as if their earlier, pleasanter relationships had returned.

Whenever Charles happened to be at home in the evening, she would sit with her sewing or mending, talking to him with casual friendliness about the children, or the latest village news, listening to him as he told her about his work, or read aloud to her the news of the day—Gladstone's Home Rule Bill, the changes in Egypt, the war between Lobengula and the British South Africa Company.

And all the time she was fighting to keep him. Even when he was away from her, and she was apparently engrossed in her household duties, she was fighting to keep him. She was wholly inexperienced in the tactics and weapons of the battle she had undertaken. She had to trust blindly to intuition. There was nothing but some deeply buried instinct to tell her that, where anger or tearful appeal would have hardened him, this apparent lack of resentment, this gentle, unprotesting acceptance of the situation, touched and bewildered him. The memory of her quiet voice, her golden head bent over some tiny garment, followed him when he went to Mrs. Payne's and persisted with him throughout his visit, poisoning the ecstasy of her voluptuous love-making. Hermione did not know this. She was like someone groping in the dark, with no idea whether her groping led her to the light or away from it. One morning she met Mrs. Payne face to face in the village. She had, of course, always been prepared for this, though Mrs. Payne now rarely left her garden. She had decided to show no emotion, but at the sight of the warm, olive skin and the curving, scarlet mouth, a mist rushed again before her eyes, and her knees felt suddenly unsteady. She mastered herself quickly, smiled, said "Good morning", then passed on her way.

"Your wife can't know, Charles," Linda Payne said that night to her lover. "I met her in the village this morning, and she was quite pleasant."

At the thought of their meeting, a hot wave of anger surged over him. He felt as if he had deliberately exposed Hermione to insult.

"Charles . . . about the divorce . . ." went on Mrs. Payne.

"That's settled once and for all," he said curtly. "I've asked her, and she's refused. I'm not going to ask her again."

A month later Mrs. Payne shut her house and went on a visit to friends in India. Hermione had realised that the affair was at an end before that. Charles had begun to spend his evenings at home. His manner was sheepish, defiant, and wary, as if he were ready to respond at once to her kindness or to fly out in anger if she reproached him.

The battle was over and Hermione had won. There was no exultation, no happiness even, in her heart. That panic terror that had been with her since Maud had so casually told her news disappeared, and with its going she became conscious of other emotions, emotions that she would have felt at the beginning if terror had not held her so completely in its grip, if the battle had not been so desperate and so urgent. She became conscious of a humiliation that seemed to scorch and sear her whole body, of a bitter, angry resentment against her husband. He had put another woman in her place. He had made her lower her pride to plead with him—not in words, but her whole attitude had been a suppliant's. He had degraded her and besmirched her so that never again could she feel as she had felt before this happened. Now that he had given her back his whole allegiance, she felt a shrinking from him that she could not conquer. He had belonged to another woman. He was not her husband any longer. She knew that her attitude was ungenerous, and she struggled gallantly to hide her feelings from him. She never blamed him for his unfaithfulness. She was pleasant and accommodating, ready to do whatever he wished, showing interest in everything he told her of his day's doings. She tried her utmost to be kind to him, but he was continually aware of her secret hostility, and felt her to be immeasurably removed from him. She spoke and smiled at him unnaturally as if from an infinite distance. She made no protest against his embraces, but he felt her slender body stiffen through its every nerve when he approached her. He saw her grow taut even when he entered a room where she was, saw her relax as he left it. The smile with which she greeted him was set and forced. . . .

He had a slight cough, and after a week or so she asked him with some embarrassment if he would sleep in his dressing-room, as his cough disturbed Nigel, whose cot still stood next their bed. His cough disappeared, and she did not ask him to return to her. She knew that she was now in the wrong, but what had been to her a sacrament had become a degradation, and her fastidiousness revolted from it. She had not thought much about Mrs. Payne while Charles was actually her lover—the fear of losing Charles had entirely obsessed her—but now whenever he came near her she saw that warm, downy, olive skin and the scarlet mouth. . . . He accepted the situation, becoming still more bad-tempered and morose, snapping at the children whenever he came across them, grumbling at her housekeeping, responding ungraciously to the superficial kindness with which she tried to quiet the pangs of her conscience. On the surface their daily relations were pretty much as they had been before Charles's affair with Mrs. Payne, but beneath the surface there was a new tension, a secret, daily widening of the gulf between them.

Charles began to avoid his home, but there was no question of his taking another mistress. He was not a sensual man, and Linda Payne's voluptuousness had sickened him long before the end of his affair with her. His love for Hermione went down to the very roots of his being, and he now accepted with more resignation than joy the fact that it would last as long as his life lasted. He began to meet his bachelor friends again and come home very late and not quite sober.

Christmas was drawing near—a Christmas on which the whole energy of nursery and schoolroom was concentrated. John was going away to school in January, and it seemed somehow especially important that this last Christmas before John went away should surpass every other Christmas of their memory. The Christmas Tree was to be dressed by Charles and Hermione on Christmas Eve. The young parents always kept up impeccable relationships before the children, never betraying the slightest hint of disagreement or irritation with each other, deferring all argument till they were alone.

The elder children had provided the ornaments for the Christmas Tree. For days the schoolroom table had been covered with crinkly paper of every shade, and even Miss Lattimer had been induced to help with the making of the paper roses and daffodils and sunflowers that were to adorn the tree.

They had all been into Fernham with Hermione to buy presents for each other. ("I'm going into this shop. None of you must come but Mummy. You must all wait out here for us. Promise on your word of honour that you'll stand with your backs to the door and not look in to see what I'm buying.")

The Christmas Tree had been set up in the morning-room. The balls, paper flowers, and candles were ready in a box on the table. The children held little piles of presents, wrapped in white paper, tied with coloured ribbon, the names neatly written on each. Charles was to fix up the decorations, then tie on the parcels one by one as they were handed to him. Then the room was to be locked up till the next day.

The children clustered at the window, watching eagerly for Charles, guarding zealously their little armfuls of parcels. Their heads were close together, all fair but those of John and Monica, who were dark like Charles. Monica and Alan knelt side by side on the window seat, while Jimmie with three-year-old persistence tried to battle his way between them to the front. Vere, as usual, looked hurt because no one seemed to want her. Hermione, holding

Gillian in her arms, joined the group at the window, so that she could draw Vere to her with her free hand—very carelessly because Vere could not bear anyone to notice when she felt left out of things.

"Here he is!" shouted Alan excitedly. "He's come in a cab."

A cab had drawn up at the gate. A man whom Hermione did not know was getting down from it. He spoke to the cabman, then a second stranger descended.

"Where's daddy?" wailed Jimmie. "Those aren't daddy."

A limp form was being lifted out of the cab and half-carried, half-supported up the walk. There was a sudden tense silence. The children's faces were masks of terrified amazement. Alan burst into tears.

"He's dead," he sobbed. "He's been run over. . . .

Hermione, still with Gillian in her arms, went out into the hall. At first she, too, thought that he had had an accident, but the sheepish faces of the men who supported him soon told her that he was drunk. She stood watching them as they carried him across the hall. The frightened children peeped from behind her billowing silk skirts.

"His room's the first door on the left at the top of the stairs," she said clearly. "I'll come up directly."

She drew the children back into the room, setting Gillian down upon her plump unsteady legs. Alan was still crying, and Jimmie had begun to cry as well.

"Don't be frightened," she said to the children. "Father's not well, but he'll be all right soon. I'll just go up and see to him."

She went upstairs, dismissed the men curtly, and put Charles to bed. He had fallen into a heavy stupor, and it was not easy to undress him, but she did not wish to call for help. Then she went down to the children.

Nurse was comforting them as best she could, but Nigel had set up his thin, plaintive wail, and Alan and Jimmie were sobbing noisily. Only Gillian, sitting under the table and tearing up a red paper rose with crows of delight, was unaffected by the atmosphere.

"It's all right," said Hermione cheerfully. "Father must stay in bed for this evening, but he'll be all right in the morning. There's nothing to worry about."

John looked at her, solemn, anxious. "Shall I go for the doctor, mother?"

"No, darling, there's no need for that. He's not really ill, you see. He's—he's just fainted."

But John, the eldest of the family, felt responsible and uneasy.

"Wouldn't it be better to send for the doctor, mother? He might have fainted because he was ill, mightn't he?"

"No, darling, it's all right. . . . Alan, I'm ashamed of you! A great boy of six crying like that! And Jimmie, you little silly-billy! Stop it at once."

She caught up Jimmie, tickling and kissing him till his sobs turned to chuckles.

"Now, come along," she said gaily, "let's get on with the tree. I'll put on the things, as father's not well."

But her gaiety was unconvincing, the atmosphere was spoilt, and the whole evening was a failure. They were all a little relieved when bedtime came.

And Christmas Day was worse. Hermione worked hard to make it successful. Charles, pale and desperately ashamed, seconded her, but from the beginning it fell flat. There was an unaccountable air of depression over everything, against which Hermione struggled in vain. The children sensed something in the situation that they could not understand. Alan, the most highly strung of them all, and as sensitive as a barometer to the domestic atmosphere, wept at frequent intervals throughout the day. Monica, an impulsive little alarmist, spread a report that father had heart disease and might die any moment, and that was why he looked so funny, and mother was only pretending to be jolly. . . . Hermione's nerves were worn to shreds by the effort of trying to dispel the all-enveloping gloom, and she was glad when the end of the day came and life could resume its normal course.

But, of course, life could not resume its normal course. Charles, drunk as he was, had been sober enough to see the group of frightened children staring at him from behind Hermione's skirts.

His shame and abasement at the memory was so acute that in the days that followed he dared hardly look at them. Hermione he avoided altogether. He began to bring home work from the office and do it in the evenings at the desk in his dressing-room, so that he should not have to sit with her in the drawing-room. His shame was so evident that somehow Hermione felt ashamed, too, and avoided him as much as he avoided her. Rather to her surprise, she felt no anger at what had happened, but it had widened yet further the gulf between them. When they were alone together, each of them felt only a desperate desire to escape. . . .

The date of John's going to school was growing nearer, and Hermione was busy with his outfit. It was a momentous occasion to the brothers and sisters. Parting gifts were presented to him, and the day before his departure a grand nursery tea was held in his honour, at which they drank his health in milk out of their christening mugs.

Hermione lay awake in bed the night after he had gone, yearning over him in her heart. He had looked so small and defenceless and plucky when he set off with Charles. Her thoughts went back to the day when she had first known that she was to be his mother. She remembered Charles's tenderness, his gentle protective care of her. Pictures came back to her . . . Charles kneeling on the floor to take off her boots for her . . . Charles carrying her upstairs and undressing her when she was tired . . . John's birth . . . Charles by her bedside, kissing her hand and leaving his tears on it . . . John's face, red and tiny, on its little white pillow. . . . And now they had sent him away from them. . . . She saw him, bewildered and frightened, among strangers—strangers who would perhaps torment him for the sheer fun of tormenting a homesick little boy . . . saw him desolate, abandoned by her, bereft of her love and comfort for the first time in his short life. Her first-born. Hers and Charles's. . . .

She got out of bed and opened the door between her room and Charles's dressing-room.

"Charles."

She heard the bed creaking as he sat up.

"Yes?"

She went across to him.

"Charles. . . . Are you sure they'll be kind to him? He's so little. . . ."

He forgot everything in the world but her need of his comfort. He stretched out a hand through the darkness and found hers.

"Of course, my dear. . . . You mustn't worry."

"Charles . . ."

She stopped. He could hear her teeth chattering. He threw back his bedclothes.

"You're cold. . . . Get in here."

She got in with him obediently, then suddenly clung to him sobbing. His arms closed round her.

"Forgive me, Hermione," he said hoarsely.

"I've been hateful," she said, through her sobs. "I haven't meant to be. Somehow I couldn't help it. Oh, let's forget it, Charles. . . ."

They lay strained in each other's arms, his lips against hers. Everything that had separated them faded away once more as if it had never been.

Chapter Ten

THE elder children had now left the nursery, and in contact with the grown-up world around them were showing decided and often conflicting personalities. It was no longer merely a question of keeping them well clad, well fed, well exercised, and in good health. The nursery lore that Hermione had so laboriously acquired ceased to be of primary importance, and she felt herself again to be groping her way blindfold in a strange land.

She needed her husband's advice and support, and Charles began to take his rightful place in the family. He had become much graver and more responsible since that Christmas Eve when his friends had brought him home drunk. Hermione knew that even after their reconciliation the memory of it was intolerable to him.

Brought face to face with a growing high-spirited family, he was at first inclined to take up the attitude of a stern and autocratic parent as involving the least trouble to himself and being in accord with the fashion of the time. Vere became unyieldingly stubborn in the face of any attempt at compulsion, and Charles soon clashed with her.

The domestic atmosphere was generally most strained on Sundays. All of them except Gillian and Nigel went to church in the morning and stayed for the whole service, which included Litany and a twenty minutes' sermon. The result was that they were tired and on edge, and inclined to be troublesome for the rest of the day. One Sunday Vere refused to eat her rice pudding at dinner, and Charles, who was also feeling tired by the long service, said angrily:

"You'll sit there till you've eaten it, then, and you'll have nothing else till you have eaten it."

Hermione glanced from one to the other, but said nothing till she and Charles had gone to the drawing-room and the other children to the schoolroom, leaving Vere alone in the dining-room, staring obstinately at her plate of rice pudding.

"It's no use, you know, Charles," said Hermione. "You can't force her to do anything she doesn't want to. We tried to do that in the nursery, and it wasn't any good. You can't sit and watch her starve."

Charles's face, set in lines of stubbornness, looked curiously like Vere's.

"They must be made to do as they're told," he said shortly.

Her eyes laughed at him.

"But, Charles, they're *people*, real people, not little puppets with strings that you make do just what you want. You see"—frowning, she searched for words—"the idea of *making* them do things is so futile. Only stupid people try to do it. Don't you see if you've made a child do something it doesn't want to, you're just where you were before? It still doesn't *want* to do it. You're worse off really than you were before, because you've hurt and angered it as well. If you can't make it *want* to do the thing you want it to do, you'd far better leave italone. You see—it should be a question of mind influencing mind, not body forcing body. If a child does something just because it knows that you'll hurt it physically if it doesn't—well, it's not even a sporting fight. Any grown-up fool can hurt a child. It's futile and despicable. If that's the only hold people have over their children, I suppose they're justified in using it, but it's a confession of weakness."

His mouth was still set obstinately.

"My father would have horsewhipped me if I'd refused to eat something he told me to eat."

Her eyes grew tender.

"Poor little Charles!"

"Even Maud came in for it sometimes. . . . As for refusing to eat . . .!"

She laughed.

"I wouldn't eat rice pudding if I didn't want it, and neither would you. Why should you expect Vere to do something you wouldn't do yourself?"

He went slowly back to the dining-room, where Vere still sat, white-faced and stubborn, before her plate of rice pudding.

"You needn't eat it if you don't want to, Vere," he said. "You can run away to the others."

She shot him an odd glance, humble, grateful, and slid off her seat without speaking.

For the rest of the day she hovered about him shyly, fetching him his pipe, his book, his slippers, almost before he realised he wanted them.

"I can't make it out," he said to Hermione. "She's got the better of me, thanks to you. I should have thought that she'd have been crowing over me like blazes."

"Why should she?" said Hermione. "She'd have fought as long as she'd breath in her little body to fight with, but she was dreading the fight. She's grateful to you for calling it off."

"Well, it's all beyond me," he said; "it's not the way I was brought up."

The children adored Hermione. They pretended to be her pages and vied with each other in running errands for her. When sent for her work-box or a book, they would bring it ceremoniously upon a cushion and present it on bended knee. Every morning she found a posy freshly gathered from the garden and put by her plate at the breakfast table. The elder ones had each a special day for getting it and zealously guarded their turns.

They missed John very much when he went to school. He had been so trustworthy and good-tempered, taking so seriously his position of responsibility as the eldest of the family. Monica, left at the head of the little band, was well-meaning but less reliable. She was a round pudding of a little girl, generous, passionate, and impulsive. When she and Vere quarrelled, as they frequently did, Vere could taunt her into such uncontrolled rages that she would scratch and bite like a small wild animal. Afterwards she would be overcome by a penitence as passionate as her rage and would inflict extravagant punishments on herself or empty her money-box to buy a peace offering for Vere.

Vere was sensitive, but so proud and reserved that she hid every sign of her sensitiveness from those around her, making herself seem hard and unresponsive. She had an unchildlike power of self-control that made her very difficult to deal with.

She seemed to stand alone against her little world, between the nursery and the schoolroom, scorning the companionship of Jimmie and Gillian, rigorously excluded by snubs or physical violence from the activities of the elder ones.

There were days, of course, when nothing happened to disturb her serenity, days when she was happy and placid and sweet-tempered. At such times Hermione found her very helpful. She was quicker, defter, more capable than any of the others. Unlike Monica, she never forgot errands and always brought back the right change, while she could set a table or dust a room as well as Hermione herself. She had unusually clever fingers and loved to make things in laborious detail—fashioning once an entire village from cardboard boxes, arranging gardens in front of the houses, with pieces of looking-glass for ponds, moss for lawns, little hedges and flower gardens and fences and microscopic garments hanging out on tiny washing lines. The joy lay in the actual making. She lacked the imagination to play any games with what she had made—unlike Alan, who was independent of his clumsy fingers because his imagination could fashion for him whatever he needed.

Charles liked his boys to be "manly", and Alan from the first was a disappointment to him. Alan was even more sensitive than Vere, but without her fierce pride and power of self-control. He wept openly at an unkind word or look. He would burst into tears on hearing an emotional piece of music. When certain hymns were given out ("Abide with Me" in particular), Hermione would resign herself to leading a sobbing little boy out of church. He was ashamed of his tears, but seemed to have no power to check them. He always preferred to play by himself rather than with the others, and had a host of imaginary companions who were more real to him than the people around him. Though he and Monica had little in common, something in his helplessness appealed to Monica's impulsive generosity, and she had constituted herself his friend and protector. Vere, in the frequent quarrels between her and Monica, had found that she could hurt Monica most effectively by hurting Alan. Miss Lattimer was his other champion, but her praise of the boy's intelligence only made him seem more unnatural to Charles, who would almost have preferred him to shirk his lessons in the normal manner of childhood. Charles felt hotly ashamed whenever he saw the boy in tears, and his undeniable physical cowardice was a constant humiliation to him.

Jimmie came nearest to Charles's ideal of "manliness". Like John he was straightforward and courageous, but he had also an elusive charm, a touch of irresponsible gaiety, that John lacked.

It was Gillian who, growing from babyhood to little girlhood, was Charles's favourite. He had felt no interest in the others when they were her age, but Gillian could do what she liked with him. Charles was her slave. He always went up into the nursery to see her before setting off for his work in the morning, and was disappointed if she had gone to bed before he came home in the evening. He carried a miniature of her about with him in his pocket, and at week-ends would patiently play with her for hours on the nursery floor. She was easy to play with, responding with ready delight to his attempts to amuse her, entering zestfully into all the games he invented for her. The others stood in awe of him, but Gillian had never feared him, and her love was a secret joy and gratification to him.

Nigel was battling his way through his sickly babyhood. He was seldom quite well and still suffered a good deal of pain. Charles was always tender and patient with him, as if to hide from himself his lack of affection for the child. Nigel's sickliness made him somehow seem not normal, and Charles shrank from anything that was not normal. He felt, too, vaguely ashamed, as if a weakly child were a reflection on his own virility. He was happier when both Nigel and Alan were out of his sight. Hermione, on the other hand, loved Nigel, her weakling, more than any of the others.

When he was a year old she took him to London to a Children's

Specialist, who examined him thoroughly, then said that there was nothing organically wrong with him, only a general delicacy that would possibly disappear as he grew older.

Soon after the visit to the specialist, Nurse's mother died, and she had to go home to look after her father. About the same time the exemplary cook left to be married and the housemaid to "better" herself, and there followed a stream of inefficient servants who turned Hermione's life into a kind of waking nightmare. She was too trusting to be a successful mistress, and she had a reputation in the village of "spoiling" her servants.

Nurse was, of course, the hardest to replace. Hermione could not hope to find anyone else with Nurse's calm efficiency, her placid imperturbability. In the end she engaged a woman who had been a hospital nurse and had found the work too strenuous. She ran the nursery on hospital lines, its details so highly organised, its appearance so clean and bare—no curtains, no carpets, no unnecessary furniture—that Hermione often longed for the old warm, cosy, hugger-mugger days. Still, Jimmie was almost beyond the nursery stage now, and Gillian, the family favourite, was so welcome both in the schoolroom and downstairs that she seemed to have escaped the nursery before she left her babyhood behind. And Nigel grew stronger and less fretful under the hospital-like régime.

The years brought their sudden terrors and heart-racking anxieties. Pictures remained branded for ever on Hermione's mind. . . . John staggering into the house, his face blackened and bleeding from a firework explosion. . . . Monica's limp form carried through the gate by two men (she had been knocked down by a horse and was stunned, but not seriously hurt). . . . Jimmie falling through the air from the breaking branch of a tree. . . . Vere limping home with a torn stocking and bleeding leg ("A dog's bitten me, mother").

The usual nursery epidemics swept them down, and the house would be turned into a hospital, with carbolic sheets and temperature charts everywhere, while they succumbed in turn to measles, chicken-pox, scarlet fever, and whooping-cough.

"Put them all together," Dr. Bannister would say. "They may as well all get it over at once."

Chapter Eleven

CHARLES rose from the breakfast table with a glance at the clock.

"Well . . . time I went, I suppose. . . ."

Immediately there was a scramble among the children, and each flew to his or her self-appointed post for the ceremony of seeing him off to work.

John, now a big boy of fourteen, home for the holidays, ran across the village green to the little shop for his morning paper; Monica got down his coat, Jimmie his hat, Vere his umbrella or walking-stick, according to the weather, Gillian a buttonhole from the garden. Alan hovered in the background with his gloves, feeling always a thrill of pride when Charles took them out of his hand. Alan was aware of Charles's impatient contempt, and, so far from resenting it, showed a humble, doglike devotion to him, looking upon him as the ideal of manhood in courage, strength, and intelligence. When in a good temper Charles would let Monica, standing on one hall chair, help him on with his coat, while Jimmie, perched upon another, put his hat on for him. When in a bad temper he cut the ceremony short impatiently. But on the whole he was flattered by this daily ritual. It made him feel vaguely important and satisfied the secret hunger for affection of which he was not even himself aware. When he was ready, Gillian walked with him to the point where he took the short cut across the fields to the station. She had done this ever since she could toddle, and no one ever disputed her right to it. She was seven years old now—still exquisitely lovely, still adored by the entire household, still unspoilt. Her sunny temper and perfect health made Hermione feel somehow detached from her. Her heart had never yearned over

Gillian in tender anxiety as it had yearned over the others. Gillian loved her, but had never needed her as the others had needed her. She seemed to be more Charles's child than Hermione's.

Hermione went into the hall where the children were still getting Charles ready. He was in a good temper this morning and was prolonging the ceremony, pretending not to be able to find the sleeves of the coat that Monica held out for him, moving his head suddenly so that the hat Jimmie was trying to put on to it fell to the floor. His clowning was very successful, and shrieks of laughter arose from the little group. At last he was ready. He kissed Hermione, waved to the children, and set off down the path, holding Gillian's hand. Hermione went back to the dining-room. The children hung over the gate, still calling "Good-bye, daddy."

From the dining-room window Hermione watched him walk down the road with Gillian. Even in the distance he was beginning to look middle-aged. He was growing stouter and stooped a little. He seemed older than his forty years warranted. She knew that he found it increasingly difficult to work with his father. The old man, of course, should have retired long ago, and Hermione suspected that the only reason why he had not retired was that he could not bear to hand over the reins to Charles. He was losing his memory and his judgment, and it took all Charles's time and energy to rectify his mistakes, but he still had not made Charles a partner, and he still seemed to find a delight in humiliating him. Hermione hated the old man so much that she now refused all Maud's—not very pressing—invitations to Mettleham Hall.

The children—except Gillian—had come back from the gate and were clattering into the house again, stampeding upstairs to the schoolroom—used as a play-room in the holidays—scuffling and shouting. She took up the letter from her mother that lay by her plate and glanced through it again. It was full of the facile expressions of affection that her mother used as naturally as breathing. Reading it, one would think that she was longing passionately to see Hermione and the children again. Hermione, however, had learnt to take such protestations at their real value. Her mother was entirely engrossed in her small social circle at Little Barnwell, with its whist drives and parties and "competition teas". She found children a trouble and inconvenience and had long since ceased asking any of the little Derehams to visit her or accepting Hermione's invitations to Ivy Lodge.

Hermione put the letter into its envelope with a rather twisted smile. There had been many occasions in her married life when she would have been glad to turn to her mother for help, but Mrs. Pennistone's genius for refusing to recognise any claim that could interfere with her comfort had served her well as a defence against such demands.

She forced her thoughts to face the day that lay ahead of her. She was without cook and must cook the dinner as well as help with the children and the housework. She felt unduly tired, and her head ached slightly. She had had a bad cough in the spring, which left her so weak that the doctor had said that she must go away for a change. She knew that it was useless to ask her mother to have her, so she had written to ask Helen if she might go down to St. Hilda's for a week. She had been wondering whether to send Monica to St. Hilda's now that she was getting too old for Miss Lattimer, and she was anxious to view the school through the eyes of what Helen always referred to as a "prospective parent". Helen had replied at once giving her a cordial invitation to St. Hilda's.

Hermione had seen very little of her elder sister since her marriage, and she felt again the familiar awe of her when they met, though she became aware almost at once that Helen had changed in some subtle, indefinable way. The impression she had given in the old days of a crusader in shining armour was there no longer, and in its place was something complacent, something—it was a dreadful word to apply to Helen's regal loveliness, but it occurred to Hermione and would not be dismissed—smug. Helen had striven hard to make St. Hilda's one of the foremost of the private schools of England, and she had succeeded—succeeded so well that there was nothing further to strive for, so she was striving no more. Hers was a personal as well as a scholastic success. The atmosphere of the place was one of feverish adoration. Her classic beauty was at its height, and she used now, in her dealings with people, a deliberate charm of manner that once she would have scorned as a weapon unworthy of her. It seemed to Hermione that she had unconsciously begun to look upon this adoration of herself as the aim of her school's existence. She had become, as it were, a priestess at her own shrine. The school held an excellent place in the educational world, but Hermione could not help feeling that this hothouse atmosphere of Helen-worship was like a canker at the heart of it. Helen was very kind to her, the standard of comfort in the school was so high that it was in some ways like a luxurious hotel, and the rest and change of air took away the last remnants of Hermione's cough, but she decided not to send Monica to St. Hilda's, though Helen offered to take her for a nominal fee.

She went slowly upstairs to the nursery. She felt depressed as well as tired. Yesterday had been nurse's afternoon out, and Hermione had had to look after the children as well as cook the dinner. When she was tired and overworked, she always felt an odd, nagging sense of resentment against Charles, as if somehow he were responsible for it all. He had come home from work and had sat reading his paper without offering to help her, while she tried to get the children to bed and cook the dinner at the same time. She knew that he would have helped her if she had asked him, but she did not ask him; something in her did not even want him to help her, because his not helping her was fuel to the sustaining fire of resentment against him that burnt so fiercely at her heart.

After dinner he had talked about the Employers' Liability Act that had just passed through the House of Lords, inveighing against it as a piece of tyranny, and going on to condemn unreservedly both free education and the Old Age Pension Scheme. As she listened to him her irritation had risen to fever pitch. Charles was, she knew, a good husband. The sowing of his wild oats—a mild enough proceeding on the whole—belonged completely to the past. He had never taken too much to drink since that fateful Christmas Eve. He had never been unfaithful to her since his affair with Mrs. Payne. She had come to depend upon him, turning to him continually for help and advice. She knew that, though often thoughtlessly inconsiderate, he would readily have given his life for her or for any of their children. But he was a man of set ideas and preconceived notions. His mind was inelastic and firmly closed to novelty of any sort. With him a "discussion" took the form of dogmatic pronouncements to which he obstinately adhered in the face of all argument. Moreover, his unspoken standpoint that because she was a woman her opinion on anything beyond her nursery and kitchen was unworthy of consideration, had infuriated her, and she had gone to bed feeling out of patience not only with Charles but with her whole life. The old sensation of having been trapped had swept over her again, and she had longed to be free, unhampered by home and children and husband. Then in the night Nigel had had one of his attacks of pain and sickness, and an intolerable sense of guilt had seized her as if her mood of discontent were the cause of it. This morning her remorseful love for Charles and the children lay like a weight at her heart.

In the nursery Nigel stood on a chair while Nurse fastened up his blue reefer coat with its brass buttons and put his sailor cap on his head. There was upon his pale face that eager smile that it always wore when the pain and discomfort of his attacks of illness had passed and he felt comparatively well again.

"Better, darling?" said Hermione, kissing him.

He smiled radiantly at her.

"*Quite* well, mummy," he said.

Gillian and Jimmie stood by him, dressed also in blue reefer coats with brass buttons, sailor caps perched jauntily on their curls. Jimmie, who was now eight, was beginning to resent having to take part in the nursery's morning walk while the elder children stayed at home to play in the garden. He looked as if he were planning some mischief, his blue eyes twinkling, a merry, impudent smile on his lips.

"You won't be naughty, will you, darling?" said Hermione.

"Not *very* naughty, mummy," he promised.

"You're such a big boy," she said, "that I like you to go with Nurse, because you can carry things for her and help her with the others."

She saw them off at the gate, then turned to see Vere coming down the path in her hat and coat.

"Where are you going, dear?"

"To Greystones," said Vere shortly. "I'm going to take Mrs. Howe's baby out for her."

It seemed to Hermione that Greystones had a persistent animosity towards her. Mrs. Payne had stolen Charles from her. Now Mrs. Howe was stealing Vere. Mrs. Howe had arrived in Abbotford a few months ago—lovely, newly widowed, with a fourteen-months-old baby. Hermione did not care for her much—she seemed so determined to extract every atom of effect from her position—but Vere, the reserved and aloof, conceived for her a schoolgirl adoration at the moment of first meeting. She hung about Greystones continually, trying to catch a glimpse of the young widow. Her greatest joy was to perform some service for her. And it turned out that there were plenty of services to perform. Mrs. Howe had only a general servant, and a willing, adoring little girl of eleven could be very useful in the house. Hermione pretended to treat this infatuation lightly, but she felt secretly chagrined that Vere should give to this second-rate stranger a love that she denied herself. Moreover, it infuriated her that the woman should use Vere as a household drudge, making her wash dishes, peel potatoes, and carry her heavy baby about. But as long as Vere gloried in her slavery, was raised to heaven by the blonde beauty's smiles and caresses, there was little that she could do. Open opposition was always useless with Vere.

"May I stay to dinner if she asks me, mummy?" called Vere.

"Not to dinner, darling. You can stay till dinner time and go back afterwards if she wants you to."

Hermione smiled wryly to herself as she watched the little figure set off at a run toward Greystones. Vere could have been very useful to her at home, now that she was without cook. . . .

She brought down a pile of mending to the verandah and sat in the sunshine with it. Endless buttons and tapes to be stitched on . . . patches . . . darns . . . Jimmie's stockings were dreadful—knees and heels right out. . . . She went into the kitchen to prepare the dinner, then, having put it into the oven, returned to her mending, still wearing her apron. . . . She heard the clop-clop of horses' hooves on the road, and soon Maud appeared in her riding-habit, one gauntleted hand holding up her skirt, the other holding her riding-crop. She looked very handsome and trim and well-groomed, and Hermione, feeling suddenly tired again, wished that Maud had not caught her like this, wearing a soiled apron, her hair coming down, her face scorched with cooking. The passing years made little difference to Maud. With her high colour and regular features, she looked as young now as she had looked five years ago. Except in the evening one seldom saw her out of her riding-habit.

"I rode over with Bobby Cornwall," she announced in her deep voice. "He has to see old Swallow about some work. He's going to call for me when he's finished."

Bobby was the youngest of the Cornwall boys. He had been a schoolboy when first they had come to the neighbourhood. He had, in fact, only left school last term, and was at present extremely mattered by Maud's notice.

Hermione moved her work-basket and a torn petticoat of Gillian's from a chair so that Maud could sit down. She was still always making good resolutions to like Maud. She could keep them fairly well as long as she did not meet her, but as soon as they were together the old antagonism seemed to spring to life at once.

"Well, how are things going?" said Maud, laying her riding-crop on the table. Hermione moved a strand of hair from across her eyes.

"Oh . . . fairly. The housemaid's *hopeless*, and we're without cook again."

"Good gracious! Why?"

"She said there was too much work and went off in a temper last week. She wasn't any good, anyway. I'm trying to get another."

"We can always keep cooks at the Hall."

"You haven't seven children at the Hall."

"Well, naturally not. . . . Children all right, by the way?"

"Yes. . . ."

"How old is Alan? Isn't it time he went to school?"

"He's nearly twelve. I don't think he's going. Dr. Bannister says he oughtn't to."

"That old granny!"

"He says that any doctor would agree with him. He's too highly strung."

"Highly strung! School's just what he needs. He wants the nonsense knocked out of him. Charles says he gets worse and worse."

Hermione's face, bent over Jimmie's stocking, flushed faintly. It always seemed to her disloyal of Charles to criticise their children to Maud. She said nothing. Maud went on: "You've spoilt him, you know, Hermione. You've made him a namby-pamby baby."

"I've let Charles try his methods," said Hermione. "I let him thrash him for telling a lie, and Alan was so sick after it that we had to send for the doctor. He was in bed two days with a temperature. Even Charles hasn't wanted to try it again."

"Lying seems to be a favourite trick of his," said Maud, with her short, hard laugh.

"He's frightened of Charles, and he always lies when he's frightened. He can't help it. Dr. Bannister says that it would ruin his nerves to send him to school."

"What does Charles say to that?"

"Charles can't help seeing that it's true. He's not exactly pleased about it, of course."

"I should think not. . . . So you're going to keep him at home?"

"Mr. Swallow seems interested in him. He says he'll coach him."

"Does he still read all the time and moon about by himself?"

Hermione laid aside a pair of Jimmie's stockings and held up Gillian's pinafore, considering it meditatively.

"It's too small for her—she's growing so fast just now—but I might as well mend it. It will do for Nigel to wear in the nursery. Poor Nigel! He's never had a new pinafore in his life. . . . Maud, I do wish you would get your father to retire."

"Why?"

"He's *hopeless* at the office. He makes life unbearable for Charles."

Maud laughed.

"So you want him to retire so that he can live at home and make life unbearable for me."

"He wouldn't. He's never been as bad to you as he's been to Charles. You know he hasn't."

"Oh, I know how to manage father," said Maud, smiling to herself. "If he annoys me he finds his Benger's half cold and his room draughty and things generally uncomfortable. Also, I'm not there when he wants me to read the paper to him, or all his things get lost and no one can find them. He minds his p's and q's with me nowadays. I suppose he's got to take it out of someone, so he takes it out of Charles."

"Charles says he's ruining the business."

"Even I, my dear Hermione, can hardly force father to give up his work if he doesn't want to."

"I suppose not. . . ."

Hermione caught a movement in the copper beech that was Jimmie's particular stronghold. She could imagine his merry, mischievous little face peering at her and Maud through the branches.

At that moment Nurse appeared with Gillian and Nigel.

"I don't know where Master Jimmie is," she said breathlessly. "He was with us till just a minute ago, then he disappeared. I can't think what's happened. Shall I go back and look for him?"

In spite of her hospital training, or perhaps because of it, the woman got ridiculously flustered when anything went wrong. She was a constant temptation to Jimmie, who was always brimming over with mischief.

"No, it's all right, Nurse," said Hermione. "He's come home. He's in his tree. Come down, Jimmie. I know where you are."

He dropped from branch to branch with an agility that made Hermione's heart stand still, then, leaping across the lawn, flung his arms around her. She felt his hot, firm little body pressed against hers, heard the strong beating of his heart, smelt the fragrant baby smell that still lingered about him. Then he released her, laughing.

"Oh, Jimmie," she smiled, "how you take away one's breath!

Say 'How-do-you-do' to Auntie Maud, then go and get tidy for dinner."

He greeted Maud dutifully, did a hand-spring (John had just taught him how to do hand-springs, and he was very proud of the accomplishment), then went indoors, jumping like a kangaroo, keeping his feet together. Jimmie was full of happy, eager, exuberant life, and his mischief was innocent of ill intent. He was becoming too much for Nurse and Miss Lattimer, however, and Hermione and Charles had almost decided to send him to school next year. He would be younger than John had been when John went to school, but he adored John and was longing to go with him to Moorcroft. Charles, too, was anxious for him to go to school. He had a vague, unformulated idea that his going to school early would compensate in some way for the disgrace of Alan's unfitness for school life.

Hermione rose and laid down her sewing on the table.

"Just excuse me a minute, Maud. I've got to put on the vegetables. I won't be a minute. They're ready prepared."

She hoped that Maud would take the hint and go, but Maud stayed on, leaning back in her chair, tapping her trim, gleaming riding-boots with her crop.

"I suppose that Vere's with Mrs. Howe," she said when Hermione rejoined her.

"I suppose so," said Hermione shortly, taking up her sewing. She had removed her apron and tidied her hair indoors.

"I hear that the woman's practically adopted her."

"What nonsense!" said Hermione sharply.

"Well, I've heard that she calls Vere her little girl, and that Vere calls her 'Mother'."

Hermione flushed hotly, and a sharp stab of jealousy shot through her heart. She had not known that. . . .

"There's no particular reason why she shouldn't, is there?" she said casually.

Maud shrugged.

"Oh, as long as you don't mind. . . . Here is the child."

Vere was coming slowly up the garden path from the side gate, her hat hanging down her back by its elastic. She stiffened when she saw Maud. None of the children were fond of Maud, but only Vere actively disliked her.

"Well," said Maud as she came up to them, "been with your beloved Mrs. Howe?"

Vere gave her a hard, defiant stare.

"Oh no," she said. "I've been for a nice brisk walk into Fernham and back."

"Eight miles?"

"I'm a very good walker."

Hermione looked at them helplessly. It was absurd to attack Vere in that obvious fashion and not to expect to get back as good as you gave. In any case, Vere always lied blatantly and deliberately when you questioned her about what she considered to be her private affairs.

"Another little liar!" said Maud pleasantly. "It seems to run in the family."

At that moment Monica and Alan came up the garden path. Alan's face was swollen with weeping, Monica's flushed and indignant.

"Mother," said Monica, "Alan saw a man kicking a dog, and it's upset him so dreadfully, and——"

Vere turned her defiant stare on to them. Mrs. Howe had dismissed her on the arrival of a friend from town, dismissed her curtly and without even thanking her for taking out the baby and washing up. She had returned home to be attacked at once by Auntie Maud, whom she hated, and now came the sight of Monica and Alan united in an alliance from which she was rigorously excluded.

"Cry-baby!" she taunted him. "Silly little crybaby!"

Monica turned on her passionately.

"Shut up, you little beast!"

"Fatty!" jeered Vere.

Monica was beginning to be painfully conscious and ashamed of her roly-poly plumpness. She lost her temper and sprang at Vere, striking out wildly. Vere, who was wiry despite her thinness, caught her wrists and held them.

"Fatty! Cry-baby! Fatty! Cry-baby!" she jeered, an exultant grin on her small pale face.

Hermione rose. The children always seemed at their worst when Maud was there.

"Vere, stop it at once. . . . *Monica!* Go indoors, all of you."

The babel ceased abruptly as they went indoors.

Maud glanced at her watch and rose.

"Well . . . I expect Mr. Swallow will have finished with Bobby. I'll go and meet him."

She drew on her well-fitting gauntlets and turned to Hermione with her hard smile.

"Good-bye, Hermione . . . I don't envy you your bear garden."

Hermione watched her unhitch Nan from the gate-post, mount, and canter off in the direction of the vicarage.

"Bear garden, indeed!" she repeated to herself indignantly, wishing that she could have thought of something clever and cutting to say in reply.

Then she went slowly upstairs to Alan's bedroom. He was lying on his bed, still sobbing convulsively. She sat down by him and drew him to her.

"What was it, Alan, darling? Tell me."

She smoothed back his hair. His brow was like fire beneath her cool hand.

"He was kicking it, mother," he sobbed, "over and over again . . . I can't bear it. I wish I could die. I shall never forget it, never all my life. I shall see him doing it always, all the rest of my life. I don't want to go on living. It was only a little one, mother, and he was kicking it, and he had great heavy boots on. . . . Oh, *mother*!"

His sobbing rose to a sharp cry as the picture came vividly before his mind again.

"Hush, darling! . . ."

He clung to her, still sobbing desolately. She knew that Charles would have pooh-poohed his distress as childish and unmanly, that John or Jimmie in his place would have attacked the man, and probably rescued the dog from him, not fled the scene in horror as Alan had done. But she knew, too, that, child as he was, the sight had so sickened his spirit of life that he did at that moment actually long for death.

She did not know how to give him comfort. To tell him that time would dull his memory of the scene did not touch the root of the trouble. The root of the trouble was that he found himself in a world where such things happened. So she said nothing, only held him closely to her, stroking his hot brow, and gradually her unspoken love and sympathy did their work, and his sobs began to die away.

Just as she was going to leave him, there came a high-pitched scream of "Mother!" outside. She ran to the door. Monica stood in the passage, white-faced and terrified, holding out a wrist that streamed with blood.

"Monica!" gasped Hermione. "What *have* you done?"

"I was cutting myself to punish myself for losing my temper and hitting Vere, and I didn't know the penknife was so sharp, and—*Mother*!" her terror rising again shrilly, "I'm bleeding to death."

"Rubbish!" said Hermione, drawing her into the bathroom. There she staunched the bleeding and bound up the cut. Having bound it, she dropped a kiss on to Monica's dark curls. "What a little idiot you are, Monnie!"

The smell of burning meat was now filling the house, and she ran downstairs. John was just coming in at the front door.

"Am I in time to help, mother?" he said.

"Oh yes, John, come along. I'm afraid everything's spoilt. Auntie Maud came, and with one thing and another—I'll dish up, and you help us carry the things in."

She was glad of John's help. You could always be sure that John would not drop anything.

She sat at the head of the table and looked round at them. The meat was not, after all, badly overdone. Nigel sat next to her on one side and Alan on the other. She always gave Nigel more than his share of gravy from the dish, but nothing seemed to make him any fatter. She had given Alan a very small helping, because she knew that after his fits of crying he always felt too sick to eat, but that he hated public attention to be drawn to the fact. Their faces were freshly washed, their hair brushed neatly back. All except John wore clean gingham pinafores. They had forgotten their quarrels and were laughing and chattering together. Jimmie was making a "country" of his mashed potatoes, with tiny mountains and valleys, and rivers and seas of gravy. . . .

Hermione's thoughts hovered over them tenderly.

"Bear garden, indeed!" she said to herself again indignantly.

Chapter Twelve

HERMIONE studied her reflection in the mirror with a critical frown. She wanted to look her best this afternoon, because she was going to Mettleham Hall to have tea with John's fiancée's people.

Though Charles's father had now been dead for four years, she could never approach the Hall without the sinking of her heart that visits to him had always meant in the old days. . . . He had been almost senile towards the end of his life, but he had persisted in his refusal to hand over the conduct of the business to Charles. Hermione suspected that Maud secretly encouraged him in his obstinacy, though Charles, who trusted and admired his sister as much as ever, was indignant whenever she suggested this. He had died just in time to save the business from failure, and Charles had had to work very hard during the last four years to pull it together again.

His chief relaxation consisted in the books of travel that still formed his only reading.

"We'll do this trip, Hermione," he would say, "when we've got the children off our hands, and can leave John to look after the business."

He consulted innumerable time-tables of ships and trains, and drew up innumerable trips complete to the smallest detail.

John, now twenty-two, had just left college and entered the business. He was, as he had always been, trustworthy and reliable, and Charles was very proud of having a son in the firm with him. In appearance John was beginning to remind Hermione of Charles as she had first known him—tall, handsome, upright. Like Charles he was limited in his outlook and slow in grasping new ideas, but, unlike Charles, he realised this, and admired those whose minds showed a quicker grasp and wider scope than his.

The business had still not quite made up the ground it had lost under Charles's father, and Charles at present could pay John only a small salary. Hermione sighed. . . . It was a pity that John had become engaged so soon. He should have waited a few years before he took on the burden of a wife and family. But he had always been the most responsible member of the family, so perhaps it would press less hardly on him than it would have pressed on most young men of his age. It had been, of course, inevitable that he should see a good deal of the new owners of Mettleham Hall and their only daughter. It was perhaps inevitable, too, that he should fall in love with the girl. She was pretty, unaffected, and pleasant. Even Hermione, with the keenly jealous eyes of John's mother, could find no fault in her. But it was difficult to know what a girl was really like when one had only seen her in the position of an indulged daughter. Both father and mother adored her, and she, on her side, seemed to be as devoted to them as they were to her, despite the fact that they belonged undeniably to the class of the "self-made", while the girl, who had been to a good school, held her own with ease in the class to which their fortune had now raised them.

Hermione frankly disliked the father. He was purse-proud and conceited, and there was about him a suggestion of "commonness" that went far deeper than mere manner and accent. The mother appeared to be negligible—a meek echo of her husband, a wraith-like worshipper of her daughter. The girl had had everything she wanted from babyhood. She would find it difficult to manage on John's salary. But that, of course, was what the trouble was about, for, though they had been engaged only a month, Hermione gathered that there was trouble. John did not wish to live on his father-in-law's bounty.

She turned to the cheval-glass so that she could see her reflection full length. She wore a dress of grey silk with cascades of white lace from the throat and wrists.

"I'm forty," she said to herself. "I can't expect to look anything but a middle-aged woman." In her heart, however, she was triumphantly aware that she looked absurdly young and pretty.

She heard the hoot of the car that told her John was ready, and came slowly downstairs drawing on her gloves. His face lit up as he saw her.

"I say, mother," he said admiringly, "you *do* look nice."

"Rubbish!" she said, though his praise delighted her. "I'm almost an old woman. I'm forty."

"You may be," he said, "but you look about twenty-one."

"Nonsense!" she laughed, as she got into the car beside him, but it made her feel about twenty-one to be told that by John.

He let in the clutch, and they set off through the village. She leant back in her seat so that she could watch him—his strong square shoulders, his stalwart figure, his clear-cut profile, the whole six feet of splendid masculinity of him. It thrilled her to think that this was her son, that she had carried him in her arms and fed him from her body, now so small and slight beside his.

They passed Greystones, where Maud lived with Susan, her maid.

Mrs. Howe had left Abbotford to be married again the year before old Mr. Dereham's death, but Vere's infatuation for her had come to an end long before that. It had ended very suddenly. . . . Standing unnoticed in the village shop, Vere had overheard her idol say to a friend:

"Yes, darling, I'd love to come. I'll get the little Dereham girl to mind Baby while I'm out. She's the plainest and most unattractive little thing in the world, but very useful."

Vere had never visited her or spoken to her after that, and had greeted her when they met in the village with a hard stare of non-recognition.

Charles had been surprised and disappointed when Maud refused his invitation to live with him and Hermione. ("It would be nice to have old Maud with us, wouldn't it?" he had said wistfully to Hermione.) He had helped her to settle into Greystones, but had disapproved of her taking with her Susan, whom he had always disliked. "Of course," he excused her to Hermione, "she's been with us donkey's years, and I suppose old Maud's too kind-hearted to send her away."

Maud was open-handed and hospitable, and Greystones had become the meeting-place of the young people—chiefly male—of the neighbourhood. There was a rumour—it never reached Charles, of course—that Maud plied her guests rather too freely with whisky, in order to work up the atmosphere of uncritical horsey camaraderie that was most congenial to her. Though still handsome, she was beginning to look slightly overblown.

The car drew up at Mettleham Hall.

The Newmans had so completely altered the interior of the house that it was difficult to recognise it. Mr. Newman was a wealthy man and he liked people to know it. It afforded him immense gratification when visitors from the neighbourhood gasped and stared and said, "But what's happened? The hall used to be half this size, didn't it? And surely the old staircase went up from the other side? . . ." Then he would see a thoughtful look come over their faces as mentally they reckoned the cost of the alterations. He always enjoyed that look. He had left the decoration of the house to his daughter, and it was unexpectedly harmonious. Cecilia had excellent taste. She seemed to have inherited nothing of her father's flamboyance or her mother's colourlessness, and yet to love and understand them both.

She came forward into the hall as soon as Hermione and John entered.

The glance of tremulous happiness she gave John as she greeted him reassured Hermione. The girl loved him, and there was no reason, after all, why the marriage should not be a success. All mothers, she supposed, felt this yearning anxiety for their children, this fear of the future, this desperate eagerness to ward off whatever blows Fate had in store for them. And John was her firstborn. Probably it wouldn't be so bad when it came to the others. Probably when Nigel was married she would accept his wife as a matter of course. That thought made her smile tenderly to herself.

Nigel had gone to school last year. He was still delicate, and both the doctor and his parents had at first been unwilling to allow him to go; but Nigel himself had pleaded so passionately and had fretted so inconsolably that at last he had worn down their opposition. Jimmie, now sixteen and an important person at Moorcroft School, had joined his entreaties to Nigel's. The kid would be all right. He was a little sport, and it was cruel to keep him from Moorcroft if he wanted to go. Nigel was certainly a little sport, and, despite his delicacy, as "manly" as even Charles would wish. Nigel's own shame of his delicacy had in fact completely killed Charles's, and his pluck and courage and constant struggle to overcome his disabilities had made his father intensely proud of him. He would boast of him to his friends.

"The kid weighs hardly anything, you know, and hasn't any stamina at all, but he'll take on anyone with or without gloves and not give in till he literally can't stand. The other day someone dared him to ride down the side of the old quarry on his bicycle—it's practically sheer—and he did it without turning a hair. It's a miracle he wasn't killed, because only one brake of the thing acts anyway, but all he got was a sprained ankle, and he walked home on it and wouldn't have told anyone about it if his mother hadn't noticed he was limping."

Hermione, of course, had held out the longest against his going to school, only yielding when it seemed certain that his fretting would harm his health far more than school life could possibly harm it. And they had been justified. He had settled down quickly and was very happy. Jimmie's popularity and the memory of John's prowess in games helped, of course, but it was the child's own pluck and gallant struggle against his physical weakness that won him the respect and liking of his school-fellows. Jimmie, who knew the signs of Nigel's recurrent attacks of high temperature and headaches, however much Nigel tried to hide them, was in friendly conspiracy with the matron, and would let her know when Nigel needed a day or two in the sick-room. Sometimes Hermione felt desperately anxious about the child, but his weekly letter always reassured her—inky, untidy, with strange spelling, full of humour, affection, and that joy of life that defied his delicacy so successfully.

She dragged her thoughts from Nigel with an effort. Mr.

Newman—short and stout, the ends of his waxed moustache standing up perkily—was telling her in detail the price he had had to pay for the alterations to the Hall. His wife watched him admiringly. Conversation on the subject was, however, difficult. Hermione murmured "Really?" and tried not to look at John. A wave of depression swept over her. The girl was sweet, but—what in-laws to have! One would, of course, inevitably see a good deal of them. It was going to be very trying.

"Now guess what it cost to put the four new bathrooms in?" Mr. Newman was saying.

"I've no idea," said Hermione.

"Well, guess. . . . I bet you don't touch it by a third."

Suddenly Hermione seemed to see the figure of old Mr. Dereham, sitting in his armchair by the fireplace gazing in horror at this upstart desecrator of his home, and for the first time in her life had a feeling of sympathy with the old man.

"We've never done any building," she said. "I'm afraid I've no idea what it costs."

John was watching her proudly as she sat there, looking so young and pretty in her grey silk dress, her rounded chin as white as the lace that fell beneath it, her hands, in their grey kid gloves, folded in her lap. There was about her an air of refinement that set her in a different World from the world to which her host and hostess belonged. His eyes turned to Cecilia. There was that same air of gentleness and refinement about her, too. She belonged to his mother's world. She and his mother would love each other. He felt a thrill of pride in both of them. He imagined Hermione as a grandmother with his child—his and Cecilia's—in her arms.

"I'll get you the estimate," Mr. Newman was saying. "That'll give you some idea of the class of work they've put into the place."

He went from the room with his prancing little step.

"He's so delighted with it all," said Cecilia, "and he's worked so hard. . . ."

Hermione felt a sudden shame, as if caught in a piece of snobbishness, and a quick generous admiration for the girl. That was the way one must try to look at him. . . .

Now that he had gone the atmosphere was suddenly pleasant and normal—just she and John and Cecilia. The mother, watching Cecilia with a fond smile, still seemed quite negligible. She looked very neat and clean—rather as a housekeeper might look. Her greying hair was plainly dressed, and her pale skin shone as if from a good wash with strong yellow soap. The girl was simple and natural and kindly, turning every now and then with a word or smile to her mother, so that she should not feel out of it. They were all laughing happily when Mr. Newman returned with the estimates. As he pointed out items to Hermione and she made conventional comments, she was thinking: "She's nice. I'm going to like her. And she loves John. You can see that every time she looks at him."

"That's the plan of the new wing," said Mr. Newman.

Hermione looked at it, but she didn't see it. She saw the picture that John had seen a few moments before—herself with John's first baby in her arms.

A butler and two footmen brought in the tea. During the meal Mr. Newman kept up an unceasing monologue in his harsh grating voice, describing to Hermione the "improvements" he meant to make in the garden and the probable cost of each. Her spirits sank again. How much was one expected to see of one's son's parents-in-law? She imagined family gatherings, Christmases, birthdays, dominated by that voice. . . .

Tea had been taken away, and Mr. Newman, placing his short stout figure in a commanding position in front of the marble mantelpiece, turned to Hermione.

"Well, Mrs. Dereham," he said, "these young people don't seem any keener on waiting than the rest of us were."

Hermione hesitated, then said in her quiet, gentle voice: "My husband thinks that it would be well for them to wait till John is in a rather better position. I know that my husband hopes to be able to increase his salary in a year or two, but till then——"

Mr. Newman waved that aside with a small fat hand.

"That's of no consequence at all."

He turned to John, and the waxed ends of his moustache raised themselves as he smiled benignly.

"Now, young man, I've got a nice little surprise for you."

John's face grew wary.

"It's something that I'd have been glad enough of, I can tell you, when I was your age and setting up house."

John still said nothing, and after a short pause the other man continued:

"Do you know what I'm going to give you for a wedding present?"

"No."

"Burnham House. Just outside Fernham. Nice and handy for all concerned."

"Burnham House," said John slowly. "I couldn't possibly afford to live in a house of that size on my salary."

Again the waxed ends of Mr. Newman's moustache lifted themselves in a benign smile.

"No one's asking you to, my boy. I'm going to give you an allowance to keep it up on."

John's face hardened.

"I'm sorry, but I couldn't possibly accept an allowance from you, sir," he said stiffly.

"How much salary does your father pay you?" asked Mr. Newman abruptly.

"He's willing to pay me four hundred a year when I marry. I'm only just learning the work, so it's generous. And he says he'll increase it as soon as the business gets on to its feet again."

"Exactly. . . . But you don't really think that you can support my daughter on four hundred a year, do you?"

"I don't see why not. We should have to have a small house and one servant, of course."

"A small house and one servant!" exploded Cecilia's father contemptuously.

"I've gathered from Cecilia that she has no objection," said John. There was an ominous quiet in his voice.

"I'd love it," put in Cecilia breathlessly. Her father waved her aside.

"You think you would. A nice disgrace it would be to us to have you living in this neighbourhood in a small house with one servant! You don't know what you're talking about, Cecilia. You've lived in a home with six indoor servants and had everything done for you ever since you can remember. Your mother and I had a struggle, and we know what it's like, and we're not going to let you go through it. What do you think I've been working for all these years? Well, I'll tell you if you don't know. To give you a home like this. Do you think I'm going to sit by and watch you pig it in a little house and slave over housework, when I've got the money to keep up half a dozen houses the size of this one? I'll tell you what I'll do. If your young man's too proud to take an allowance from me, I'll make it to you. I'll give you the house as a wedding present and money to keep it up as a yearly allowance."

There was a set stubborn look on John's face that made him very like Charles.

"I can't allow Cecilia to accept it."

The little man's face grew purple. He began to rock himself to and fro upon his small fat feet. The mother watched them in obvious distress, her thin hands clasped. Hermione's heart began to beat unevenly.

"You can't allow—?" repeated Mr. Newman explosively.

"No," said John shortly. "If you like to give Cecilia a small allowance for pocket money, that's a different matter, but I'm not going to live in a style that isn't justified by my own salary, and I'm not going to live in any house that I can't pay for myself."

The little man's eyes seemed to be starting out of his head with fury. Hermione rose quickly.

"I think that it's useless to discuss this just at present," she said. "The young people must think it over quietly. There's plenty of time. In any case, John and I must go now Good-bye, Mrs. Newman. Good-bye, Mr. Newman. Good-bye, Cecilia."

Cecilia came to the door with them. She looked pale and unhappy.

"If only I could make them understand each other . . ." she whispered to Hermione as John went to start the car. "Daddy means so well."

"Don't worry," said Hermione; "things will come right. Have patience."

The girl kissed her impulsively, then accompanied her down the steps to the car. John still looked stubborn, and their leave-taking was formal and constrained. Hermione, turning at the bend of the drive, saw her standing—a small disconsolate figure—in the magnificent doorway. Hermione waved to her, but John did not turn round.

"I know just how you feel about it, darling," said Hermione, as they drove along the country road, John's profile above the steering-wheel looking very set and grim, "but, you know, it's quite usual for the bride's father to make a settlement on her."

"That's not the same thing," burst out John. "He wants to manage the whole show as if it belonged to him. He adores his money. He can't bear to spend a penny without everyone for miles around knowing about it. Can't you see him strutting about our house and telling everyone how much he'd spent on it? I know I was rude to him, mother, and I'm sorry, but I've been seeing rather a lot of him lately, and he's got on my nerves. He wouldn't give us a moment's peace. He'd splash his money about on us, he'd engage our servants for us, he'd buy everything he thought we ought to have whether we wanted it or not, and behave generally exactly as if the house were his own, and I shouldn't be able to say a word. I do love Cecilia, but, honestly, I couldn't go on loving her if once I gave in to his keeping us like that."

"What does Cecilia think of it?"

"We've never really discussed it. We begin to, and then I forget everything but what a darling she is. Of course, the old man's never made himself quite as objectionable over it as he did this afternoon."

"I don't think that you and Cecilia ought to consider getting married yet awhile, John. You're both too young. A long engagement doesn't do any harm, whatever people say. You ought to wait till you've been in the business four or five years. By that time probably all these difficulties will have solved themselves."

"Oh no, they won't, mother. He's got the idea into his head, and he'll never let it rest now. There'll be nothing but endless discussions and quarrelling over it every time we meet. He's at a loose end now he's retired, you know, and he's just beginning to get bored with the alterations at the Hall. We shall be a godsend. He'll probably start looking at houses for us to-morrow and knocking them about next week. No, I think the best thing is to get the fight over."

They had reached Ivy Lodge now, and, as he pulled up, the sombreness left his face, and he shot her a sudden grin. "And you needn't talk about long engagements, mother. Yours was short enough."

The romance of her short engagement, of her and Charles's falling in love with each other at first sight, was a tradition in the family.

John followed her into the hall and took up the letters that lay upon the table.

"One from Alan," he said, handing it to her. "Well, I'll run into Fernham and fetch father."

Chapter Thirteen

SHE went slowly upstairs to her bedroom, opening Alan's letter on the way.

Alan—now in his first year at Oxford—was spending part of his vacation reading with a friend in Somerset. He had done well with Mr. Swallow, missing a scholarship to Oxford by only a few marks.

"He's one of the quickest, most responsive boys I've ever taught," Mr. Swallow had said. "Mind you, he's not a scholar. Don't expect him to end up as a Fellow or Professor or anything like that—but he's got more originality and imagination and a quicker grasp of things than nine out of ten boys of his age."

Alan had long ago grown out of his childish fits of hysteria, but he remained painfully shy, especially with strangers. Under the mellowing influence of university life, however, he was fast losing his self-consciousness. He played no games—he had always disliked games—and the river meant to him only lazy afternoons in a punt, but he had at once been admitted to the artistic set of his college, and for the first time in his life was living with people whose scale of values was the same as his own. He was gaining a new poise and assurance and had already lost the air of bewildered shrinking that he had had before he went there. He was dimly conscious that he possessed creative powers and was blindly fumbling for an outlet for them. He had written several poems that were enthusiastically acclaimed by his friends.

To Charles, of course, his college career had been as great a disappointment as his boyhood. He had secretly hoped that it would "make a man" of him. John had played rugger for his college and had rowed in the Cambridge boat. It had been the proudest moment of Charles's life when he heard that John had won his blue, and nothing could have been in Charles's eyes more despicable and unmanly than the life Alan led—taking no part in games or sports, mooning about with a set of unhealthy "muffs", as Charles scornfully called them. Curiously, Alan still retained his childhood's admiration of Charles, admiring in particular that very "manliness" whose lack in himself was the chief cause of his father's contempt.

In her bedroom Hermione sat down in an armchair by the window to read his letter.

> "DARLING—Mellor's had to go home because his mother's ill, which is a nuisance, and I'm in bed with a cold, which is another. It's not bad, of course, and I'm well supplied with books. I think I'll stay on here another week in any case. It's wonderful country, and I'm getting through a lot of work. I hate writing in bed, so good-bye, darling. All my love.
>
> ALAN."

The heavy weight of anxiety that any illness of her children, however slight, always brought to her, fastened itself at her heart. Alan ill . . . only a cold, but—perhaps his bed had not been aired; perhaps he was not being properly looked after. She saw him lying neglected, tossing feverishly on an untidy bed in a squalid room, while his landlady sat drinking in a neighbouring public-house. It was, she knew, a ridiculously exaggerated picture, but there might be a grain of truth in it.

She took off her hat and gloves, tidied her hair, and went slowly downstairs again. Passing the schoolroom, she heard a murmur of voices and knew that Vere and Gillian were doing their home-work there. They cycled every day into Fernham to a Girls' High School that had been opened six years ago.

Vere had passed her matriculation last year and was now working for a scholarship to Girton. She was not naturally studious, and Hermione suspected that it was the desire to go one better than

Alan, who had just failed to win a scholarship, that inspired her efforts. She was good at games and a very capable organiser, but she was not popular at school. She maintained her childhood's reputation for "bossiness", and, though acutely sensitive to slights herself, was strangely obtuse to the susceptibilities of other people. Yearning passionately for friendships, she had a precipitate and rather bull-like way of setting about them that defeated its own ends. She would fix on the desired friend and thrust her company upon her on all occasions, separating her from all other companions and insisting on arranging every detail of her life, till the friend, at first flattered, then bewildered, then finally indignant, broke off the affair. The road of Vere's school life was strewn with such abortive friendships, and she suffered deeply on each occasion. The fact that she was generally proved to be right in the final quarrel increased her resentment.

Her latest friend was Valerie Edwards, a pretty and very charming girl who had left school last term and who therefore could not be as completely monopolised by Vere as her other friends had been. Framed snapshots of Valerie with tennis racquet, with hockey stick, with cat, with dog, in indoor dress, in outdoor dress, covered the mantelpiece of Vere's bedroom.

Vere opened the schoolroom door just as Hermione passed it. She looked very neat in her long navy blue skirt and plain white blouse, her hair drawn back austerely into its thick schoolgirl plait.

Through the door Hermione could see Gillian's lovely profile bent over her work.

"I'm going to get the ink-bottle from the dining-room bureau," said Vere in her brisk, business-like tones. "There's only one here, and we need one each. I hate stretching over yards of books to it."

"Yes, that's all right," said Hermione. "I'll get an extra bottle to-morrow."

Gillian heard her voice and looked up with her radiant smile.

"Hello, mummy. Did you have a nice tea?"

"Yes, thank you, darling. Did you?"

"No. It's always hateful when you aren't here. You look so sweet in that dress. I must just come and kiss you." She ran to the door and gave Hermione a childish hug. "Did Cecilia look nice?"

"Very."

"John says I must be a bridesmaid when they get married. Won't it be fun? Though I shall hate John going away, won't you?"

"Yes. . . . How's the home-work getting on?"

"I've only got a French exercise after this, and then I'll have finished. Did you like French exercises when you had to do them?"

"I don't think so. . . . It's such a long time ago."

Gillian laughed.

"Oh, darling, don't pretend to be *old*! Everyone at school says how young you look. You know that when you came with John to the sports someone said how pretty my sister-in-law was."

Hermione stroked the silky golden hair. Though the child still seemed to belong to Charles more than to her, she loved her very dearly.

"What rubbish! . . . And oh, my darling, what fingers! Ink all the way up. Mind you get them clean before supper. There's a new piece of pumice-stone in the bathroom."

"Oh, pumice-stone's no use . . . sucking's the best."

Vere had returned with the bottle of ink.

"Come on, Gillian," she said shortly, holding the door open with an air of importance.

Vere was rather apt to parade her school authority over Gillian at home, but Gillian submitted to it philosophically and with a good grace.

Hermione went to the morning-room and took up her never-ending task of household mending. Her thoughts returned to Alan, and the heavy load of anxiety weighed down her spirits again. Soon she heard the sound of the car outside, and Charles and John entered.

"Hello, darling," said Charles, dropping his perfunctory home-coming kiss on to her soft cheek. "I wonder if I've time to develop those plates before dinner. . . ."

Charles had taken up photography and was unbearably fussy over it, as indeed he was over most things. Charles never seemed to be able to do anything quietly by himself. His turning the bathroom into a "dark room" and developing his plates was a nerve-racking, world-upheaving affair, every available member of the family being pressed into his service. Next came the printing—frames propped up at every window, and Charles fussing from one to another, tormented with anxiety lest they should be under- or over-exposed; then the fixing, when no one could use the bathroom hand-basin because it was full of floating prints; and lastly the pasting of the prints into an album, an elaborate process in which Charles measured out each space with maddening accuracy and became inextricably entangled in his adhesive paste. He hated working without an interested and admiring audience, and was disappointed and slightly aggrieved if Hermione did not watch every stage of the process.

"Oh yes, I think there's time. You're back a little earlier than usual."

"I'll begin now. . . . Could you spare the time to give me a hand?"

Her conscience raised its head and murmured: "He wants you to come: he'd sooner have you than anyone." But she dealt with it firmly. "You know how sick I am of that wretched developing business. I simply *can't* go through it again. Besides, I am busy. . . ."

"I'm afraid that I'm rather busy," she said, trying to put a suitable note of regret into her voice. "I think Gillian could come. . . ."

She still felt somewhat guilty as she went to the foot of the stairs and called "Gillian".

The schoolroom door opened.

"Yes, mummy."

"Would you like to help daddy to develop his plates, and leave the rest of your home-work till after supper?"

"Oh, I'd love to," said Gillian, eager and excited.

Gillian really enjoyed helping Charles with his photography.

As soon as she had settled down to her mending again, Monica burst into the room with that headlong impetuousness with which she did everything. She had been playing in a match for the Fernham Ladies' Hockey Club, which she had joined immediately on leaving school. Her skirt was mud-splashed, and her hair was coming down, but her cheeks were glowing, her eyes sparkling with the exercise.

"Hello, mummy," she panted.

"Hello, darling," said Hermione, looking up from her darning. "Did you win?"

"Yes, rather!" said Monica breathlessly. "Ten goals to five. I ran all the way from the station. That's why I'm so puffed."

"Why ever did you run from the station?"

"Oh, I just felt like it. . . ."

Hermione smiled at the thought of the twenty-one-year-old Monica running along the main road from the station, mud-stained and untidy, brandishing her hockey stick.

"My mother used to call me a tomboy," she said. "What she'd have called you——!"

Hermione's mother had died six years ago.

"I'm not really a tomboy," said Monica, becoming rather dignified, "but I *am* dirty. Can I have a bath?"

"I'm sorry, dear. Father's in the bathroom, developing."

"Oh, blow! . . . I'll get some hot water from the kitchen and just wash, then."

Hermione heard her filling a water-can at the kitchen tap, then plunging upstairs with it noisily.

Monica's adolescence had been a turbulent affair of exaggerated emotions and swiftly changing moods, of painful self-consciousness and fits of passionate despair. Her personal appearance had caused her agonies of humiliation in her 'teens, for though her features were good she was fat and shapeless, with a pallid complexion apt to break out into pimples. She would spend hours in tense and nerve-racked preparation for a party, torturing incipient spots into acute inflammation, putting up her thick brown hair and tearing it down again frantically, till at last her attempts ended in an outburst of hysterical tears. . . . She wouldn't go to the party at all. . . . She looked awful, and no one wanted her, anyway. . . . Vere must go without her. . . .

Vere, who shared her bedroom, was little help on those occasions.

She herself was devoid of personal vanity, and, having finished her own quick dressing, would sit on her bed watching the storm and stress of Monica's toilet with irritating detachment. The joint interests of school life had drawn the two girls together superficially, but Monica's tempestuous abandonment to her every passing mood and emotion outraged something reserved and austere in her sister, and she would retaliate by a deliberately assumed expression of contemptuous amusement that goaded Monica to further fury. Novelty always stimulated and excited Monica, so that she was at her best with new acquaintances—charming, eager, vivacious—and this in some way deepened the obscure resentment that Vere felt against her, for Vere's reserve made her constrained and brusque with strangers, and she never shone in company as Monica often did.

The last two years, however, had wrought great changes in Monica. Her figure had lost its shapelessness and now looked firm and well formed, with the seductive roundness of healthy young womanhood. Her complexion had cleared and had gained a warm glow, her brown eyes were big and lustrous and dewy, her red lips moist and curved like a cupid's bow. She was, in fact, beautiful in a very provocative fashion. When she went into Fernham men often spoke to her in the streets, and she was inclined to respond with friendly naïveté, despite Hermione's warnings. ("But, mother, he thought he'd met me before, and then by the time he'd found that he hadn't we'd somehow got to be friends. . . .")

Only last week, when she was going into Fern-ham to do some shopping, a stranger had spoken to her in the train, asking her if she had ever been to the new Fernham picture-house. She said that she had not and asked if he had. He replied that he wanted to go but did not like going alone, and had no one to go with. On an impulse of pity for his loneliness, she offered herself as his companion and actually went to the pictures with him that afternoon. His subsequent attempts at love-making infuriated her, and she came home to tell the story to Hermione aglow with righteous indignation. Hermione's attitude threw her hotly upon the defensive. "I can't go about being beastly to everyone and not answering when they speak to me. . . . He seemed a nice man and I was sorry for him because he said he was so lonely. . . ."

Further protest drove her into a passion of despair and self-pity. "You all hate me. . . . No one ever tries to understand me. . . . I wish I'd never been born. . . ."

Hermione realised that there was something sensual about the girl of which she herself was wholly unaware. While as yet amorousness of any kind frightened her, she instinctively and unconsciously tried to attract every man with whom she came in contact, and this worried Hermione, because, though her ideals were almost morbidly high, she had very little self-control.

Chapter Fourteen

HERMIONE laid down her sewing and, going up to the bathroom, tapped lightly on the door.

"Charles, you'll be out in good time before dinner, won't you, so that the children can wash?"

"Yes, yes," said Charles impatiently.

"Oh, daddy, look!"—in Gillian's sweet excited voice—"it's coming!"

Hermione returned to the morning-room. John stood by the fireplace, frowning gloomily.

"John," said Hermione, "how would it be to ask your father to speak to Mr. Newman?"

"That wouldn't be any good," said John morosely. "They'd be at loggerheads in two minutes."

Just then there came the sound of the front door knocker, and a moment later Cecilia entered. She looked pale, and it was obvious that she had been crying.

"I had to come and see you, John," she said breathlessly. "No, don't go, Mrs. Dereham. I want you to help us. There's been the most dreadful row at home. John, how *could* you treat father like that?"

"I'm sorry if I was rude to him," said John stiffly, "but if I marry I intend to support my wife myself."

"John, do listen, do be reasonable"—she was standing close to him, her hands clasped, looking up at him beseechingly—"do try to see father's side of it. He was furious after you'd gone. And mother"—her voice wavered suddenly—"John, mother's been crying ever since. She says it will break her heart and father's if you don't let them help us. She says it would kill father, and she'd never forgive me." (So the mother isn't negligible, thought Hermione.)

"You see," she went on—"oh, if only you'd try to understand. I don't want their money. I only want you, but—don't you see?—I'm all they have. They've—*lived* for me all these years. All the time father was making his money he was thinking of me. The only thing he *really* wants it for is to make me happy. It doesn't make me happy, but I can't explain that to him. John, I know how you see father, but he isn't like that really. He's such a darling—so sweet—so easily hurt. He's been bitterly hurt over this. I'm everything to him. Oh, *can't* you understand? Won't you just let him help? John, if you love me do this for me."

John's face was still set and rigid.

"It would be far easier for me to give in to you than stand out," he said slowly. "I love you, and I want to please you. But I see more clearly than you what would be the end of it. I see that it would be—impossible. I've got to make the stand now. Once I give in, our happiness is over."

"How is our happiness over just because you let them help us? John, I've *tried* to make father understand. I've got him to give up the idea of Burnham House at any rate. He suggested—he wondered—" She faltered.

"Yes?" said John, not very encouragingly.

"What about our living at the Hall with them and your paying father the rent you'd meant to pay for the little house? It wouldn't be the same as their *giving* us a house, and you'd feel independent, and they'd still have me. John, I can't *think* what they're going to do without me, if I go right away. They'll be lost. I've—made up their lives for them for so long. I've been with them all day and every day. They depend on me so."

"You went away to school."

"I know, but that was different. They'd got the holidays to plan for and look forward to all the time. Would you consider that, John?"

"Not for a minute," he said grimly.

"Well, then, he made another suggestion—that he should buy

us a smaller house and furnish it for us and pay for one maid, so that we'll have the two maids. John, darling, I'd love the tiny house and one maid, but the thought of it hurts him, and—I can't bear to hurt him. John, what *does* it matter? I think you're being so—ungenerous." She turned suddenly to Hermione. "Mrs. Dereham, won't you advise us?"

Hermione made a little helpless gesture.

"I can't. It's a thing that only you two can settle."

Cecilia turned back to John. His face still wore the set stubborn look that made him so like Charles.

"John, how *can* it hurt you for father to give us a house?"

"It isn't that," burst out John. "He doesn't want just to give us a house. He wants our house to belong to him. He wants to go on managing your life for you. He knows that, if he buys this house, he's got me bound hand and foot. How can I tell a man to mind his own business when he's paid for the very ground I'm standing on?"

She went white and flinched as if he had struck her, then turned from him and, covering her face with her hands, burst suddenly into tears. He was aghast and contrite. He had never seen her cry before.

"Cecilia, I'm sorry. Darling, don't cry like that. I'm a beast. I'm sorry. I didn't mean to say that. . . . Cecilia, darling, forgive me."

He took her in his arms, kissing her wet cheeks, and Hermione slipped quietly from the room. She knew that she could not help them in this crisis. She liked the child, but her sympathies were with John.

Soon they came out. John's arm was round Cecilia. They had forgotten the quarrel in the reconciliation.

"I'm just going to take Cecilia home, mother," John called.

Hermione came to the hall and kissed Cecilia.

"Good-bye, darling. . . ."

The girl clung to her.

"Don't worry about us," she said. "We love each other, and things are bound to come right when people love each other."

Hermione watched them dreamily as they disappeared into the

dusk. She was roused from her dreams by the opening of the bathroom door and Charles's voice shouting: "Hermione! Come up and look at these plates."

He had taken down the red blind and was holding the plates up to the light. She studied them one after another.

"Awfully good, Charles," she said, making an effort to put the right amount of enthusiasm into her voice.

"Well, I do think," said Charles, "that I have a pretty good average of successes on the whole. Would you mind printing them for me to-morrow, Hermione? The light's gone by the time I get back from the office."

"Yes, I'll see to them," she answered.

She hated the business of printing—putting the frames at all the windows, turning up the little corners at frequent intervals to see how they were getting on. Charles was very particular as to the exact amount of exposure each should have. It would take the whole afternoon.

"I simply love it when it just begins to come on the plate like a ghost," laughed Gillian. "It always seems like magic."

Vere came from the schoolroom and stood in the bathroom doorway.

"I don't think that Gillian ought to be allowed to leave her home-work half done like this," she said severely.

The sound of their talking together in the bathroom and of Gillian's laughter had made her feel obscurely hurt and "out of it".

"She's going to finish it after supper," said Hermione soothingly; "she's only got a French exercise. . . . We'll just put these things away."

"I'll do that," said Charles. "Don't you bother."

But she knew that he would either forget to do it altogether or call her up to help him half a dozen times.

"No, I'll do it," she said. "Gillian, wash your hands, darling, then go and start the French exercise."

Slightly mollified, but still disapproving, Vere returned to the schoolroom.

Hermione tidied the bathroom, then went downstairs to Charles. Anxiety about Alan lay like a physical oppression at her heart. Suppose he were really dangerously ill and the woman had never even thought of getting a doctor. . . .

Charles had got out his album and was carefully measuring a page for the new prints.

"I think that the effect of that one of the summer-house will be very good," he said; "I took a lot of trouble over it."

She made no answer, and he said suddenly:

"Who was it who called when we were developing?"

"Cecilia. She wanted to see John."

"What on earth did she want to see John for? He was there this afternoon, wasn't he?"

"He'll tell you when he comes in. . . . I've had a letter from Alan, Charles."

He made the gruff, unsympathetic sound that he always made when she mentioned Alan.

"Mellor's had to go home, and Alan's in bed with a cold. I've no idea what sort of room or landlady he's got. He's probably much worse than he says." She came to a sudden decision. "Charles, I must go down to-morrow and see whether he's really ill."

He was silent for a minute, then said gently:

"If you're worried, of course, you must go."

"I'll come back at once if he's all right."

He looked at her, and she saw the deep tenderness for her that underlay his often irritating exterior.

"My dear, if he's all right and the place is comfortable, stay there a few days yourself. A change will do you good."

Having given her permission to go, he became suddenly gloomy and sorry for himself.

"Though, Heaven knows, we shall all be uncomfortable enough with Mon housekeeping."

His gloom deepened still further as he added:

"And I suppose the prints won't get done till the week-end now."

Chapter Fifteen

WHEN she saw the cottage—spotlessly, fragrantly clean—and Alan sitting up in bed with a red nose and watery eyes, but otherwise well and cheerful, she laughed at herself as a fussy mother hen.

"It's heavenly to have you," said Alan, holding both her hands as she sat on the bed. "Your post card this morning saying you were coming completely cured me, but I've been holding on to the end of my cold like grim death ever since, because I couldn't bear the thought of your going away. I had horrible visions of you just throwing one glance at me, saying, 'He's all right; he's just a humbug,' and rushing back to the station to catch the next train home. You won't do that, will you?"

She laughed.

"Father said I could stay for a few days even if you were all right."

"That's splendid!"

"He didn't really want me to. He hates being without me."

"Well, so do I, and I've not had you for ages. . . . It seems too good to be true. The doctor said I could get up to-morrow. I'm absolutely well, really, you know—just a complete fraud. I might have done it on purpose to decoy you down here. I didn't, as a matter of fact, but only because I never thought of it. . . . Mother, you will stay, won't you? Mrs. Prettyman's got a bedroom ready for you with her best linen sheets and every crochet mat she possesses, and the very best text over your bed."

"Which is the very best text?" she smiled.

"I've forgotten the wording, but it's framed in plush, and the others are only framed in wood. . . . Well, you will, won't you?"

"Of course."

Looking back, the next week always seemed like a dream to Hermione. She had never before had a holiday apart from her family. On the rare occasions when they went away they took a furnished house by the sea, and Hermione's life was a breathless rush of housekeeping, of preparing and organising excursions, of keeping the children happy and occupied in unfamiliar surroundings.

But it was not the peace of Mrs. Prettyman's cottage, and the welcome respite from household duties, that made the fortnight stand out in Hermione's memories. It was the adventure of getting to know Alan. When they came in from a walk together on the third day of her visit, Alan said: "Do you know, mother, this is the first time in all my life that I've ever had you to myself."

She realised that it was true. He had been always one of the crowd of children, so shy and sensitive that she had never noticed him except when his obvious unhappiness claimed her hastily given comfort and sympathy. And now they walked together through the country lanes and woods, took their meals together in Mrs. Prettyman's old-fashioned parlour, spent the long, quiet evenings together. Hermione would sit by the fire just outside the circle of the lamplight, her hands idle in her lap—there was to her an almost sensuous pleasure in mere idleness, because it had so little part in her ordinary life—and Alan would sit at her feet, his head resting against her knee. Sometimes he would read aloud to her from one of the slender volumes of poetry that he always had with him. His voice was quiet and beautifully modulated, and Hermione found an exquisite pleasure in surrendering herself to its spell. He restored her to her oldest love, poetry, opening new worlds to her, introducing her to the "modern" poets—Sturge Moore, John Drinkwater, W. H. Davies. Or they would talk together—the desultory talk of perfect friendship interspersed with long, comfortable silences.

At first Hermione tried to talk of the others, but the others had become unreal, somehow. A spell seemed to have been laid on her, so that even John's love-affair became unimportant, so that not even the thought of Monica could stir the old nagging anxiety at her heart.

Looking down at his clear-cut, delicate features, she noticed suddenly one evening how good-looking he was growing.

"Alan, darling," she said, "I'm just beginning to realise that you're grown up. You aren't a little boy any longer."

"I'm glad I'm not," he said dreamily. "I think that childhood is a very overrated condition, don't you?"

"I suppose so. . . ."

"People say 'as happy as a child', but children aren't happy, you know."

"Weren't you happy?"

"Just now and then—not often."

"You make me feel very guilty. I ought to have made you happy."

"It wasn't you. You were always heavenly. It was just that when you're a child you can't see beyond the thing that's actually happening, so that if one thing goes wrong there seems nothing left to live for. When you get older you can see beyond the thing that's happening, and it's not quite so bad. . . ."

"You're happy now, aren't you, Alan?"

"Yes. . . . I was horribly scared at first. When I went to Oxford, I mean. I didn't know how to make friends with people. I was terrified of their speaking to me, and when they did I was so nervous and so afraid of not responding properly that I was horribly effusive. It must have been painful for them. Then suddenly I found that there wasn't anything to be frightened of. You see, I was always trying desperately hard not to be—different. But at college I found that people didn't mind your being different, because they were different too—or rather a good many of them were. I've suffered agonies trying to talk about games to John's and Jimmie's friends. I'm glad those days are over."

"That's the best of college life, I suppose. There are so many types there that you're sure of finding the type you understand among them."

"I wouldn't say understand exactly. Nobody really understands anyone else, do they? Nobody ever understands himself, I suppose. And, of course, one changes so. One's never exactly the same to two different people, is one? It's as if in everyone there were a little empty space left for the person they're with to fill up, and that little bit makes all the difference, so that one's identity seems actually to change according to the person one's with."

"You mean that if you're very sympathetic you can't help taking some of the colour of the person you're talking to, seeing things from their angle. . . . You'd feel incomplete on a desert island. . . ."

"Yes, but in some ways I'd love it; wouldn't you? I hate civilised life. I think it's degrading. I always feel wretched and abject with waiters and cloak-room attendants and people like that. I'm not a socialist, but I hate sitting in state at a little table while another man—twice as good as me, probably—runs about waiting on me. I avoid meeting his eye *and* can only just stop myself apologising to him."

She smiled.

"You're still a little boy, Alan, after all. I believe you always will be."

He rubbed his cheek affectionately against the cool silk of her dress.

"I've always loved your dresses," he said dreamily. "You had a blue one once that was a great comfort to me because Mon had a dreadful pink affair, all over trimming, at the same time, and whenever I saw it I used to shut my eyes and think of yours."

"I remember. . . . She bought it with her first dress allowance and wouldn't let me help her."

"It made me so wretched. I was so terrified of showing her how much I hated it and hurting her feelings that I kept telling her I liked it and saying how nice she looked in it. . . . I didn't want to and I hated myself for doing it, but somehow I couldn't help it. I decided that if ever I were a king I'd make a law that everyone in the world must wear dresses just like yours."

"What are you going to be, Alan?"

He stared dreamily into the distance. "I thought I was going to be a poet not very long ago, but now I know I'm not."

"I loved your poetry, Alan. . . ."

"It wasn't poetry," he said and, smiling, quoted: " 'Only, overmastered by some thoughts, I paid an inky tribute to them.' "

"What do you want to be, then?"

"Don't laugh at me, will you?. . . I think I want to be an actor."

"An actor!" She was dismayed. "Have you acted at all, Alan?"

"Just once—in an informal thing we got up at college. But—it came to me quite suddenly last week. Don't take it seriously or mention it to anyone. I don't feel absolutely certain yet. It may be just one of those flashes of insanity that come to one sometimes. Father would hate it, of course," he added wistfully.

Her eyes were fixed upon the fine lines of his young profile.

"You're all growing up," she said. "It frightens me to think of it. . . . It seems only a week ago that you were all babies in the nursery, and here's John engaged. . . . I shall be having grandchildren before I know where I am."

"People who marry and have children are like God, aren't they?" he said dreamily. "They make a world and people it, and they rule it either wisely and kindly like a good god, or else cruelly like an evil god. . . . I don't know how people dare get married. . . ."

She smiled.

"It takes you by surprise," she said; "it doesn't leave you time to think."

"That's as well," said Alan. "No one would dare to do it in cold blood."

One afternoon on the last week of her visit they had decided to go out for a walk, but while she was putting oh her hat in her bedroom the sky became so black and overcast that she went into his room and said:

"Shall we go, after all, Alan?"

He was standing at the window and did not turn or answer, did not indeed know that she was there. His eyes were fixed upon an apple-tree in full bloom in the garden. The pink-and-white blossoms seemed to shine as if with a light of their own against the darkening sky, and there had come to him one of those moments of ecstasy that had come to him at intervals ever since he could remember—moments in which his whole being seemed to be intensified, moments that swept him up into a strange, unreasoning rapture. They passed as suddenly as they came but left in their train a feeling of exultation, a sustaining sense of power.

Hermione came and stood by him, and suddenly the ecstasy swept her up too, bringing a sudden catch to her throat. How long was it since Beauty had sent this sword-like message to her heart, transforming the whole world? It belonged to the days before household cares had dulled her eyes and drugged her understanding. But—a wave of exultant joy swept over her again. It didn't matter. She need never feel again that resentful sense of having been trapped, betrayed. The girl she mourned was not dead. She lived in this boy beside her.

Becoming aware suddenly of her presence, he reached out for her hand and crushed it in his, still without taking his dazed eyes from the flaming loveliness outside.

As the end of her visit came nearer, she began to shrink from the thought of returning home.

There was a dreamlike glamour about this holiday. She had recaptured her youth, she had formed a new friendship, precious, fragile, that perhaps would not survive the atmosphere of normal home life. She felt that something beautiful had come to an end when Alan took her down to the station, carrying her bag. She would miss poignantly his tenderness, his understanding, his little lover-like attentions.

"Good-bye, darling," he said, as he put her into the carriage. "It's been the happiest fortnight of my life."

Chapter Sixteen

THEN two days after her return home came the telegram.

"Nigel seriously ill. Pneumonia. Come at once."

For the rest of her life Hermione shrank from the memory of the next week ... the hurried journey to Moorcroft with Charles ... Nigel, his eyes feverishly bright, his hair plastered damply on to his brow, fighting for each breath he drew, looking up at her in an easier moment with the ghost of his old smile, whispering, "How nice of you to come, mummy—but you shouldn't have bothered. I'm all right. Really, I'm quite all right. ..." Jimmie, white-faced and self-reproachful, for Nigel as usual had hidden and defied his illness till it could be hidden and defied no longer. "I ought to have noticed, but somehow I didn't see the kid at all last week. We had two matches, and I was swotting for an exam. I'd have noticed if I'd seen him. I can always tell when he's feeling rotten. ... It's all my fault. ..." A horror-stricken silence over the whole school ("Dereham Minor's *frightfully* ill, you know. His people have come down"). ... Boys creeping past the sick-room in bedroom slippers, throwing glances of sympathetic enquiry at Hermione when they met her in the passage. ... A friend of Nigel's thrusting a penknife into her hands ("Please give it him, will you? It's got a thing for taking stones out of a horse's hoof. I know he'll like it").

Everything that could be done was done. Two nurses were in charge of the sick-room, and a specialist arrived from London the same time as Hermione and Charles, but the child had no reserve of strength, and had stood out too long against his illness. He loved to have Hermione sitting by his bedside, stroking his hot brow with her soft cool hand. He lay with his feverish eyes fixed on her face, as though the sight of her were an amulet against his suffering. He was uneasy and restless whenever she went out of the room.

He died while he was asleep so quietly that Hermione, sitting by the bedside watching him, did not know at first that he was dead.

Jimmie was sent for from his classroom, but it was Charles who consoled him with broken words of comfort, holding the boyish form closely to him. "Don't, old fellow . . . steady, now . . . it wasn't your fault. . . it would probably have been just the same if they'd caught it earlier . . . poor old chap . . . there now. . . ."

Hermione, kneeling by the little bed, was unaware of both of them. She could not take her eyes from the waxen face that had been Nigel.

There was something furtive and horrible in the way they left the school. . . . The coffin was brought after dark up the backstairs, and they departed with it before light the next morning. The headmaster was very sympathetic, but he wished his boys to see as few signs of the tragedy as possible.

Hermione had at first no time to indulge her own grief. She needed all her energy for the comfort of the others. Monica's grief was, of course, loud and tempestuous, but it was Gillian—Nigel's old nursery playmate—who was the most heartbroken by his death. Hermione slept with her the night they brought him home, holding her in her arms and comforting her till morning. Vere, who probably felt his death less than any of them, took her sorrow to Valerie for consolation, and was not seen in Ivy Lodge except at meals. Alan came home, very quiet and unobtrusive. That strange new confidence between him and Hermione seemed to have vanished. Hermione felt almost guilty now when she thought of it. She had forgotten the others completely in that fortnight she spent with Alan. While she walked in the woods with him and sat talking to him in the lamp-lit cottage parlour, Nigel was even then fighting his illness with a courage that had cost him his life. She felt as if her absorption in Alan had somehow contributed to the cause of Nigel's death, as if her thoughts might have saved him.

She did not break down till the night after the funeral when she was alone with Charles. He soothed her with clumsy tenderness.

"We oughtn't to have let him go to school," she sobbed. "He wasn't strong enough, and we knew he wasn't."

"We did the best we could for the child, darling. He wanted to go, and he was happy there. . . . The doctor said it was the best thing to do, the only thing to do. He'd have fretted his heart out at home."

"But he wouldn't have died."

"You can't say that, my dear. . . ."

"I can, Charles. I'd have seen at once when he wasn't feeling well."

"You couldn't have kept him in a glass case, you know. You mustn't blame the school."

"I don't. I blame myself."

"Look here, Hermione . . . let's try to get it straight. The child's gone, and it's damnable for us—for you and me and the other children. I'd somehow never thought. . . . You know what I mean. I'd taken for granted that the children would all grow up with us. I know that this knocks you far harder than it knocks me. But—well, you surely don't believe that he—doesn't exist any longer. It isn't as if we didn't hope to see him again sometime. I mean," he ended almost shamefacedly, "there's the Bible and all that."

"Oh, Charles, I know, I do believe it. I'm sorry. I'm so tired. I've not slept since we went down to Moorcroft."

He helped her to bed, and she lay in his arms, still sobbing wearily.

"My sweet," he whispered, "my poor little love . . . there, there. . . ."

She slept that night for the first time since she had received the telegram.

For the next few days she could not endure Charles to leave her. Only his presence could keep away that overwhelming nightmare of grief and desolation, that terrible sense, unreasonable though she knew it to be, of having killed Nigel by her neglect.

She had a dream one night that drove her overwrought nerves

almost to breaking point. She and Alan sat talking in Mrs. Prettyman's parlour, while outside there raged a storm of wind and rain. Suddenly Nigel's figure appeared at the window, cold and drenched, beating at the pane with his thin hands, crying to them in his little high-pitched voice to let him in. Alan did not see or hear him, and she was powerless to move or to draw Alan's attention to him. She had to sit in the nightmare grip of paralysis, watching him and listening to his cries for help.

Only Charles could keep these terrors at bay. He had no suspicion of what she suffered, his comfort was clumsy and awkward, but she had an obscure feeling that, because she and Charles had brought Nigel into the world, then as long as she and Charles were together all must be well with him. He was very patient, staying away from his work to be with her for a week after Nigel's funeral. When he went back to it she would at first go into Fernham every day to meet him for lunch, because she could not face a whole day away from him.

Then she seemed to settle down to her normal life again. Charles could not know, of course, that her thoughts had turned to the baby Nigel and dwelt with him continually. She locked herself in her bedroom and took out his baby, clothes, smoothing them on the bed, cradling them in her arms. She went about her duties in the house, but they were unreal and dreamlike. Only Nigel was real. She would sit idly, her arms folded in her lap, and Charles was glad to see her resting. He could not know that she was holding the baby Nigel in her arms, soothing him to sleep. She would go into the old nursery and stand as if watching him playing with his toys on the patchwork mat before the fireplace. Sometimes she would lock the door and kneel down to play with him as she used to do, speaking aloud to him.

"Let's make a farm, shall we, Nigel? . . . You make the pigsties, and I'll make the cow-sheds. Here are the bricks."

The child became so real to her that often she thought she actually saw him. He filled all her thoughts, and she cared nothing for the others.

Outwardly the household had returned to its normal ways. Jimmie had gone back to school and Alan to college. Nigel's death had at first brought John and Cecilia together again, making their quarrel seem futile and unworthy. But, as the weeks went by and life resumed its ordinary tenor, their relations became strained once more. The mother, whom Hermione had thought so negligible, was the foremost actor in the little drama. She shut herself into her room, refusing food and weeping continually. Cecilia was breaking her heart and her father's ... she couldn't bear it ... she wished that she had died, she said, before she'd seen their child cast back in their faces all they had done for her.

John and Mr. Newman had several interviews, but they always ended stormily. Cecilia, who loved the three of them, soothed and pacified each, only to see all her efforts nullified at their next meeting. The proffered gift of a house had become magnified out of all proportion to reality. To the father and mother the refusal of it had become equivalent to a complete disowning of them by their child. To John the acceptance of it had become equivalent to a complete surrender of his independence. Both sides held out doggedly, becoming more bitter and nerve-racked as the weeks slipped by. After a particularly stormy interview John told Cecilia that she must choose between him and her parents. Cecilia's loyalty would not allow her to disown her parents, and, indignant at his attitude, she returned his ring to him.

John felt half relieved at the ending of a situation that had become intolerable—he and Cecilia had not met without quarrelling for weeks—but he felt also bitterly hurt and angry. He had finished with women, he told himself. ... Despite all her protestations, Cecilia had preferred her father's money to his love.

As always when he was in trouble his thoughts turned to his mother. She was a rock in the shifting sands of his life. She was unlike any other woman who had ever lived. After his final interview with Cecilia, he sought her out in the morning-room, where she usually did her mending or sewing after tea. She sat by the fire, looking very pale and thin in her black dress. Her mending basket was by her side, but she was not working. Her hands were folded in her lap. She turned to him as he stood in the doorway, an odd hostility in her expression. Nigel had been climbing into her lap, putting tiny arms round her neck . . . and then John came in and interrupted them. Why was he standing looking at her like that? In thought she was holding Nigel tightly to her, whispering, "Don't leave me, my baby. He'll go away in a minute."

"What is it, John?" she said in a flat, dull voice.

He came into the room and closed the door behind him.

"Cecilia and I have broken it off, mother."

He saw that her eyes wore that strange dazed look that they had worn ever since Nigel's death. His heart began to beat unevenly, and a sudden terror clutched him by the throat. The world couldn't go on if she were going to fail him. They looked at each other in silence for a moment. Then the desperate appeal in his hurt young eyes pierced the mists of luxurious self-indulgent grief in which she had wrapped herself—pierced and dispersed them. John needed her. John, her first-born. She made a little gesture that seemed to cast aside for ever the morbid play-acting by which she had sought to cheat her sorrows and turned to him again, the old Hermione, loving, tender.

"Darling, I'm so sorry. Come and tell me about it."

Chapter Seventeen

In 1909, when John was twenty-six and Gillian eighteen, Sir Lionel Amhurst died at Aix-les-Bains and his nephew took up his residence at Abbotford Manor.

The new Sir Lionel and Lady Amhurst were young, good-looking, and high-spirited, and the Manor became the centre of the youthful life of the neighbourhood. They entertained freely, giving tennis parties, garden parties, and dances, and organising amateur theatricals, in which Lady Amhurst was especially interested.

Many other changes, too, had taken place in Abbotford. The Kendalls and Bannisters had left the village. Greencroft, where the Kendalls had lived, was occupied now by the Pettigrews—a large noisy family who fraternised readily with the young Derehams—and Brightmet, where the Bannisters had lived, by the Carews. Mrs. Carew was a handsome, arrogant, affected woman, who dressed extremely well, but was reputed to be very mean in her dealings with tradesmen and servants. She had one daughter, Sylvia, a girl of eighteen, who unconsciously copied her mother's manner when she was with her, but who, away from her mother, was unaffected and likeable. She, too, was very friendly with the young Derehams, and Hermione, having heard that the food at Brightmet, though served with great ceremony, was inadequate in both quality and quantity, gave the girl an open invitation to meals at Ivy Lodge, of which she took full advantage.

The young people went about together—John, Monica, Vere, Sylvia Carew, and Bobby and Linda Pettigrew. Bobby, the eldest of the Pettigrews, was a youth of nineteen, tall, fair, athletic, with a disconcertingly deep voice and an equally disconcerting habit of uttering sweeping judgments on subjects of which he could not possibly know anything at all. He generally looked rather vague and untidy, and Vere took him in hand, "mothering" him (the younger members of Mrs. Pettigrew's flock absorbed all her maternal instinct, leaving none over for the elder ones), and bullying him, and generally improving his manners and appearance. They all joined tennis, hockey, and badminton clubs in Fernham, going to and fro on bicycles. There was a hard frost about Christmas, and Lady Amhurst gave skating parties every night, turning the boat-house into a refreshment buffet and hanging Chinese lanterns on the trees around the lake.

The village was gayer, more full of young life, than it had been for years.

Cecilia Newman had gone to stay with a friend in India soon after her engagement with John was broken, and the visit seemed to be stretching itself out indefinitely. A rumour had reached the village that she was engaged, but had been contradicted afterwards. Relations between the Derehams and the Newmans were still strained, and they met, whenever they had to meet, on very formal terms.

Vere had not won her scholarship to Girton, though she took a creditable place on the lists. Having failed to win it, she lost all interest in a college career. There was in Vere—unacknowledged even by herself—a secret longing to shine and be admired, a longing that she instinctively concealed both from herself and others by a deliberate curtness of manner and a determined refusal to cultivate any personal or social graces. She would have pretended to despise the kudos that the winning of the scholarship would have brought to her, but secretly she craved for it. It was this secret longing for admiration that made her, quite unconsciously, jealous of the radiant charm of manner that was Monica's instinctive reaction to any social gathering, whatever storms may have attended her preparation for it.

The friendship between Vere and Valerie Edwards had lasted longer than Vere's friendships usually lasted. Hermione suspected that Valerie had little affection for Vere, but that she pretended still to be devoted to her because she liked going about with the Derehams and their friends.

Valerie's father had been an ironmonger in Fernham, and, despite her good looks and irreproachable manners and accent, she had had no footing in the local society till she made friends with Vere. Monica ignored her—for the sisters, though they had little in common, were always jealous of each other's friends—but John was gradually becoming her recognised escort on all their joint expeditions. She was certainly pretty enough to attract any man. Her hair was so pale as to be almost silver, her skin was dazzlingly fair, and her eyes a pale forget-me-not blue. Only a very keen observer would have noticed that the little red mouth was just too small and the forget-me-not eyes just too close together. Hermione felt puzzled by the girl. Her charm, was like an armour both protecting and concealing her. One could never get through it to anything beyond. Though she had been Vere's friend for three years and was in and out of the house with the others continually, Hermione felt that she knew her no better than on the day when Vere had first brought her to Ivy Lodge.

Gillian was now head girl of Fernham High School and extremely popular there. Her childhood's promise of beauty was fulfilling itself, but she was shy and quiet, taking her duties and responsibilities very seriously. She was still Charles's favourite, and he loved to tease her about her position of importance at school, pretending to be afraid of her authority.

Charles had worked very hard the last few years, and the business was now doing so well that he could afford to relax his efforts. His chief anxieties were his baldness and his stoutness. He tried innumerable hair restorers, and twisted himself into contortionist attitudes every morning in the hopes of reducing his girth. Hermione would often find him examining his head in the mirror with an air of chagrin.

"I don't think that last stuff I got's any better than the others, do you?" he would say gloomily, caressing his bald crown, and she would reassure him mechanically, as she would have reassured one of the children.

Their relations had settled down into a sort of jog-trot harmony. They never quarrelled, but they never discussed anything more intimate than superficial household affairs. Though Hermione occasionally felt a flash of the old irritation with him, she was always restless and ill at ease when business took him away for a few days. Her normal feeling for him was the protective tenderness that she felt for the children, but a wave of depression would sometimes surge over her when she realised how completely her old passion for him had died.

Charles had been bitterly disappointed by Alan's decision to go on the stage. To the end he had clung tenaciously to the hope that college would after all turn Alan miraculously into a second John. He had a secret longing to have his three sons in his business.

"Damned nonsense!" he had said, when the idea was first broached to him. "The fellow ought to have been a girl. Stage-struck at his age! Good Lord!"

He refused obstinately to give his consent, but Alan distinguished himself so brilliantly at an O.U.D.S. performance that he was offered a part in Benson's company, and Charles reluctantly agreed to his joining it. He was deeply offended by Hermione's attitude.

"I didn't think that you'd have supported the boy against me," he said. But he had now reconciled himself to the idea, and was pinning his hopes on to Jimmie, who was to leave school in the summer. Jimmie wouldn't want to go on the stage. It would be Dereham & Sons when Jimmie came into the firm. Hermione knew that Charles's disapproval had hurt Alan, and at first she tried to soften it by interesting Charles in the boy's career and reading extracts from his letters. She soon found, however, that this was worse than useless. It roused afresh Charles's contemptuous indignation. She could not rid him of the idea that play-acting, as he called it, was unmanly.

"I gave the boy every chance," he would say, "and this is his gratitude."

The company in which Alan was playing visited Fernham one week, and Alan came over to Ivy Lodge for the afternoon. Hermione had asked him to bring some other members of the company with him. She thought that the visit—his first since he had become a professional actor—would pass off more easily and naturally if he had friends of his own to support him. She realised as soon as they arrived that she had made a mistake. Charles was polite to his guests—he even made an effort to welcome Alan heartily—but his secret disapproval hung over the assembly like a black cloud. And his stiffness was reflected in the bearing of the rest of the family. These people whom Alan had brought down with him belonged to a world that was a strange and alien world to the Derehams. The Derehams eyed them askance and with suspicion. They were too free-and-easy in their manners and expressions ("My God," said one, "it was a hell of a long wait"); the girls were too obviously made up, and one of them addressed Alan as "darling".

The Derehams had always been a united family, and with unconscious jealousy they now resented the terms of familiarity that existed between Alan and his new friends. Alan belonged to them, and it was as if in some way his friendliness with these aliens were a deliberate disloyalty.

John's manner was almost as aloof as Charles's. Monica, after a few half-hearted attempts at flirtation with the most handsome of the strangers, surrendered to the general attitude of disapproval. The guests, aware of the constraint of the atmosphere and taking it as an expression of censure of themselves, became, as if in self-defence, defiantly exuberant, bandying stage jokes, using stage nicknames. Two of the girls began to smoke, with only a casual "You don't mind, do you?"

Charles held old-fashioned views on women smoking—as on most things—and could hardly contain his anger.

Hermione tried to help Alan to bridge the gulf, but without success. Somehow she seemed to belong to both sides, and to be held powerless in the middle by the opposing forces. Alan made vain efforts to draw his family into the chaff and jokes that his friends, rather too aggressively, kept up. He looked pale and unhappy. He loved his family and was proud of them, and they were treating him as a stranger. His father's attitude hurt him most. As if for consolation he looked forward to the fame that he confidently believed would come to him, but it seemed suddenly savourless. He felt an intolerable loneliness, like the loneliness of a nightmare. Hermione managed to get him to herself for a moment in the morning-room before he went.

"Alan," she said breathlessly, "it's been so lovely to have you. . . . Come over whenever you can."

He took her in his arms and held her closely.

"Darling, it's been hateful. Everything's gone wrong, you know it has. Father will never understand now. Mother, they're not a bit as they seemed to you. They're so jolly and generous and—understanding. You do know, don't you?"

"Yes, of course I do. I liked them so much, darling."

"The others didn't."

"It was rather overwhelming, I suppose. It's all my fault. I oughtn't to have asked you to bring them the first time you came like this. It takes father a long time to get to know people. . . . Alan, darling, I'm so proud of you. You know that, don't you? And—you'll come again soon?"

"Yes . . . don't let me slip away from here, will you, mother? I'd hate to, you know. Even if I got famous, nothing would ever make up for that."

"I understand."

"You understand everything in the world. You always did."

"And you'll go on writing to me? I want to know everything about you. Remember that I look forward to your letters all week."

She had charmed away the worst of the loneliness, and by the time he reached the station his mind was again full of dreams of the future. He would work hard, he would be famous, he would make them proud of him yet.

Charles said nothing till he and Hermione were going to bed that night, then he burst out:

"I'll never have those play-acting fellows in my house again."

He spoke breathlessly, partly from indignation and partly because he was engaged in doing his exercises that he had not had time to do in the morning.

"Charles, don't be so silly," said Hermione impatiently.

She was tired, and felt self-reproachful because she had not been able to help Alan more.

"You'd have thought the house belonged to them," he went on, panting with exertion. "There wasn't a gentleman among them . . . and those girls . . . *painted*, I tell you . . . and smoking . . . *smoking* in my house. . . . I could hardly bear to see Gillian in the same room."

"I thought they were delightful. People who're on the stage are always unconventional."

"*Unconventional!*" he exploded. "I suppose you call swearing in front of the girls unconventional?"

"Oh, Charles, what does it matter? They're young, and actors are always free-and-easy. They live on such intimate terms together. They lose all that formality that ordinary people have."

"I wish I'd been firm and made the boy come into the business. He was always a fool, and now I suppose he'll be a cad as well."

Her anger rose hotly, and she opened her mouth to reply, then closed it without speaking.

Charles looked somehow so pathetic, standing there in his pants, his face red with exercise and indignation, laboriously bending his thick trunk backwards and forwards. . . .

Chapter Eighteen

JOHN became engaged to Valerie at the beginning of the next year. It was one of those engagements that make little stir, because they have been foreseen for so long. Hermione could not feel very enthusiastic about it. She had no fault to find with the girl, but she still seemed curiously unreal, despite her never-failing charm. There was no doubt, however, that she and John were in love with each other, and Hermione was glad to see John happy again. It had taken him a long time to recover from his broken engagement.

Hermione might, perhaps, have worried more than she did over the affair if all her anxiety had not been absorbed by Monica. Monica had entered a stage of hysterical religious fanaticism, bringing to it all the tempestuous energy that she brought to everything she undertook.

Old Mr. Swallow, who had long been too old and frail to perform his duties properly, had died at the end of last year. He had grown deaf and practically blind, and latterly his memory, too, had begun to fail, so that he would omit large portions of the service. His parishioners had conspired to hide this state of things from his ecclesiastical superiors, as they liked the old man and wished him to end his days, if possible, in the home he loved so dearly. He had died suddenly one Sunday in the vestry, as he was taking off his surplice after a morning service at which he had recited Evensong with unusual accuracy.

His successor, the Rev. Arnold Rothwell, was about forty years old, but he looked so much younger than his age, and his wife looked so much older than hers, that strangers generally took them for mother and son. He was tall and handsome, with auburn hair that curled crisply, a straight nose, well-cut lips, and a cleft in his chin—the type of face that looks extremely well in profile against a stained-glass window. His wife was a colourless, badly dressed little woman, with a strong North-country accent and a patent lack of education. As if aware of her unsuitability for any prominent position, she took no part in the parish activities, confining herself to the care of her home and husband. Neighbouring clergymen paying their first call at Abbotford Vicarage usually thought that she was the housekeeper.

Immediately after their arrival at Abbotford Monica began to attend daily services at the little Norman church. A few weeks later she set up a *prie-dieu* in her bedroom, and after that regularly spent the greater part of her pocket-money on subscriptions to missions and the purchase of devotional books. Her life became uncomfortably austere. She observed all the fast-days, refusing food ostentatiously at every meal; she gave up games and parties as unworthy of the seriousness of life; she went over to the vicarage every evening to borrow or return a book (she was laboriously reading the Early Fathers) or to ask for help in some religious difficulty. She began to go to Confession. . . . There was nothing subtle or introspective about Monica. She honestly believed that the ecstasy that seized her when she sat looking into the vicar's grey-blue eyes and listening to his low gentle voice was a religious ecstasy. He had offered to teach her Greek so that she could read the New Testament in the original.

Hermione felt peculiarly helpless. To suggest to Monica that she was in love with the man would not only hurt and alienate her, but would rouse all her obstinacy and make her in very loyalty persist in the new friendship.

She did her best, gently and unobtrusively, to discourage Monica from her frequent visits to the vicarage, but, once Monica had set her feet in a path, she was impervious to suggestion, command, or ridicule.

When the family teased her—as they did unmercifully—Monica welcomed their ridicule, looking upon it as religious persecution and feeling vaguely that it raised her to the rank of a martyr.

"Mon, dear," said Hermione one evening, glancing at the address of a letter that Monica was carrying through the hall, "need you write to Mr. Rothwell so often? You see him nearly every day."

"It's something that I don't quite understand in a book he lent me," said Monica, with dignity. "I thought that I'd better write it down while it was fresh in my memory. . . ."

Hermione noticed that it was one of Monica's best pink envelopes, freshly scented. Monica's attempts to allure were as instinctive as her breathing.

The Greek lessons had now begun, and Monica went to the vicarage every morning, giving much care to her appearance in preparation for the visits. She was blossoming into a fresh, seductive loveliness; there was a subtle, if unconscious, invitation in the dewy eyes and the full red lips. Hermione would have felt less worried had she not suspected that the man was deliberately encouraging her. He must have had enough experience of the world to know that the girl was falling in love with him, and to have stopped it if he had wished to stop it.

Vere, however, took her thoughts from Monica by suddenly announcing her engagement to Bobby Pettigrew.

Though John's absorption in Valerie, and Monica's absorption in her "religion", had thrown the two of them into each other's company a good deal lately, the announcement of their engagement took everyone by surprise. Bobby was two years younger than Vere, and Vere had always been so aloof and matter-of-fact that the local gossips had not included her in their matchmaking speculations. She tried to carry off her engagement with her usual nonchalance, but it was obvious to everyone that she was passionately in love with the boy. She could not hide it; did not, after the first embarrassment of the announced engagement had worn off, even try to hide it. She lost the hardness that had been her chief characteristic, becoming soft and young and radiant. Her eyes grew bright, her pale cheeks glowed with a rosy bloom, so that she was beautiful for the first time in her life. For the first time in her life, too, she began to take pains with her appearance, surrendering the austerity on which she had prided herself, dressing her hair in the latest fashion, studying the latest styles in dress, spending all her allowance on her clothes, thinking hours of preparation well repaid if Bobby said that she looked pretty. Though she had always hated needlework, she began to make her trousseau, working laboriously at the endless "dozens" of hand-made underclothes that the fashion of the time demanded.

Hermione watched her with an aching tenderness. The child was letting down her defences so completely, and the boy did not seem good enough. He was a nice, ordinary, good-tempered, decent boy, but she would have liked someone splendid for Vere, just as she would have liked someone splendid for John.

"I suppose that the people one's children marry never do seem good enough," she said wistfully to herself.

Monica sat on the seat in the vicarage garden that was half-hidden by the trees, her Greek book on her knee, her teacher by her side. It had been very hot, and the vicar had suggested this shady seat that could not be seen from the house or the road. The lesson was over. It had been rather a desultory lesson, as indeed all the lessons had been lately. Teacher and pupil seemed to have so much to talk about. Mr. Rothwell was leaning towards her. His arm was stretched along the back of the seat behind her. Occasionally it touched her, setting every nerve in her body a-tingle.

"I can never keep any good resolution," Monica was saying. "I get into horrible tempers and rage and storm at people. I'm selfish and beastly and bad-tempered. . . ."

But she was talking at random, not listening to what she said. She did not know what was happening to her—only she knew that all their friendship had been leading by strange, circuitous ways to this moment. He placed his hand on hers and a delirious excitement seized her. Her heart was beating wildly as if it had been a bird in her body trying to get out.

"Look at me, Monica," he said.

She turned her eyes slowly to his. . . . Once she and John had been on the river and had taken the boat too near the weir. She had the same feeling now of being drawn by some irresistible force towards a whirlpool. . . . John had just saved her then. There was no one to save her now. . . .

His voice came to her through a mist, half-drowned by the throbbing of her pulses.

"You must never talk like that, child. I know you better than you know yourself. I know your sweetness, your——"

The arm that had lain on the back of the seat closed round her. . . . Her pulses pounded suffocatingly in her throat.

Then quite suddenly, as it seemed, the plain, drab figure of his wife stood before them. So quickly had the man replaced one hand upon the back of the seat and taken up the Greek primer in the other, that it seemed impossible that she should have seen anything. There was no embarrassment in his face. He spoke in his usual pleasant voice.

"Yes, my dear?"

She looked at him with her pale, expressionless eyes.

"It's the man from Frankson's," she said. "He's mended the chair in your study. Was there anything else you wanted him to do?"

"No, thank you. . . ."

The woman went back towards the house. The man turned to Monica with a smile, obviously intending to encircle her again with his arm, but she sprang to her feet and spoke in a choking, breathless voice.

"I'm going . . . good-bye," she said, and hurried down the drive to the gate without waiting for him to speak. She ran home as if she were being pursued. An intolerable sense of shame possessed her. . . . She went to her bedroom and sank on to the floor, holding her hands to her eyes as if to shut out some horror. It was not his love for her that horrified her. It was the sudden, blinding knowledge of her love for him. So she was like that—loving a married man—a clergyman—and pretending that it was God she loved.

She heard a sudden stir of excitement downstairs and the words "Mrs. Rothwell" in Mrs. Pettigrew's high-pitched voice.

She crept to the top of the stairs.

"It only happened a minute ago. . . . I was there when the message came for the doctor. . . . She'd fallen out of the attic window. . . .

She'd gone up to clean it . . . she'd got the cleaning leather in her hand. . . . It's a miracle she wasn't killed. I believe it's only a broken leg. The bush by the door broke her fall. . . ."

Monica waited, her hands across her mouth, her eyes bright with terror, till Mrs. Pettigrew had gone. Then she called "*Mother!*" and Hermione came running upstairs.

"Whatever's the matter, Mon?"

Monica told her the story, sobbing convulsively as she told it, for Monica was no Vere to hide her trouble from those around her.

"Don't you see, mother? It wasn't an accident. . . . She saw us. . . . He'd put his arm right round me. . . . She saw us and went straight up to throw herself out . . . she took the cleaning leather so that it should seem an accident. . . . Mother, I hate myself. I'd let him put his arm round me and I'd have let him—do anything. . . . I'd been in love with him all the time, but I didn't know it till now . . . honestly, I didn't know it, mother. And now I know it, and I *hate* him and myself. . . . Oh, I'm so beastly, so *beastly* . . . I loathe myself. I wish I could die."

Hermione comforted her as best she could, relieved that things were, after all, no worse.

The news of the accident spread through the village, but no one suggested that it was anything but an accident. The next day Mrs. Rothwell's sister came down to help to nurse her. She was uncompromisingly a working woman and inclined to be garrulous. She confided her sister's history to Mrs. Binks of the general shop, and within an hour it was common knowledge in the village. Mr. and Mrs. Rothwell had been mill hands when first they became engaged, though Mr. Rothwell had always been more the "gentleman" than his fellows. The girl had been passionately attached to him, and, on his telling her of his secret ambition to become a clergyman, had insisted that he should at once begin the necessary training. In order to pay his fees for him, she had taken in washing as well as working at the mill, and had half-starved herself in her efforts to earn money for his training. She had paid his fees—with help from a local fund—and they had been married when he was given his first curacy. Mrs. Rothwell, said her sister, still worshipped her husband, but the sister seemed to have no very high opinion of the man for whom these sacrifices had been made.

That night Monica entered Hermione's room tempestuously before Charles had come to bed.

"Mother . . . I want to go into a nunnery."

"A *what*?" said Hermione, startled.

"A nunnery. . . . I want to join a sisterhood. Mother"—with sudden passion—"I can't face life—ordinary life—now with the feeling that I've done this awful thing. I *can't*. . . . I shall never be happy again, never for a single moment all the rest of my life. Mother, he—he sort of hinted to me that his marriage was a tragedy because she belonged to a different class from his. He didn't actually say so, but he *hinted*. I can't bear to think of it. I can't bear to think of her face as she stood there looking at us, but—don't you see?—if I enter a sisterhood, I'll feel that I'm doing penance for it. I *want* to do penance for it all the rest of my life. . . . I can't face my life now any other way. I loathe myself too much."

"Oh, Monica," smiled Hermione, "what an exaggerated person you are! Listen, darling. You've been foolish, but you're young and inexperienced. The whole blame was his. And mine. I saw the danger, and I ought to have prevented it somehow. You've done nothing wicked, darling."

"Yes, I have," persisted Monica. "I—I'd have done anything he wanted me to, if she hadn't just come along then, and she tried to kill herself, and she'd have done if it hadn't been for a tree. Mother"—her voice rose hysterically—"I'm a murderer. Can't you see I'm a murderer? I'll kill myself if you won't let me join a sisterhood. I *must* do penance."

"Listen, darling," said Hermione again patiently. "You must go away—right away from here—for a few weeks. You aren't in a fit state to know what you want. When you come back you'll see things sanely, and if you still want to join a sisterhood, we'll consider it seriously. But you must go away first to rest and think things out. Will you?"

"Where shall I go?"

"I'll write and ask Aunt Helen if she'll have you for a few weeks. Will you go, darling? Because I want you to?"

"Yes," sighed Monica resignedly.

When Charles came up, Hermione told him that Monica needed a change, and that she suggested sending her to St. Hilda's. He acquiesced without much interest. He was worried about his business. Professional agitators were busy with his work-people, and he was threatened with a strike.

Chapter Nineteen

JIMMIE had been eager to come straight into the business on leaving school. He said that he did not want to go to college, and Charles, who cherished a deep suspicion of colleges since the O.U.D.S. had opened the way to the stage for Alan, had readily agreed. Jimmie was anxious to arrive quickly at man's estate, in order to catch up with John, whom he had worshipped from babyhood. He longed to take his part in the home life of Ivy Lodge. School holidays there had been affairs of fun and parties, of hilarious gatherings of young people, of expeditions, bicycle rides, dancing, and "musical" evenings, when the countryside for miles around had re-echoed to the choruses from the *Scottish Students' Song Book* and *Songs of a Savoyard*. That meant home life to Jimmie. The thought of belonging to it permanently thrilled him, and the thought of working under John, his idol, seemed the summit of earthly happiness. His boyish face was flushed with pride and excitement the first morning he set off to the station with Charles and John.

Monica was still at St. Hilda's. At first her letters had been full of passionate misery and self-reproach. She would never know another moment's happiness for the rest of her life. . . . Why had not Hermione let her join a sisterhood at once? . . . She would not feel any differently about it when she came home. . . . Then gradually their tone became more cheerful. She was beginning to enter into the life of the school, to make friends with the elder girls and young mistresses. She was beginning to forget the tragedy that had sent her there. Helen was glad of her services in the capacity of unofficial secretary. She wrote to Hermione: "She is as unmethodical as—pardon me, my dear—one would naturally expect a daughter of yours to be, but she is willing and hard-working and responds quickly to instruction. I am finding her quite useful."

Vere was still radiantly happy in her engagement, but she was beginning to make the same mistake in that as she had made in all her friendships, trying to manage the boy's affairs for him and order his life. It was the old fault of "bossiness" that had alienated the other children in the nursery. Hermione noticed that, though still in love with her, Bobby was at times sulky and restive, as if he resented her domination, however affectionately exercised. She gave Vere a tentative hint, but Vere took it in bad part, becoming offended and on her dignity. "That's my business, please, mother. Bobby and I understand each other."

"It's dreadful," thought Hermione, "how little you can help the people you care for most. . . ."

Bobby was just finishing his training as an engineer, and it was understood that an uncle in India would find a post for him there as soon as he was ready.

John and Valerie were married early the next spring. John had insisted on Gillian's being chief bridesmaid, though Valerie raised several not very convincing objections. She had been jealous of John's affection for Gillian from the beginning. Often, when he brought home presents for Gillian, Hermione had seen Valerie's small mouth tighten ominously and had been depressed by the sight, though it was natural enough, she told herself, for a man's fiancée to be jealous of his sister. Absurd as it now seemed, she had once been jealous of Maud. . . .

The marriage took place in Abbotford church, and the ceremony was performed by the new vicar—an elderly bachelor whose whole interest was concentrated on the growing of the mammoth chrysanthemums for which he won prizes at all the local flower-shows. Mr. Rothwell had applied for an exchange as soon as his wife was well enough to leave Abbotford.

At the reception Hermione noticed that Jimmie was paying marked attention to Sylvia Carew, and paying it in rather a self-conscious manner as if showing off the new manhood and independence that still gave him such pride.

"Mother," he said that night, "do you like Sylvia?"

Hermione considered. The girl had always seemed pleasant enough when she was not imitating her mother's manner.

"Yes. . . . I think she's quite nice."

"I mean—would you like her for a daughter-in-law?"

"Jimmie, you mustn't dream of getting married yet."

"Why on earth not? John has."

It was as if he could not hurry enough to catch up John, to be on equal terms with his hero.

"John's six years older than you. You aren't twenty-one yet."

"I'm nearly twenty-one."

"You couldn't possibly afford to keep a wife."

"I know I couldn't, yet. But there's no harm in being engaged, is there? Then we could get married as soon as I could afford it. I think a man ought to settle down."

"You aren't a man yet. You're only a boy. You wouldn't have left college if you hadn't insisted on coming straight into the business from school. Have you proposed to her?"

"No," he muttered sulkily.

"Jimmie, don't be silly. You know I only want you to be happy. It's such a terribly important thing. The happiness of your whole life depends on it. Sylvia may be the right woman or she may not. You're both too young to know."

"You were only seventeen when you married."

"Your father was much older," she said, but she spoke with less assurance. She had, of course, little right to discourse on prudent marriages. . . .

John and Valerie went to Devonshire for their honeymoon, then took up their quarters at Broom End, a small Georgian House—rather like a miniature of Ivy Lodge—just outside Fernham. The Newmans had come home soon after John's marriage. There was a certain awkwardness in the first meeting between John and Cecilia, but Cecilia no longer mixed much with the young society of Fernham and Abbotford. Her mother had had a series of heart attacks while she was abroad and was now an invalid, demanding constant attention from her daughter.

Charles and Hermione gave a dance to celebrate Jimmie's twenty-first birthday, and Jimmie proposed to Sylvia while sitting out the first extra, bringing her at once to Hermione to announce their engagement with a sort of defiant excitement.

"I did mean to wait, mother," he said, "but she's such a darling that I couldn't."

He looked so young and eager and confident that Hermione's heart yearned over him. She kissed Sylvia, trying to put into the kiss more affection than she felt. Another nice ordinary girl, not good enough for Jimmie, just as Valerie had not been good enough for John or Bobby for Vere. . . . They were all leaving her. . . . John had married; Monica had come home for Jimmie's dance, but was going straight back to St. Hilda's to-morrow; Alan had not been home since his ill-fated visit last year; Vere would soon be joining Bobby in India; now Jimmie wanted to go. . . . Only Gillian was left, and Gillian was so lovely that they could not expect to keep her long. If only she could have felt more sure of their happiness. . . . She said to Charles that night: "When they're children you torture yourself with anxiety. . . . You feel that if you can bring them safely through their childhood all will be well. Looking forward, you think that if they grow up happily, healthily, that's the end . . . and then they grow up happily, healthily, and you find that it's only the beginning. You've got to torture yourself all over again."

Charles, who was deep in his evening paper, merely grunted.

The house seemed very silent and empty nowadays. Vere had no interests apart from Bobby, and spent most of her time at the Pettigrews', Jimmie was generally out with Sylvia, and John's new home had such an irresistible fascination for Gillian that she often went there directly after breakfast and did not return till bedtime. Though Valerie was jealous of John's affection for his sister, her visits broke the loneliness of the day for the young wife, and she found the child very useful about the house. The old friendship between Valerie and Vere had long since come to an end. Safely engaged, to John, Valerie had no longer troubled to keep up her pretence of devotion to Vere.

For so many years Ivy Lodge had been an eager, noisy hive of childhood and youth that Hermione found it hard to accustom herself to its sudden silence and emptiness.

In their nursery days and schoolroom days her children had adored her, and now quite suddenly she found them absorbed in their own love affairs, and herself relegated to the second place in their affections. She was continually being hurt by evidences that she no longer counted as a primary factor in their lives. They still loved her, of course, but between them and her was the gulf that inevitably separates one generation from another. She could not share their experiences. They did not even want her advice, for youth everywhere prefers—and rightly prefers—to make trial of life itself rather than to accept experience second-hand in the form of advice.

It should have been the moment for husband and wife to draw closer to each other, to form a new friendship that would replace their old passion and their recent absorption in their children. But Charles was gloomy and morose. The bulk of his employees were on strike, and he was carrying on business with the minimum of work-people, and with the prospect of having to close his works altogether. John, of course, was a great help to him. John could turn his hand to any job in the factory, and do it as well as the most skilled workman. But John, though he worked indefatigably, was distrait and absent-minded and, Charles felt, did not take the situation seriously enough. Valerie was now expecting a child, and John's whole attention was focussed upon that event, while to Jimmie, of course, the strike was a colossal "rag".

Charles would come home in the evening, tired and depressed, wanting only to forget his worries in Hermione's love and kindness. And Hermione, for the first time in her life as it seemed to him, was failing him. She insisted on discussing the strike with him—what had led to it, what exactly the men were demanding, whether or no they had any real grievance, how best it could be brought to an end. And he didn't want to talk about it with her. He wanted to forget it with her. His attitude hurt her as much as hers hurt him. Hurt and affronted her. . . . Did he really think her incapable of discussing his affairs with him intelligently? Did he put her on such a low level that she was fit only to minister to his creature comforts, that her mind was of too inferior an order to grasp a serious problem?

The subject of Women's Rights was in the air, and the militant suffragettes were opening their campaign of violence. Monica's letters from St. Hilda's were full of it. "Aunt Helen's terribly down on the Cause, and no one here dare mention it, but all the some most of the staff are in sympathy. . . ."

"Disgusting exhibition!" commented Charles, reading of their exploits in the newspaper.

"Men got the vote by rioting," Hermione reminded him.

"Women are different. . . ."

"Evidently," said Hermione ironically.

"Do *you* want a vote?" he challenged her.

"Why not?"

"What use would you make of it?"

"As good a use as a drunken farm labourer who can't spell his own name."

He clung as usual to his ready-made views and was impervious to argument, but he felt hurt and bewildered because she did not agree with him. It was, he felt aggrievedly, her duty to agree with him. . . .

Left alone with Charles in the house that had once seemed too small and now seemed so much too large, Hermione for the first time in her life began to develop nerves. Everything Charles said or did irritated her. His little mannerisms, his slow deliberate movements, his ineradicable little fussinesses, even the sound of his rather harsh voice, jarred her nerves intolerably. Sometimes when she saw him performing some quite ordinary everyday action—winding up his watch, brushing his hair, folding his newspaper carefully into its original folds—a sudden flash of hatred of him would seize her, so that she could hardly endure to be in the same room with him. One part of her had never belonged to Charles, and now it seemed to have come to the fore, to be pulling the rest of her along with it. Sometimes she even played with the idea of leaving him, of making a life for herself as so many women were doing. The children did not need her any longer. . . . Then would come, unbidden, some memory of Charles—helping her with the children when they were little, waiting on her with clumsy tenderness when she had a headache—and remorse would surge over her. Middle age was bringing her a second adolescence—stormy and turbulent as her first had never been. She had moods of black depression and often wept in secret for no reason. Even Charles, imperceptive as he was, noticed that she was not well, but his blundering solicitude only increased her irritation.

It did not improve matters that Monica was sent home from St. Hilda's in disgrace, having been heard by Helen openly championing the militant suffragettes.

Helen, who had scorned the conventional lot of women and had, unaided, made a career for herself, might have been expected to be a staunch supporter of the Rights of Women. But she was not. She herself occupied a position of privilege, but it would cheapen positions of privilege should too many women occupy them. The ordinary woman ought to marry and have children, ran her teaching nowadays. The vote would bring women into the dusty arena of politics, unsex them, take from them the higher, more potent weapon of their aloofness. This attitude was, of course, partly forced upon her. There were, after all, only a limited number of Advanced Parents. The majority of her parents wished their daughters to become Ladies. As Ladies, her old pupils pulled occasional political wires, but on the whole kept apart from politics and concentrated on the Home. In the Home they recommended her to their friends, and sent their daughters to her.

"The vote for women must come, I suppose," said Helen, "but when it comes it will not prove the panacea its supporters seem to expect it to prove. It certainly had better not come at all than that women should turn themselves into wild beasts for it."

So, when she heard her own niece openly advocating militant tactics in the staff-room, she packed her off by the next train.

Monica arrived home, not abashed or shamefaced, but a-thrill with the enthusiasm of a martyr who has suffered for her cause.

She had completely forgotten that a few weeks ago she had wished to enter a sisterhood. She had almost forgotten the tragedy that had made her wish to enter one, except in so far that it had been caused by the Perfidy of Man. For Monica was now a man-hater. She would discourse for hours on the general inferiority of man to woman, and on the millennium that would result when women won the vote.

Hermione noticed that this attitude was not incompatible with her receiving frequent letters addressed in a bold, masculine handwriting—written, Hermione gathered, by a Leonard Ashton, the uncle of one of Helen's pupils, whose sudden interest in his niece's education had coincided with Monica's visit to St. Hilda's—and despatching in reply the familiar pink scented notes.

She argued vehemently on the subject of Women's Rights with Charles in the evenings, cornering him so successfully at every turn that even Hermione pitied him.

But the atmosphere of her own home now rasped her nerves continually, and she looked forward eagerly to Alan's weekly letter. It seemed to bring into her life the breath of another world. Alan was succeeding. He had appeared in a West-End Shakespeare production, and, though his part had been a small one and the play had been a comparative failure, it had brought him into touch with several important people in his profession. One of them, Gervais Lynne, had given him the part of understudy to the hero in a modern comedy that he was producing, and had invited him to share his flat during the run of the play. He was a much older man than Alan, but Alan had always seemed in many ways older than his years, and a real friendship had sprung up between the two men. Alan, of course, was still young enough to be a hero-worshipper, and his letters were full of praise of his new friend. "You'd like him, mother, he's our sort."

One week there came a short, excited note instead of the usual long letter.

"Gervais is going away for a few days, and he suggests that I ask you to stay here while he's away. Do come, darling. It would be lovely to have you. Tell father that I'll take the greatest care of you. . . ."

She glanced round the room. Vere was at the Pettigrews'; Jimmie was out with Sylvia; Gillian had gone to Broom End to help Valerie drape the cot, and had arranged to stay the night there; Monica and Charles were carrying on their unending squabble about Women's Rights.

She sat down at her bureau and wrote to Alan, telling him that she would come.

Chapter Twenty

It was a continuation of the friendship she had formed with Alan during that visit to him in Somerset. The constraint that always overlay their relations in the home circle vanished completely when they were alone together. They were continually discovering new ideas and tastes in common. Hermione had lived in a backwater of life, but she was naturally open-minded, quick-witted, and receptive. She had never subscribed to the hide-bound attitude of her generation towards the problems of the day. She found her intercourse with Alan even more exciting and stimulating than she had found it on her other visit. It was strange, she thought, that the only real friend she had ever made should be her own son. Charles had been her lover, but never her friend. . . .

The depressing sensation of having grown old before her time left her, and she began to feel like a young girl again.

"I simply can't believe that you're my mother in the way other men's mothers are their mothers," said Alan. "You seem to belong to my generation, not father's. I can talk to you just as I'd talk to someone I'd been at school and college with. I feel that you're at my stage somehow—I mean the stage of being interested in everything, wanting to know . . . not turning new things down because they're new. You're so young and alive . . . and, oh, my dear, you're so pretty."

It was years since Charles had told her she was pretty.

"Alan, darling," she laughed, "I'm getting old. I'm forty-five. . . ."

"*Old*!" he said. "What nonsense! You're a little older than Gillian but years younger than me."

She studied herself carefully in her glass that night. Yes, she was still pretty, she decided, but her country clothes made her look old-fashioned and badly dressed. A sudden revolt against middle age and dowdiness seized her, and the next morning, while Alan was at rehearsal, she went out and spent money recklessly, buying one of the new Directoire dresses that had just come into fashion, and one of the enormous hats that were being worn with them. It was an absurd costume, of course, but it showed off her slender, graceful figure perfectly, and Alan laughed in delight when he saw her.

"You're adorable," he said. "How much younger do you want to look?"

She had only visited London before on hurried shopping expeditions, generally with the children—she knew and hated the Zoo and Madame Tussaud's—and Alan's London was a new world to her. He showed her the hauntingly lovely bits of old London that linger here and there, undiscovered by the ordinary tourist; he took her to the churches that are in themselves complete histories of England—All Hallows, St. Alban's, St. Bartholomew's, St. Olave's, St. Saviour's, St. Helen's. They visited Clifford's Inn, Staple's Inn, Fountain Court, and Chelsea's quaint garden of herbs.

He was interested in early editions, and she accompanied him on what he called his "hunting expeditions", searching old book-shops in out-of-the-way places for treasures. While Hermione was with him he found the missing volume of his First Dublin Edition of *Cecilia*, and bought it for four shillings. He taught her the love of old furniture. Together they bought a Queen Anne wall mirror with a canopy top and charming gilt shell for Hermione's bedroom.

"Isn't it thrilling," said Alan, "to think of all the beaux and belles in powder and patches who must have looked into it?"

In the evenings, when he came back from the theatre, he loved to sit on the floor at her feet, his head against her knee, the room lit only by the firelight, talking to her. . . . Sometimes he would say: "You must meet Gervais, mother. He's such a good sort. . . . I should think he's about your age—perhaps older—but he's like you; he doesn't belong to any generation. He's just young and alive. And awfully kind and simple and unspoilt."

She would say evasively: "Yes, I'd love to meet him sometime." But she did not really want to meet him. A third person, she felt, would spoil the friendship between her and Alan. There were few things in the flat to remind her of its owner. It might have belonged to Alan. There was nothing in it that Alan would not have chosen. Even the books, though the name "Gervais Lynne" was written in a small cultured hand on the flyleaf, were Alan's books. . . .

But one afternoon, two days before the end of her visit, when she was sitting in the flat waiting for Alan to return from a rehearsal, there came a knock at the door, and a man entered—tall, spare, stooping, with a thin, lined face, and deep, kindly, humorous eyes.

"I'm sorry to barge in like this," he said. "I'm Gervais Lynne. You're Alan's mother, aren't you? I got my business finished a day sooner than I expected. I ought to have stayed away till the end of your visit, in any case, but I wanted to meet you. I'd heard so much about you from Alan. . . . Will you put up with me? I promise I won't be any extra trouble."

She laughed, though an odd perturbation had seized her at his entry. She knew this man, had known him all her life, longer than all her life. . . .

"Do come in. . . . It's your flat, after all, isn't it? I ought to be the one to apologise. I've enjoyed my visit here so tremendously. . . ."

Then Alan burst in, pleased and excited by his friend's return. And close on Alan came tea, brought in by Gervais's factotum, grinning a welcome at his master.

Gervais and Alan at once began eagerly to discuss the play, which was still drawing full houses. Hermione, her heart beating unevenly, pretended to be busied over the tea-table. She did not look again at the new arrival, but, even though her eyes were turned away from him, she could see him plainly. Every line of his face, every swiftly changing expression of it, was familiar.

"You're mad," she was saying to herself. "You can't be in love with a man whom you've only known for a few minutes. . . ."

Alan went out to get his copy of *Cecilia* from his bedroom, and they were left alone together. Hermione summoned all her forces and turned to her host with a casual question about his holiday. But as soon as she met his eyes, the words died away. They looked at each other in silence. . . .

Hermione never knew how long Alan was away. When he returned, he at once began to talk to Gervais, showing him the book. Hermione sat gazing into the fire. She was trembling slightly. The whirlpool that had seized her had seized him too. That one look into his eyes had told her that. Even now, though he was talking easily and naturally to Alan, he was pale and shaken. She belonged to a generation that regarded love outside the marriage bond as sin in whatever guise or circumstance it came. Bewildered, her emotions in a tumult, she clung to the certainty that she must fight this thing as long as there was breath in her body. He must never know what had happened. Somehow or other he must be made to believe that she was in love with her husband. . . .

It often seemed to her one of the strangest things in her life that Charles should have come that evening. She had written to Monica to ask her to send some things that she had left behind, and Charles had come into Town to bring them. He was missing his wife poignantly in the long evenings and felt vaguely aggrieved by her absence.

He looked curiously out of place in the little book-lined room. As he came in and sat down, the whole scene became suddenly unreal and dreamlike to Hermione—the three men, herself, the firelight flickering on the polished surface of old wood, and on the mellow bindings of old books. . . . But even in the dream she and Alan and the other man were bound together indissolubly, and Charles was a stranger. . . . He was sitting in the armchair that his host had drawn forward, looking round distrustfully as if he, too, suspected that he was in an alien world. His eyes rested finally on Hermione. . . . He did not realise that she was wearing a new dress and that her hair was arranged more fashionably in a mass of "sausage curls" behind her head instead of her ordinary coils. But he thought that she looked different somehow, and it increased his obscure feeling of resentment. He wanted to say to her, "Come home with me. I hate it without you." Instead, quite unaware that he was scowling at her ungraciously, he said, "Well, how are you? Having a good time?"

"A wonderful time," she said, and, trying to shake off the dreamlike languor that possessed her, told him of her expeditions with Alan, of the book and the little Queen Anne mirror. It meant nothing to him, of course. Old furniture to Charles was old furniture—nothing more. Old books were old books. Dirty and insanitary. You never knew who had had them. He preferred his things new. . . .

With an increasing sinking of her heart, she said: "And how are things going at home?"

"Oh, Mon's still on at the wretched Women's Right business," he said, and, because he could not resist having his say in peace now that Monica was not there to pull him up at every word, continued:

"She can't or won't see that a woman's place is the home. As soon as a woman leaves that she loses everything that makes womanhood a power in the world."

"But surely," said Gervais Lynne, smiling, "only a comparatively small proportion of women can afford to remain in the home. There are thousands of women workers shamefully underpaid who—as non-voters—are negligible to politicians. It isn't worth anyone's while to right their wrongs as long as they haven't got a vote."

"So you agree with them?"

"Absolutely."

Hermione broke in to ask Charles if his disagreement with the work-people were settled yet. She realised, as soon as she had said it, that it was a mistake. It drew from Charles a long tirade against Trade Unions, and Gervais defended them quietly, unanswerably. "They're absolutely necessary to ensure the working man justice and a living wage. He's up against a strong organisation—official or unofficial—of employers, and he has to have an organisation of his own to deal with it."

"So you approve of strikes?" glowered Charles.

"When justified, yes."

The antagonism between the two men was growing more evident every moment. Hermione watched and listened helplessly. She was saying silently to Charles: "You ought to have pretended to be different. He'll know now. . . . That was the only hope, that he shouldn't know."

At last Charles rose and took his leave. To Hermione, despite that curious feeling of despair that his visit had brought her—as if she had cried out to him to save her and he had merely turned away—there was something pathetic in his big stooping figure as he set off alone from the flat. She knew that he missed her and wanted her to go home with him.

There was a moment of constraint when he had gone. Then Alan said: "Father's old-fashioned, you know, but he's a real good sort."

Charles, away from Ivy Lodge, had startled Alan somewhat but had not shaken his loyalty.

"He's always been good to his work-people," he went on, "and he feels awfully hurt that they should strike."

Gervais was looking about the room. "What have you done to it?" he said to Hermione. "It looks different—more like a home, somehow."

"I've done nothing. . . . Only put some flowers about."

"That's it, I suppose. . . . I must remember flowers in future.

"I've got hold of rather a good play," he went on after a moment's pause, "and there's a part in it for this young man. I'm going to put it on as soon as *King's Men* comes off."

"What's the plot?" said Alan.

"It's a fairly ordinary plot," said Gervais slowly. "It's the old story of an uncongenial couple and the inevitable tragedy."

Hermione began to speak quickly, breathlessly.

"But—don't you see?—there isn't any inevitable tragedy. It needn't matter so terribly that a husband and wife are not congenial. It's not being congenial that binds a husband and wife to each other. It's the things they've been through together. It's—" She paused, reaching for words; she felt that it was vitally important that he should be made to understand this: "You see, they've been through things that—make them part of each other. . . . No one else could ever take their place, because no one else could ever have gone through those particular things with you. . . . Being congenial isn't as—frightfully important as people think. Other things matter more. If they've been kind, if they've loved you. . . ."

"I don't quite agree," said Gervais. "We're talking of an uncongenial husband and wife, of course. Suppose then the wife leaves her husband for another man—a man she loves. They, too, go through things together—the same things probably. It forms a bond between them stronger than the original bond, because in their case there is deeper understanding and sympathy."

In the silence that followed she seemed to feel again Charles's tears upon her hand after John's birth, his hand upon her shoulder by Nigel's deathbed. . . .

"No," she said slowly, "it couldn't be the same. You see—they couldn't be just the same things. You could never have your first child again. You could never—lose a child for the first time again. You couldn't go through just those things with anyone else. However much you loved the other man, however—congenial he was, you'd be haunted by—memories—all your life. . . ."

Alan stirred in his chair. He felt drowsy and happy. He was in this little room he had come to love so well, with the two people who were dearest to him of all the world. He was not listening to what they were saying. He had known from the first that they would like each other. He was aware that already the three of them were old friends. He took up the poker and lazily stirred the fire. The blaze flickered up, showing him his mother's face—pale and beautiful in the sudden light.

"You look tired," he said solicitously.

"I am," she said. "I think I'll go to bed now. . . . Good night."

She did not sleep, of course. A strange excitement possessed her. She had thought that she was growing old, and here was life, youth, love, offered to her in rich abundance. At the memory of him—his eyes, his voice, his mobile sensitive lips—every nerve in her body seemed to thrill. The something in her that had been trapped and cheated cried out to her to let it free, now at last, after all these years. "Don't cheat me a second time. . . . Here's the chance. It will never come again. . . . Your life with Charles is a farce, a makeshift. . . . This is your last chance, your last chance. If you let it go, there's nothing for you but a dreary old age. . . . If you take it, there's youth and love and the whole world before you. . . ."

She lay with lips tight and brows drawn sharply together as if in pain. "You're at a dangerous age," she told herself sternly. "Women do foolish things at your age and regret them all their lives. Even suppose you'd be happy—what is your happiness worth in comparison with your children's? It would destroy their belief in goodness, perhaps in God. . . . You'd be ashamed all your life when you thought of your children. Charles is dull, and you don't love him as you love this man, but he's given you his youth. He's always been kind. You couldn't have gone on living without him when Nigel died. You loved him like this once, too, but it went. How do you know that your love for this man won't go? . . ."

Lying tense and rigid in the darkness with closed eyes and set lips, she fought till the sweat stood out on her brow against the sweet, soul-shattering languor that assailed her; prayed desperately, doggedly, monotonously: "Oh, God, please help me. . . . Please help me . . .," and, ridiculously as she knew even while she said it: "Please don't let Nigel know. . . ."

She did not appear for breakfast the next day till after Gervais had gone out, and to Alan's surprise and disappointment she insisted on going home before lunch.

"But, mother, Gervais is being in for lunch. He's expecting to see you again."

She left polite messages for Gervais and went back to Abbotford by the early train.

Chapter Twenty One

VALERIE'S baby was born the day after Hermione reached home, and Hermione went to Broom End immediately to take over the housekeeping and help with the baby. She was glad to have the hours so fully occupied that she had no time to think of the strange and terrifying thing that had happened to her. "You were mad," she said to herself sternly; "you must never think of him or meet him again. . . . You're a grandmother. Remember that, and don't make a fool of yourself."

As a matter of fact, it thrilled her to realise that she was a grandmother. The child was a girl—healthy and well formed. John was, of course, delighted. He had bargained before the birth that, if a girl, it was to be called after his mother. Hermione loved to look after the child, and she encouraged the nurse to devote herself to Valerie, who indeed demanded a good deal of attention. Charles was absurdly proud of his first grandchild and called at Broom End every day on his way to and from work. He was feeling and looking much happier. The strike had petered out, leaving remarkably little ill-feeling in its train, and his business was forging ahead again. His only worry was that Jimmie, though he worked well enough, seemed to be losing the keenness he had shown when first he joined the firm. And, of course, he missed Hermione. She had only been at home a day between her visit to Alan and her visit to John.

He came from work with John one evening and found her bathing the baby by the bedroom fire, wearing a mackintosh apron, her sleeves rolled up above her elbows.

He watched her, smiling.

"Seems like old times," he said, and added, "I think it suits you to be a grandmother."

"It's ridiculous to think of her as a grandmother," said John. "Just look at her."

"Does it make you feel any older?" asked Charles.

"No, younger," she smiled. "I feel as if I were beginning my own babies all over again. . . ."

"Which is she like?" said Charles, looking down at the tiny being she handled so deftly.

"She's like John, of course," said Valerie from the bed.

"I think she's a mixture of all of them," said Hermione.

When Charles went, the nurse took the baby from Hermione, so that Hermione could go downstairs to see him off.

"When are you coming home?" he said.

"Valerie seems better," she answered. "I think I could come to-morrow."

Upstairs Valerie was saying to John peevishly: "Really, anyone would think, by the fuss you all make of her, that it was your mother who'd had the baby, not me."

Hermione went home the next day, and was gratified and somehow remorseful at the obvious pleasure of the children in her return. She was still fighting this new love that strove so ceaselessly and insidiously to enter her heart, still battling against every thought or memory that could weaken her resistance.

Curiously enough, the irritation with Charles that had tormented her nerves before she went away had disappeared. She felt instead a nagging compunction, as if she had deliberately wronged him, an ashamed desire to make up to him for it by additional kindness.

Bobby Pettigrew had finished his training as an engineer, and his uncle had obtained the promised post in India for him. The salary would not be enough to marry on at first, so he was to go out alone and send for Vere after a year or two. The faint exasperation that he had begun to show to Vere vanished as the day of his departure came nearer. Meekly, even gratefully, he allowed her to make all his arrangements, and preparations for the voyage.

He seemed bewildered and aghast at the thought of being parted from her.

"I'll send for you the second I've got enough to marry on," he said. "I can't bear the thought of leaving you. You won't forget me, will you, darling?"

Vere grew more and more curt in her manner to him, and Hermione knew that she was needing all her power of self-control not to break down. The boy, who, in spite of his dependence on and love for her, understood her hardly at all, was hurt by her brusqueness, and they almost quarrelled the night before he sailed.

"I don't believe you care for me a bit," he burst out; "I believe you're glad to get rid of me."

So nerve-racked were they both that Hermione felt relieved when the moment of sailing was over. Vere accompanied him to Tilbury, and returned looking pale and red-eyed. She disappeared for the whole of the next day, then went about her work as usual.

Lady Amhurst was organising a dramatic performance for Christmas. She was producing it herself, and she had asked Jimmie to be the hero and Gillian the heroine. Jimmie was rather bored by the idea, as indeed he was rather bored by most things nowadays. Secretly he was bewildered and frightened. He had been so impatient to follow his hero John into man's estate, to enter the business like John, to be engaged to be married like John. He was fond of Sylvia, but had it not been for John's example he would never have thought of proposing to her. The grown-up world had been bathed in glamour in his eyes. He had entered it with high hopes, as one would enter an enchanted land, expecting he did not quite know what, but something transcending all his boyhood's experiences. And he found it uninteresting, uneventful, narrow. He felt angry and resentful as if someone had deliberately trapped him. John was no longer the god who had been games captain of Moorcroft and had rowed in the Cambridge boat. He was kind and patient, and Jimmie was fond of him, but there was little glamour about him now. His interests seemed to be bounded on all sides by his own domestic affairs, and Jimmie, who disliked Valerie, seldom visited his home. His work was not thrilling and absorbing as he had thought it would be. It was dull and monotonous. He didn't feel proud and important any longer as he set off with his father in the morning.

And this affair of being engaged was the worst of all.

"What's the matter, Jimmie?" said Hermione one evening when they found themselves alone in the drawing-room. She had noticed his depression ever since she came home from her visit to Alan, though he obviously did his best to hide it.

"Nothing," he said shortly.

"Is it Sylvia?"

He was silent for a minute, then burst out, "I'm sick of being engaged to her."

"What do you mean? Do you want to get married?"

"Good Lord, no."

"Aren't you fond of her?"

"Yes. I'm quite fond of her. But—I'm sick to death of going about with a girl. I'm sick of her mother and going there to tea and going round to visit her relations. I've got to take her wherever I go. I want to join a football club in Fernham, but I can't because I'm expected to take her about at the week-end. I've not had a good walk or a good game of any sort since I left school. I want to go about with boys and take up games again. This girl business is footling. And she's beginning to ask if I'm getting enough salary to be married on, and saying that she wouldn't mind a little house and doing her own housework. It's the devil."

"Poor Jimmie! Well, what's to be done?"

"Nothing, I suppose. I must just go through with it."

"I don't see how you can if you feel like that."

At that moment Sylvia entered. She kissed Hermione, then seated herself on the sofa end, and looked at Jimmie in silence for a moment.

"I thought you were coming in to-night, Jimmie," she said at last.

"Did I say I would?"

"Yes."

"I'm sorry. I forgot."

"We were going to fix up what day we should go to see Aunt Charity. . . . Perhaps you've forgotten that you'd promised to go to Aunt Charity's with me."

"Oh, hell, did I? . . . Sorry."

"You needn't be so beastly about my people, Jimmie. They've been awfully nice to you."

"I know. I'm sorry. . . . It's just that"—he buried his head in his hands and spoke indistinctly—"I'm sick of everything."

There was a long silence, then she said, "You mean you're tired of me?"

He said, "Of course not," but he said it three seconds too late. She took off her ring and handed it to him.

"I've known for some time that you were," she said quietly. "I've just been—trying to pretend that things were all right."

"Sylvia, don't be a fool. I——"

"Nothing in the whole world would make me marry you now," she said. "Good-bye."

She left Jimmie, crimson-faced and abashed, staring at the ring that lay in the palm of his hand.

They heard the sound of the front door closing. Jimmie started forward, but Hermione put her hand on his arm.

"Don't, Jimmie. . . . Better leave it as it is. She's quite right. You are tired of her. Things would be worse than ever if you patched it up. . . . You felt it a drag and nuisance. Now you're free of it."

"Yes . . . I know. But"—he still looked flushed and miserable—"you see it isn't only that. It's—everything."

"How do you mean—everything?"

"Oh—everything. The business. It's so *deadly*. Just the same things day after day. When I think of going on with it from now till I'm old—I can't bear it. I feel somehow as if I were in a trap. I don't suppose you understand."

"Yes, I do understand. You were in too much of a hurry, weren't you, Jimmie?"

"I suppose I was. I thought it would all be different, somehow."

"I know. . . . What do you want to do?"

His air of depression left him. He looked suddenly boyish and eager again.

"Mother . . . do you know what I'd like to do? I'd like to join the South African Mounted Police. . . . I want real *life* with real adventure in it. But"—dejection engulfed him again—"I should never dare to tell father I feel like that. He's been so decent to me and taken such a lot of trouble with me since I went into the business. He'd never understand."

"I'll try to make him," said Hermione. "Leave it to me."

She approached Charles on the subject that night. Though disappointed, he took it better than she had thought he would. He had liked having two sons in his business, he had been pleased by Jimmie's quickness and capacity for hard work, but the boy's attitude was one that he could understand, one that he could feel proud of. The longing for adventure was a healthy, manly longing—not like Alan's namby-pamby hankering after play-acting.

He gave his permission with a fairly good grace. Jimmie applied to the Chartered Company, was accepted, and joyfully set about getting his kit.

Chapter Twenty Two

MONICA no longer spent her time quarrelling with Charles about Women's Rights. She was now Secretary of a Women Suffragists' Society in Fernham and was very much occupied in organising meetings and demonstrations. Her own family she had come to consider unworthy of the Cause and scorned even to discuss the subject with any one of them. Jimmie, whose boyish high spirits had returned now that he was definitely leaving the work he had begun to dislike, teased her unmercifully and occasionally succeeded in rousing her into one of the old flaming tempers. Her correspondence with Helen's pupil's uncle still continued, and the week before Jimmie sailed he appeared at Ivy Lodge, a plain, short-sighted little man, whose paternal manner to Monica set at rest the vague fears that Hermione had occasionally felt with regard to the affair.

Vere had joined a school of domestic economy in Fernham and went there every day for lessons in cookery and laundry work, practising what she had learnt in the kitchen at Ivy Lodge, to the mingled scorn and amusement of the cook. She even learnt dressmaking and studied books on the care of babies, determined to qualify herself at every point to be a perfect wife to Bobby. She spent all her leisure time writing to him, or working laboriously and with frequently pricked fingers on her trousseau.

The short period of quiet—almost of emptiness—that had come to Hermione when first her children began to live their lives independently of her was over. She was now drawn into the turbulent whirlpool of their love affairs. And her own love affair was most turbulent of all. It had been such a nebulous affair—she had spent only an hour or so in Gervais Lynne's company and had not exchanged one word with him in private—that she had hoped that it would seem like a fantastic dream when she came home. But it did not. . . . It seemed the most real, the most vital thing that had ever happened to her. The love that had sprung to birth so quickly seemed now to be part of her very being. She had not abated her struggle against it, trying continually to discipline her mind and thoughts and memory. She was of the generation that looked upon a woman's "virtue" as an essential part of her husband's honour. Had Charles been brutal, vicious, or a confirmed drunkard, she would still have considered it her duty to stay with him. But it was a hard struggle. . . . She dreaded and yet longed to meet Gervais again. Alan had written to ask if he might bring him over to Ivy Lodge, but she had put him off with some rather unconvincing excuse. She threw herself with renewed energy into the work of her household and the interests of her children. Only so could she gain some respite from the struggle that seemed to exhaust her body as well as her mind.

Preparations for the Christmas play had begun at the Manor, and Gillian as heroine had to go there for frequent rehearsals. She was not a good actress, but her loveliness made it impossible to consider anyone else for the part. There was still something touchingly childish and innocent about Gillian. Despite her nineteen years she retained the shy seriousness of a little girl. Hermione was glad that she should have this new interest. She had been going to Broom End every day lately to help Valerie with the baby, and Hermione considered that Valerie exploited the child, making an unpaid nursemaid of her. Once or twice she had thought of protesting, but she knew that Valerie made John suffer for any fancied slight put upon her by his family, and so for John's sake Hermione always avoided friction with her daughter-in-law.

Jimmie, of course, was to have been the hero of the play, and his departure for South Africa a fortnight before Christmas upset all the arrangements. At first Sir Lionel took the part, but he was a poor actor, and handed it over with relief to a cousin of his wife's who arrived unexpectedly a few days before Christmas, and who had had much experience in amateur theatricals.

Humphrey Scales was about forty years old-tall, strikingly handsome, with an assured and rather arrogant manner. Charles disliked him on sight, and was annoyed that he should be playing hero to Gillian's heroine.

"If I'd known Jimmie wasn't to be the hero, I shouldn't have let Gillian take the part," he grumbled. "I don't like the fellow, and I can't bear to think of him pawing her about."

It was the first time that Hermione had known him to be uneasy about any of the children in that particular way.

"It's only a play, Charles," she reassured him.

"He paws her about in it."

"No more than if they were dancing together."

"Well, I'd hate them to dance together. I don't like him. He's the sort of chap to make love to every girl he meets."

"He's going as soon as Christmas is over."

"He can do enough harm by then. . . . Why didn't they have Mon for the heroine? She can look after herself all right."

"I'm not so sure of that. . . . Anyway, just at present nothing on earth would persuade Mon to act in a play that had a single male character in it."

He went to the play and sat through it glumly, fidgeting about in his seat and muttering angrily whenever Scales made love to Gillian.

"Don't be silly, Charles," Hermione said to him that night. "You can't keep the child in a glass case all her life."

"I don't like the fellow," he muttered again.

But the next day Scales called to take Gillian for a walk, and Hermione also began to feel slightly anxious. He was too handsome, too experienced, and there was an elusive but unmistakable suggestion of dissipation about him. Even his acting had shown a man skilled in the art of making love.

Charles came home from Fernham that evening, his face set and grim. He had met a man who knew Scales and was surprised to hear that he had been received at Amhurst Manor.

"He's a blackguard all round," reported Charles. "He was co-respondent in a divorce suit some years ago and then refused to marry the woman. He's not fit to be in the same room as any decent girl. . . . He's got through all his money and lives by gambling. I'll tell Gillian when she comes in that she's never to speak to him again."

Soon Gillian came in, her violet blue eyes soft and dewy, her creamy skin flushed.

Charles delivered his ultimatum, unsmiling and with heavy authority. Her eyes looked through him, beyond him; she spoke in a far-away voice, her lips curved into a smile.

"But, father, he's just asked me to marry him, and I've said I will. . . ."

Charles went crimson. He raged and spluttered, but nothing could break through Gillian's gentle, dreamy resolution.

"But, father, I love him and he loves me. . . . Yes, he told me all about that. He said that he was going to be quite different now he's met me. . . . Love changes people, father. It's changed me even in this short time. . . . I don't care about anything in the world now but him. . . ."

"You're under age, and you can't marry without my permission," said Charles finally, "and I shall never give you permission, so you may as well put the man right out of your mind."

The next morning Humphrey Scales himself arrived and asked to see Charles. The interview was a short one, and the man went away looking flushed and angry, though not so angry as Charles, who, Hermione gathered, had lost his temper completely. In the afternoon she went with Charles to Amhurst Manor to see Lady Amhurst. They found her pale and distraught. Her cousin had just told her that he had proposed to Gillian, and she had at once ordered him to leave the house.

"I blame myself more than I can tell you," she said. "I haven't seen or spoken to my cousin for years till this Christmas. He arrived unexpectedly and asked if he might spend Christmas with us. I didn't like to refuse him at Christmas, and he made himself very useful. He took over Lionel's part, of course, among other things. . . . I never thought—I wish to God now that I'd sent him away."

"Then I take it that what I've heard about him is true?" said Charles heavily.

"I don't know what you've heard about him," said Lady Amhurst, "but the thought of his marrying a girl like Gillian is impossible. He says he's in love with her. I've no doubt he is. He's been in love with other women. He's utterly unreliable—worse than unreliable—in every way. I shall never forgive myself for this . . . never. If there's anything I can do . . ."

"There's nothing anyone can do," said Charles. "She's under age, and I shall never give my permission for the marriage. You say the man's gone?"

"I told him to leave the house within half an hour and he went. I don't suppose he's gone far."

He had gone, they discovered, to an hotel in Fernham, and he had met Gillian that afternoon while Hermione and Charles were at the Manor.

Hermione pleaded tenderly with Gillian, trying to make her realise what such a marriage would mean to her. The memory of her own recent love made her more understanding than she would have been otherwise. But Gillian was immovable. For the first time they came upon the bedrock of firmness that underlay her sweetness and docility. She did not weep and protest as Monica would have done. She was not defiant and aggressive as Vere would have been. She was enclosed in a wall of gentle remoteness.

"Gillian, darling, it would break your father's heart."

"I can't help that, mother. Humphrey comes before everyone now. It would break his heart if I didn't marry him."

"Wait till you're twenty-one, at any rate."

"I can't wait, mother. Anything might happen. . . . Suppose he died, or I died, while we were waiting. . . ."

Charles spoke to her, telling her all he had heard of the man, appealing to her loyalty and obedience, but could draw no more from her than the gentle:

"I know he's not lived a good life. He's told me so. But he's going to be different if I marry him. He loves me, you see. . . . Yes, father, I know you've always been good to me, but he must come first now. I love him. . . ."

Hermione used all her resources to get through to the loving, responsive child they had known, but she seemed to have gone from them for ever. It was as if the man had stolen her away already, leaving only this dreamy wraith of her behind.

"Mother, I *do* love you and father—you know I do—but, you see, I love him more."

She came into the morning-room one afternoon when Hermione sat there sewing, and said: "Mother . . . if you and father won't let me marry Humphrey, I'm going to him without marrying him."

The sewing dropped from Hermione's hands. She caught her breath.

"*Gillian!* You don't know what you're saying."

"Yes, I do. I don't see that words said in a church make so very much difference. I belong to him for ever and ever whether we marry or not."

Hermione's heart was beating wildly.

"Gillian, you wouldn't—you couldn't——"

"You don't understand, mother," said the sweet, childish voice. "You don't know how I love him."

"But, Gillian"—Hermione laid a trembling hand on the girl's arm and tried to speak steadily—"it would be wicked. You know it would be wicked."

The violet eyes, set wide apart in the exquisite heart-shaped face, met hers unflinchingly.

"No, it wouldn't be wicked, mother."

Reasoning, pleading, were useless. The girl remained adamant beneath her gentleness. At last Hermione gave up the effort in despair.

She did not see Charles alone that night till they were going to bed. Then she said wearily:

"You'll have to give in to this marriage, Charles."

"Why?"

"Gillian says she'll go away with him if you won't let her marry him."

He stared at her and set his lips more grimly.

"I shan't give my consent to the marriage in any case."

"But, Charles, she means it. . . . She'll go with him if you don't."

"Then she must go with him."

She went white.

"*Charles!* You can't force her to do that."

"I'm not forcing her. No one can stop her going with him if she wants to, but at least she won't go to him with my consent as she would if she married him."

"How can you compare them," burst out Hermione passionately, "marriage and—immorality? You must be out of your mind. I can't believe it. . . . You *can't* let Gillian do this. It's wicked."

"How can I stop her?"

"By giving your consent to the marriage."

"I shall never do that. . . . Listen, Hermione," he said slowly. "If she goes to him she can come back to us when she wants to. He'll have no hold on her. If she marries him her life will be one long slavery and degradation."

"Degradation!" burst out Hermione. "What worse degradation could there be than—Charles, it's *horrible*. I won't believe it. And you pretend to love her!"

"I do love her. That's why I won't let her marry this man."

"You can't love her. You're wicked, inhuman. You shan't do it." For the first time in her life she was becoming hysterical. "You shan't drive her to what's a thousand times worse than death. I wish she'd died, like Nigel, before this happened."

There came a knock at the door and Gillian entered. She wore a long blue wrapper; her golden curls fell loose over her shoulders.

"Have you told father, mother?"

"Yes."

Gillian turned her steady eyes to Charles.

"Well?"

"If you're so mad as to go to this man, I can't stop you, Gillian," said Charles, speaking very deliberately, "but I shall never give you my permission to marry him."

"You don't mean that, Charles," panted Hermione.

Charles's face was grey. He seemed suddenly to have turned into an old man before their eyes.

"I do mean it," he said. "Gillian's place here will always be waiting for her whatever happens, but nothing will make me give my consent to this marriage."

"Gillian, he doesn't mean it," burst out Hermione. "He doesn't know what he's saying. . . . Gillian——"

But Gillian's eyes were fixed on Charles's face.

"You do mean it, don't you, father?" she said.

"Yes."

She breathed a soft little sigh, said "Very well," and went out, closing the door quietly behind her.

Hermione turned to her husband. She was not crying now. Her eyes were blazing in a set, white face.

"Charles, if you force Gillian to do this, I'll never forgive you as long as I live."

He made no answer, and they got into bed in silence. Heartsick, she lay awake through the long night, planning, scheming. . . . She would talk to Charles again in the morning. She would *make* him give his permission for this marriage. She would plead with Gillian again. . . .

But in the morning Gillian had gone.

Chapter Twenty Three

It would have seemed impossible that life should go on after this, but it had to go on. Meals had to be ordered, food for the meals had to be bought, the routine of the household had to be kept up and supervised. Hermione did all this mechanically, like some clockwork figure wound up to perform certain actions.

A black cloud, thick and suffocating, seemed to brood over the whole house. The children went about silent and horror-stricken, but soon the natural resilience of youth asserted itself. Gradually their usual interests began to fill their lives again, and they thought about Gillian a little less each day.

John, of course, felt it more than any of them. Gillian had been his favourite since the days when he guided her first unsteady steps in the nursery.

Hermione and Charles lived together in the house as strangers. Charles looked old and broken, but Hermione hardened her heart against him. Their quarrel went deeper than Gillian. Hermione held the Victorian woman's attitude towards marriage. She herself had experienced love outside the marriage bond, but she had fought against it relentlessly, had never looked on it as other than a sin. Upon the sacredness of the marriage bond depended the purity of the home and the whole status of womanhood. By deliberately allowing Gillian to go to her lover without marriage, Charles seemed to her to have poured scorn openly upon chastity itself, to have degraded not only Gillian but every other woman in the world. She felt herself so insulted and outraged by his attitude that she could hardly bear to look at him or speak to him.

To Charles her attitude was incomprehensible. In defending

marriage from such a union as Gillian's would have been with Humphrey Scales, he considered that he had upheld its sanctity, had vindicated the position of honour in which Hermione and women like Hermione were held.

Both were desperately, bitterly unhappy, and neither of them could understand the other's point of view.

Once Hermione said to him:

"Are you trying to find Gillian, Charles?"

"Why should I?" he replied. "She knows that her place here is always waiting for her if ever she wants to come."

"How can she come? She'll be too much ashamed. . . . This would never have happened if you'd let her marry him."

"Worse than this would have happened."

Hermione, like Charles, looked years older since Gillian's flight, but, like Charles, she had to pick up the threads of her ordinary life again.

Monica had been deeply distressed by Gillian's love affair. It upset the always precarious balance of her emotions, and she volunteered, unknown to Charles and Hermione, to go to London and make a demonstration at a public meeting, feeling vaguely—she was never a very clear thinker—that by doing so she was somehow helping to avenge Gillian.

It was an ugly meeting. The interrupters were many and noisy, and the police had received orders to try the effect of rough handling on them. Monica, among others, was arrested, and Charles, furious at the incident, had to go up to London to bail her out. He made her promise never to take part in a demonstration again, and she gave her promise with secret relief, for she had been rather badly mauled.

On hearing about Gillian, Cecilia had come over to Ivy Lodge for the first time since her engagement to John had been broken. She walked into the room where Hermione was sitting and, without a word, put her arms about her and kissed her. Hermione clung to the girl, while a sudden unexpected gust of tears shook her. After that Cecilia came to see her frequently, and Hermione found in her a comfort that she could never have found in her own daughters. They were too near her, and their own grief was too acute. With them she had to pretend to a cheerfulness she did not feel, in order to reassure and console them. With Cecilia she could relax, could talk about Gillian, could tell her of the visions that haunted her night and day—visions of Gillian ill-treated, deserted, but ashamed to come home.

John, too, had begun to visit Ivy Lodge more regularly since Gillian had left home. He and Cecilia now met frequently, and a friendship, deeper, more real than the old one, seemed to have sprung up between them. Hermione realised that there was danger in it, but she could not bear to deprive John of whatever comfort Cecilia might give him. She could guess by what ceaseless pinpricks Valerie would make him suffer over the affair. Though Valerie had been ready enough to accept Gillian's help in house and nursery, she had always been jealous of her, and she would be glad now to use her elopement to hurt John in the loyalty and affection that was his most vulnerable point. She was an expert in little wounding phrases and covert sneers.

Life, however, would not give Hermione time to grieve her fill for Gillian. It hustled her along, making its never-ceasing demands on her. It was Vere who needed her next.

Bobby Pettigrew had been writing rather irregularly for some time. No letters had arrived now for several weeks, and Vere was watching every post with an anxiety that she vainly tried to conceal from the others. At last the evening post brought an envelope addressed in Bobby's sprawling boyish handwriting. Vere tore it open, turned white, then went quickly from the room. Hermione followed her to her bedroom. It was a pathetic little letter. Bobby was horribly sorry . . . he knew he was a cad, but he couldn't help it. He'd fallen in love with a girl on board ship on the way out. He'd meant to do the decent thing and try to forget her, but it had turned out that she was staying with some people who lived quite near his uncle. He'd seen a lot of her, and he was now engaged to her. He was a rotter, and he knew he was, but somehow, he repeated, he couldn't help it. . . . They would be married by the time Vere got this letter.

For once Vere did not repulse Hermione's sympathy.

"Mummy. . . . Oh! mummy, what shall I do? I can't bear it. . . ."

Hermione stayed all night with her, sleeping with her in the narrow bed as she had slept with Gillian when Nigel died.

The next morning Vere was hard and composed as ever. She packed up the trousseau she had made with such loving care and sent it off to a jumble sale—a gesture of scornful defiance in the face of Fate. She gave up attending lessons on domestic economy, and, instead, threw herself energetically into the organising of a band of Girl Guides in the village. She was a little harder and more "bossy" than ever, but otherwise the broken engagement did not seem to have affected her.

The new play in which Alan had a leading part was an immediate success, and Alan's performance was specially praised by the critics. He came down to Ivy Lodge occasionally, but his visits were unsatisfactory to both sides. Individually he got on well with each member of the family, but when he met them together there was a tension and constraint in the atmosphere, against which he fought doggedly and in vain. In consequence of it he behaved in a self-conscious and unnatural fashion that the others interpreted as conceit at his rapidly increasing fame.

Sub-consciously they resented his success, taking for granted that it would spoil him and separate him from them, and they were unduly sensitive to his manner, frequently mistaking his shyness for superiority, his overtures of friendliness for patronage. They could not realise that, when with them, all he wanted was to be accepted as one of them and to forget his other life. John in particular treated him with uneasy suspicion as a creature from another world. None of the family except Hermione could take his profession seriously, involving, as it did in their eyes, ludicrously short hours and no hard work at all.

Charles, however, went up with Hermione to see the play, and he was so much impressed by Alan's acting that Hermione began to hope that the gulf that had existed between them since Alan's childhood might at last be bridged.

Soon after their visit to the play Alan wrote to her to say that he was taking the hero's part in Ibsen's *Ghosts* at a private Sunday performance, and asked her if she would care to come up to see it.

It was arranged that she should go up to Alan's flat for tea and that Charles should join her later for the performance.

She knew, of course, that she would have to meet Gervais Lynne again, but she had persuaded herself that the turmoil of emotion that had seized her when she met him before and had tormented her ever since was a symptom of her age, and that when she saw him again the evil would be exorcised. He would be merely a pleasant middle-aged man. In any case, she could not hope to keep in touch with Alan if she avoided his friend. He was, she knew, a busy man, and she hoped that he would not be at home that particular afternoon.

But when she was shown into the little sitting-room of the flat he was there alone, and as he rose and came forward to meet her she knew that she had been deceiving herself. This was no passing emotional phase. She loved this man with a love that she had not known existed. For a few moments they talked of Alan's success, then both became silent.

"You're not looking well," he said at last.

The sympathy and tenderness in his voice broke down her defences, and she turned her head away quickly so that he should not see the tears that had sprung to her eyes.

Suddenly he was on his knees by her side, comforting her brokenly.

"Let me take you away from it all. From the minute I saw you I knew I loved you. . . . I can't let you go now I've found you. I can't bear to see you so unhappy. I love you so. . . ."

"I know," she breathed.

"Tell me you love me. I can't live without your love."

She turned to him. There were traces of tears on her face, but it was set and stony.

"I love you so much that I must never see you or speak to you again after to-day."

"Don't say that, Hermione. A love like this can't be evil. . . . Do you remember those lines of Rossetti's?—

Even so when first I saw you seemed it, love,
That among souls allied to mine was yet
One nearer kindred than life hinted of.

I thought of them as soon as I saw you. You belong to me. . . . You know you do. . . ."

"It's too late."

"It's not too late. We love each other, and we're neither of us old. We can start life all over again."

"We can't. It would be a sin."

"Why would it be a sin?"

"I don't know. I can't explain. Only I know that it would."

He pleaded passionately, but she withstood him. Yet, even as she withstood him, the bitterness against Charles stirred in her heart like poison. She thought: "It would serve him right if I went with Gervais, as he let Gillian go with that man. Why should I tear my heart out for his honour when he cares nothing for honour or purity, when he let Gillian do what Gervais wants me to do, though he could have stopped her by a word?"

Alan returned while Gervais was still pleading with her. He was nervy and on edge, as always before a performance, and he was depressed by Hermione's pallor and lack of vitality. She had not looked well since Gillian went away, and he suspected that, though she never now mentioned the affair, she brooded on it ceaselessly. Gervais, also pale and unusually silent, did little to help matters. It was not a successful tea-party.

Charles was already in his seat when Hermione took hers, and the play began almost at once. Neither of them had known anything about the play beforehand. The subject shocked Hermione, but her admiration of Alan's performance conquered every other feeling. She realised for the first time how fine an artist he was, and she felt a glad exultant pride in him. She was only vaguely aware of Charles grunting and fidgeting beside her.

Alan received a great ovation at the end. He made his way down to them as quickly as he could, however, accompanied by Gervais.

He was flushed with excitement, but there was an air of exhaustion about him as if the part had been too great a strain.

"Well," he said, "what did you think of it?"

Charles's face was set in grim angry lines

"It was a filthy play," he said, "and I don't see how any decent man could take part in it."

Alan went white.

"I see . . ." he said quietly.

Charles turned on his heel and began to make his way to the door.

Hermione threw out her hands with a little pleading gesture.

"He doesn't understand, Alan."

"I know," said Alan. "Don't worry about it, mother."

He had suddenly begun to tremble, and the strained jerky smile on his face reminded Hermione of his childish attacks of hysteria.

"The whole thing's been too much for him," said Gervais. "It's a most exhausting part. I'll get him home out of this crush."

Hermione watched Gervais make a way for Alan through the friends who crowded round to congratulate him, then turned to the door where Charles was waiting for her.

They went home in silence.

Chapter Twenty Four

FOR a year Charles and Hermione vainly watched and waited for a sign from Gillian. Hermione would often slip downstairs in her dressing-gown in the early morning when she heard the postman's knock. She would take the letters from the letterbox and hold them for a moment in her hand before she examined them, saying silently, with closed eyes, "Please, God, let there be one from Gillian," then turn them over one by one very slowly, so as to prolong the hope as far as she could. Often when the telephone rang and she took down the receiver, she would be silently pleading, "Let it be Gillian. . . . Please, God, let it be Gillian." A knock at the door late at night would set her heart racing wildly, and several times, when dusk had fallen and the curtains were not yet drawn, a movement of the shadows in the garden outside sent her to the front door, peering into the darkness, calling "Gillian" softly beneath her breath.

Charles had been to ask Lady Amhurst if she knew where her cousin was, but it turned out that Lady Amhurst, feeling wretchedly responsible for the whole thing, had tried herself to find them, but had failed.

"He's always been a rolling stone," she said. "He disappears for years, then suddenly turns up again. I hadn't seen him or heard of him for five years when he turned up last Christmas. He's generally at some gambling place abroad. . . ."

Then, about a year after Gillian had gone, came the telegram "Come immediately". The address was a nursing-home in London. They set off at once, but Gillian had died a few minutes before they reached it. The baby, who had been born dead several hours before, lay beside her. Hermione stared hungrily at the girl's face as if trying to wrest from it the history of the year that had passed, but it told her nothing. It was a beautiful mask, the features set in expressionless immobility. So tiny was the baby, so innocent and immature the face of the young mother set in its frame of shining golden curls, that she might have been a child asleep with her doll beside her.

Scales's manner to Charles and Hermione was resentful and defiant.

"She must be buried at Abbotford," said Charles.

"Very well."

"You'll come to the funeral?"

"No. She's gone. . . . What's left of her is yours."

"What are you going to do?" said Charles vaguely.

"That's no concern of yours. You tried hard enough to keep her from me. I've been a year in heaven. Now I'll go back to hell."

His eyes were red and bloodshot. Either he had been drinking or he was half-crazed with grief.

They buried Gillian next to Nigel ("Gillian, beloved daughter of Charles and Hermione Dereham, Aged 20 years"). It was strange, thought Hermione dully, that they had lost the two youngest first. But Gillian's death was very different from Nigel's. Nigel's death had drawn her closer to Charles. Gillian's widened immeasurably the gulf between them.

Charles was so grief-stricken that Hermione could not withhold her pity from him. Almost mechanically she gave to him the comfort that he silently asked of her, but the bitterness in her heart against him was intensified. She felt that he was somehow responsible for Gillian's death. She was convinced, though she knew her conviction to be unreasonable, that, if Gillian had been allowed to marry, she would have lived a happy life near them, with children growing up around her, and a devoted, reformed husband. She felt illogically certain that, if Gillian had been married, neither she nor the child would have died.

Chapter Twenty Five

In the lives of the Derehams, as in the lives of many other families, the outbreak of war in 1914 had the effect of a bomb, uprooting them from their homes and scattering them over the earth.

Alan and Gervais Lynne joined up at once and went out to France together in the Artists' Rifles.

Hermione had not seen Gervais since that last interview before the performance of *Ghosts*. He had written several letters of passionate pleading, but she had not replied.

Jimmie, who was still in the South African Police, was kept out there on active service. Mettleham Hall was turned into a hospital, and Monica served in it as a V.A.D. nurse. She was an indifferent nurse, but she flirted indiscriminately with her patients and was extremely popular. Maud, who was strong and healthy despite her sixty years, put on breeches and "went on the land", working at a farm in Kent.

John did not volunteer at once, as Valerie was expecting her second child and Charles needed him in the business, but, realising gradually that the war was not going to be a few months' affair after all, he joined up in 1915 and was sent to Mesopotamia.

Vere joined the Women's Legion and later the W.A.A.C. Her training in domestic economy, her Girl Guide experience, her air of authority and her undeniable efficiency, brought her to the front, and she was soon Unit Administrator in charge of the largest W.A.A.C. camp in England. She was a great success in the work, dealt with every crisis (and there were some strange crises to be dealt with) promptly and competently, and—no small achievement—exacted unqualified respect and obedience from the heterogeneous gathering around her.

Charles and Hermione went down to see her, seeking a respite from the suspense that was an hourly torment to them now that their three sons were at the war, but they found her so aloof and official even with them that they were secretly relieved to return to Ivy Lodge and their anxious daily scanning of the lists of killed and wounded.

One morning Charles, looking up from his paper, said:

"That man Alan lived with is killed. . . ."

He saw Hermione's face drained suddenly of colour, and added solicitously:

"Not Alan. I'm sorry, darling. I oughtn't to have mentioned Alan's name. Only that friend he used to live with. Gervais Lynne, you know."

The next week Hermione read the name of Humphrey Scales among the list of killed.

Alan was badly wounded in the hip and was sent home to a hospital in London, where Hermione visited him daily. He recovered, but limped slightly and was rejected from further active service. He then collected a party of artists who for one reason or another were also unfit for service, and took them out to France, where they gave entertainments at the base camps. Charles was proud of him and considered that the war had at last "made a man of him". Alan, on his side, responded politely to Charles's new affability, but Hermione knew that Charles's overtures of friendship came too late to heal the breach between them.

John's second child, a boy, was born during the first year of the war, and his third, also a boy, in the last year of it.

Hermione felt light-headed with relief when the end of the war came, and her three sons had survived.

Jimmie returned home, bronzed and cheerful. He said that he had enjoyed South Africa, but that he had had adventure enough to last him for the rest of his life, and that all he wanted to do now was to settle down quietly. He went with Charles to the office the day after he got home, and proposed again to Sylvia the next week. Sylvia accepted him at once, and abandoned the masculinity of dress and manner that she had affected since her broken engagement, becoming very feminine and dependent, doing her hair the way that Jimmie liked it done, wearing the sort of dresses that Jimmie liked her to wear, needing Jimmie's help continually, though she had apparently managed her affairs perfectly well without him while he was away. They were married a month after Jimmie's return.

Monica had now attached to her a string of good-looking young officers whom she had nursed at Mettleham Hall, but while everyone was speculating upon which one she would marry, she suddenly announced her engagement to Leonard Ashton, the uncle of Helen's pupil. It was as if her experience with the Rev. Arnold Rothwell had destroyed forever her trust in man's good looks and charm, for her fiancé was conspicuously lacking in both. Their marriage took place soon after Jimmie's and Sylvia's. Ashton's work was in London, but they bought a house just outside Fernham, and he went up and down by train.

Vere returned home, resumed her Girl Guide work, and was soon appointed District Commissioner.

Maud did not return to Abbotford after the war. She took a flat in London with a girl of twenty-two whom she had met when engaged in land work. Maud had cut her hair as short as a man's, and kept it cropped, wearing always a dark coat and skirt with stiff collar and cuffs. Her striding gait and deep voice increased the impression of masculinity. The girl was of the ultra-feminine type with fluffy hair and saucer-like eyes. They went everywhere together, and were on cloyingly affectionate terms. There was nothing wrong with the *ménage*, but its atmosphere was vaguely unhealthy, and Charles, who now disapproved of his sister as strongly as he had once admired her, did not like Hermione or the girls to visit her much.

Alan returned to the stage. His limp was so slight that it was almost imperceptible, and did not prevent his taking the part of *jeune premier* again. He played the leading part in two successful comedies, and was engaged in writing a play himself. He was too busy to pay many visits to Ivy Lodge nowadays.

After the deaths of Gillian and Gervais Lynne a sort of lassitude had begun to creep over Hermione, as if nothing that happened could now affect her very deeply.

The years suddenly began to pass by with a bewildering speed. I'm growing old, she told herself.

Chapter Twenty Six

JOHN'S marriage with Valerie had been followed by a slow and gradual disillusionment. He found his wife to be self-centred, small-minded, and essentially second-rate in her outlook and ideas. Long after discovering this, however, he continued to be in love with her pink-and-white beauty. She, on her side, found the marriage almost equally disappointing. She had fretted and chafed at the lower middle-class circle into which she had been born, and had intended to shake it off when she married John. She had always been deeply impressed by the comparative luxury of Ivy Lodge and by the terms of friendliness that existed between Hermione and the neighbouring "county". She expected to have in John an eternally devoted wooer ready always at hand to satisfy her slightest whim. She had, in fact, expected to take everything and to give nothing. And she was disappointed on all scores. John refused to drop Valerie's mother, whom Valerie had always regarded as a barrier to her social progress. She was rather a pathetic little figure, proud of Valerie but afraid of her, who made unceasing but unavailing efforts to conquer the faults of accent and manner that betrayed her origin, and against which Valerie continually remonstrated. As a matter of fact the old lady would have been quite content to be dropped by Valerie upon her marriage with so eligible a match as John Dereham, and it was perhaps rather stupid of John to insist upon his mother-in-law's being invited to the house when they gave any sort of function. John was in many ways as obtuse as Charles, and he persisted for a long time in accrediting Valerie with the same admiration of her mother that he had always felt for Hermione.

Altogether John failed as a husband to come up to the high

standard that Valerie had set him. He was not the eternal wooer she had thought he would be. He did not seem to think it his highest privilege to wait on her and load her with gifts. He often came home from work tired and depressed, receiving her peevish complaints without even a pretence of sympathy. So far was he from loading her with gifts like the ideal husband of her imagination, that only a month after their marriage he began to remonstrate with her on the amount of money she was spending. She had nothing to do but spend money. Her servants did all the work of the house, and she had no intellectual interests. On the days which failed to provide any definite social distraction, she "went shopping" as a matter of course and irrespective of whether her purchases were necessary or not. She had very little idea of the value of money, and though she had known John's salary before she married him, she had expected to live on a much more luxurious scale than actually it allowed her to. At first John was very gentle in his remonstrances, but even then there were constant scenes. Valerie was proud of her sensitiveness and seemed almost to welcome anything that she could construe as lack of understanding or sympathy on John's part.

Despite her desire for a large circle, she made few friends. Unquestioning admiration was the sole qualification for friendship with her, and sooner or later she would always say that she had "come up against a blank wall" in her friends, and the friendships would end abruptly. John came to know that ominous phrase well and to understand its meaning: it meant that the new friend had begun to rebel against the unspoken understanding that all Valerie's affairs were of supreme importance and her own of no importance at all.

Valerie had early discovered that she could hurt John most effectively by disparaging his family, and in particular Hermione. She was indeed really jealous of Hermione, for John made no secret of the fact that his mother was his ideal of womanhood. During their engagement he had foolishly talked about her a good deal, and though at the time Valerie had pretended to share his admiration, after marriage she made him pay for the boredom and annoyance it had inflicted on her by sneering at Hermione as "old-fashioned" and "stuck up". They had their first quarrel over that. . . . But it was after Gillian's elopement that their relations became definitely strained. Valerie affected virtuous disgust, and in expressing it displayed a vocabulary whose extent and force John had never before suspected. On hearing foul words applied to the sister who even now seemed to him a figure of radiant purity, he turned on his wife and for the first time lost his self-control with her. She shrank in terror from his anger and never again dared to speak against Gillian in his hearing, contenting herself with sneering remarks of general application, whose reference nevertheless he could not help guessing.

She knew that he was seeing Cecilia frequently at Ivy Lodge, but, though she now depreciated Cecilia on every opportunity in the hopes that it would wound him, she felt no real jealousy. She placed an utterly disproportionate value on her beauty and, comparing Cecilia's quiet good looks with her dazzling fairness, thought that no man who possessed her could possibly fall in love with Cecilia.

After the outbreak of the war she took up V.A.D. work at Mettleham Hall as soon as the birth of her second child allowed her to. She liked the work at first but soon tired of it and was secretly chagrined by Monica's popularity. Moreover, she missed John's kindness and protection as a background to her life and began to look forward to his leaves, making herself pleasant and attractive to him once more and welcoming the series of gaieties with which he, like so many others, tried to dull his memories and fears.

He fell in love with her again, and, when at the end of the war he returned to his home, he hoped that a new life of understanding and sympathy was opening out before them.

Chapter Twenty Seven

JIMMIE and Sylvia were a typical post-war couple. They had a son in 1920, a daughter in 1922, and decided then that the family was complete. They were happy and irresponsible, avowedly fond of pleasure, and excellent companions. Jimmie was proud of Sylvia's looks and liked her to be in the van of every changing fashion. They went up to London regularly, staying at a smart hotel, "doing" the theatres and frequenting night clubs.

So high-spirited and good-tempered were they, so whole-heartedly devoted to enjoyment and to each other, that Charles and Hermione looked forward eagerly to their visits to Ivy Lodge, though Charles felt it his duty to remonstrate frequently with Jimmie.

"Why are you and Sylvia always gadding about to dances and things? I don't like it at all. Your mother and I were content to stay quietly at home. And it's time you started putting something aside for a rainy day."

"Why encourage rainy days by preparing for them?" laughed Jimmie.

"Does Sylvia never look after the children at all?" said Charles, changing his point of attack.

"No. She's rotten with them. They bully her. . . . They're angelic with Nurse, so it seems only sensible to leave her to it. And when Nurse is out, the housemaid sees to them. She can manage them far better than Sylvia can."

"I don't like the way she puts stuff on her face," grumbled Charles once, after a visit from Sylvia. "You girls never used to do it."

Monica, who had come over to Ivy Lodge for the day, laughed.

"No, I always used to bite my lips and rub my cheeks just before I went into the room if visitors were there. Sometimes I rubbed geranium petals on to my cheeks, and then I'd cry all night, and be quite certain that I was going to hell."

Alan had been gradually gaining ground in his dual profession of actor and playwright, and in 1922 he wrote a play that brought him to the front rank. The play ran for three years and was translated into most European languages. His name was now familiar in every normal household. There were frequent articles on him and photographs of him in magazines and newspapers, and he had to engage a secretary to cope with his post-bag.

Charles was immensely proud of him and had completely forgotten that he had ever opposed his going on the stage. Alan paid occasional visits to Ivy Lodge. His manner held a suave, universal urbanity, so that on the surface his visits were more successful than formerly, but Hermione knew that it was because he had ceased his old, unhappy efforts to bridge the gap between their lives and his. He was very charming, showing always a flattering interest in their concerns, but he was a stranger. Sometimes, beneath the suave man of the world, Hermione would catch a glimpse of the eager, sensitive boy she had known, but Alan, like Vere, had had to forge an armour against Life, and its wearing had become so habitual that he had forgotten how to take it off.

Hermione was worried about John and Valerie. After the war they had seemed to settle down happily together again, but the happiness was short-lived. As the novelty of the situation wore off, Valerie's old attitude of boredom and discontent had reasserted itself. Even the existence of her three children was a grievance, and she alternately neglected them and used them as a weapon to hurt John. She often tried to turn them against John by giving them biassed accounts of their continual disagreements.

Mrs. Newman had died during the war, and Mr. Newman had had a stroke on the day of her funeral. He was now bedridden, and Cecilia nursed him devotedly. John paid regular visits to her at the Hall, and the situation was causing a good deal of local comment. Hermione taxed him with it one day.

"John, is there anything between you and Cecilia?"

"Only that we love each other."

"Nothing else?"

"No. . . . Cecilia loves me, but she can't leave her father, and I can't leave the children." He gave a short, bitter laugh. "Don't worry, mother. Our friendship's quite platonic. God help us!"

"Is it wise to see her so often, my dear?"

"I can't live unless I see her," he said. "I don't care a tinker's damn what people say. . . . Mother, you've never loved anyone but father . . . you don't understand, you can't understand. . . ."

She took his hand and pressed it in hers without speaking.

Chapter Twenty Eight

MONICA seemed to have turned the whole stream of her rich, emotional nature to child-bearing. She had a child each year, and the process seemed actually to improve her health and to serve as an outlet for her turbulence. She was still excitable and full of vitality, but there was a new background of serenity in her life. Her husband was a quiet, unassuming little man of limited intelligence, but unlimited optimism and good-nature. He had a fund of irritating little *clichés* and trite tags of philosophy such as "Keep smiling", "Think of those who're worse off than we are", "We've all got to do our bit", "We're put into the world to help each other". But he actually lived up to his philosophy. He was unfailingly kind and good-tempered and unselfish. The paternal instinct seemed to be as abnormally developed in him as was the maternal instinct in Monica, and he welcomed almost ecstatically the children with whom she so frequently presented him. He liked to be surrounded by his children, to have them growing up around him like flowers at every stage of growth—toddling, walking, learning to talk, going to school. Stupid and unintelligent with grown-ups, he was exquisitely tender and understanding with children. Sometimes Hermione wondered if Monica's experience with the Rev. Arnold Rothwell had gone deeper than even she herself realised, So deeply that it had made her shrink from sexual love and choose for a mate a man who was father rather than lover.

She was a slap-dash, unmethodical housewife, and, though wrapped up in her home, failed to instil much order or even comfort into it. She had occasional wild bursts of extravagance, followed by what she called "orgies" of economy. Every New Year's Day she made resolutions to keep accounts, but they never lasted beyond the middle of the month. Her husband loved her with her foibles and imperfections, and it never occurred to him to try to alter her in any way. He would indeed not have loved her so much without her failings, and Monica, on her side, would have been miserable with a man who tried to make her prudent and sensible and methodical. Her energy was inexhaustible. As the children grew older, she was continually arranging expeditions for them, herself as eager and excited as any. She entered wholeheartedly into their games and, disagreeing with them over some point, would quarrel with them as passionately as if she were herself a child.

Hermione went to tea with her every week—a tea that, like all the meals in Monica's house, partook of the nature of a picnic.

One afternoon at three o'clock Hermione found her just taking a *soufflé* out of the oven. Her hair was coming down as usual, and her now shapeless figure was made still more ungainly by the overall that she seldom troubled to take off even in the afternoon. But she looked beautiful and happy and eager, and somehow very like the little girl Monica of nursery days.

"It was a recipe in this morning's paper," she explained, raising her laughing, heated face. "I hadn't time to do it for lunch, and I simply couldn't bear to wait till supper. Do have some. . . ."

"Not at three o'clock in the afternoon, darling."

"I suppose it is an odd time to be making a *soufflé*. I never thought of it. I just wanted to try the recipe. I suppose that it won't do for any meal now, even tea, if it's to be eaten hot, and it's much nicer hot." She tasted a teaspoonful critically. "Yes, it is awfully nice. I'll call the children. . . ."

She called them in from the garden, and they carried off the *soufflé* with whoops of triumph to the tent that Leonard had put up for them at the bottom of the garden. Hermione watched them through the window as, having finished the *soufflé*, they began to climb the trees and walk along the top of the high brick wall.

"Darling, I can't *bear* to see them doing such dangerous things," she protested at last.

Monica looked out at her children placidly.

"Oh, they're all right," she said. "I never bother. . . ."

"Mon, you aren't going to have any more children, are you?"

"Yes, we are," said Monica defiantly, "we're going to have as many more as we can. Till there isn't another inch in the house for one to sleep in. And then we shall buy old tram-cars and things. We love having children. We don't want motorcars or clothes or servants, or any of the things other people spend their money on, but we adore children. Leonard and I can get through all the work of the house, and the elder children are awfully useful now, and we grow all our own vegetables, and—well, I'm happier than I've been in all my life and I mean to have dozens more—so there!"

Alan was married in 1925. He married Moyna Lane, an actress, who had made her début in his first play and was now famous.

He had brought her over to Ivy Lodge to meet his family soon after the engagement was announced. She was very beautiful and so fashionably dressed that she made even Sylvia look provincial. Hermione studied the lovely face anxiously. . . . It mattered so terribly what this girl was like. In the charming, courteous, distinguished-looking man who was Alan there lived a boy who could be desperately hurt. The beautiful face, however, told her nothing. It wore the inscrutable mask of youth. Then suddenly she saw their eyes meet across the room, and between them there passed a look of such complete love and understanding that her heart leapt.

Hermione's grandchildren were now in and out of Ivy Lodge continually, and she enjoyed having them about her: Monica's noisy happy young savages, Jimmie's rather correct and conventional couple, John's two healthy boys, and the gentle fifteen-year-old Hermione, whom everyone called Hermy. John's boys were close friends and allies, engrossed in their out-of-doors activities, wholly unaffected by their parents' disagreements. Hermy, however, acutely sensitive from childhood, was already nerve-racked by the atmosphere of dissension in which she had grown up. She was passionately devoted to John, despite all Valerie's attempts to secure her allegiance.

With the coming of her grandchildren the lassitude that had settled on Hermione's spirit after Gervais Lynne's death gradually left it, and she was drawn irresistibly into the current of their eager young lives. Because she felt less responsible for them, she could enjoy them as, despite her love, she had never enjoyed her own children, becoming, when with them, like a child herself, and entering zestfully into their games and imaginings. Indeed a new serenity, childlike, trusting, seemed to have come to her, a serenity that could be shattered, of course, by certain memories, but that had learnt the wisdom to shun those memories.

With Charles she had settled down once more to a quiet humdrum life. She was happy with him, yet there were things in the past between them for which a secret resentment still smouldered in her heart. Whenever she thought of Gillian, the familiar wave of angry bitterness against him would surge over her again. On the whole, however, she felt towards him as one feels to a beloved child, forgiving his blunders, accepting his limitations, grateful for his devotion. When she had a headache, he would allow no one else to go near her, but would wait on her himself tenderly, solicitously, using the old endearments, "My sweet ... my little love", though she was over sixty and he nearly seventy.

Vere, of course, lived with them, and was much occupied in organising Women's Institutes in Abbotford and the neighbouring villages. She was very capable and authoritative and awe-inspiring, a past-master in the art of official procedure as well as in the humbler arts of raffia work, leather work, and soft-toy making. She had tried to instil some order into Monica's disorderly household, but Monica had firmly and good-naturedly withstood her attempts. Monica always referred to her younger sister as "Poor old Vere".

Hermione had for some time been feeling uneasy about Helen. In the van of progress before the war, Helen had lagged behind the new ideas and schools of thought that had arisen since, resenting the whole age as lacking in refinement and reticence. Just as in the old days she had been deliberately "enlightened", so now she became deliberately old-fashioned, refusing to admit new systems into her school, refusing even to allow her girls to take the new examinations.

For a long time the school had lived on its reputation, but its numbers were now decreasing rapidly, from term to term. Helen had saved no money. In the days of her success she had made £3000 a year, but she had put it all back into the school, building on a large scale, adding a wing here, building a sanatorium or games pavilion there, always with a complete disregard for expense. The housekeeping was on a lavish scale. There were five gardeners, and the meals, both for staff and pupils, were luxurious and unstinted. She was worried by her decreasing income, but refused to listen to her solicitor when he pointed out that times had changed and she must change with them. She had always prided herself, she said, on "having the best", she had always been noted for "keeping a good table". . . . Times might change, but she was not going to change with them. She had been an autocrat for so long that to be offered advice galled her and roused in her a stubborn obstinacy. Though her overdraft at the bank was now over £1000, she continued to run her school in a recklessly extravagant fashion.

She was at last persuaded to appoint a headmistress to bring the school more into line with modern requirements. But she could not endure to see any of her arrangements altered; least of all could she endure to watch anyone else win the popularity that had once been hers. For years she had governed her school by her beauty and personal charm, and she could not reconcile herself to the loss of the adoration that, in the old days, they had never failed to secure her.

Her beauty had gone completely, and to the new generation of schoolgirls she was not an idol but a fussy old nuisance, who demanded from them a standard of manners and deportment that was ridiculously old-fashioned.

She dismissed three head-mistresses in quick succession, then took over the reins herself again, though she was now quite unfit for the work. It was at this point that her solicitor wrote in despair to Charles, asking him to come down and try to "make the old lady see reason".

Charles went down to St. Hilda's and had a fruitless and very uncomfortable interview with her, in which she was majestically indignant at his interference, and from which he came away feeling rather like Gladstone after an interview with Queen Victoria.

Chapter Twenty Nine

In 1928 Charles and Hermione went on the round-the-world trip that Charles had been planning and looking forward to ever since they were married. He was, however, now over seventy, and though he would not have admitted it even to himself, he did not enjoy it as much as he had thought he would, or as much as he pretended to.

He had always disliked what he called "strange cooking", and his liver was continually being upset by meals in foreign hotels or on board ship. He grew tired, too, of the constantly changing scenes, and became poignantly home-sick for Ivy Lodge, though he did not acknowledge this even to himself.

On reaching home again, his memories readjusted themselves, blending with his anticipation, so that after a month or two he firmly believed it to have been the most enjoyable episode in his life.

Early in the next year Valerie left John for a man who had originally scraped acquaintance with her in a London restaurant, and who had turned out to be both wealthy and tractable.

John divorced Valerie, and, as old Mr. Newman had died of his third stroke the year before, everyone thought that John and Cecilia would now marry, but they did not. They had weathered the stormy crisis of their relationship, and had conquered the urgency of their passion. There was left between them a deep but unemotional friendship that seemed to be satisfied by John's regular bi-weekly visits to Mettleham Hall.

Hermy, just eighteen, took over the direction of John's household. She was old for her years, pathetically devoted to John, and proud of her position of trust. She proved herself a very capable housewife, managing her two high-spirited brothers with tact and understanding.

Soon after his return from abroad, Charles was sent for again to St. Hilda's. A large country house in the neighbourhood had been turned into a girls' school, and had taken the few local day girls who were all that remained of Helen's life-work. Helen was left with an almost empty school, an overdraft of £2000, and ruined health. She still stubbornly refused to face the situation, and began to order goods of all kinds for the school on such a lavish scale that it soon became clear that her mind was affected.

Charles brought her back with him to Ivy Lodge, and the school was sold to pay her debts. Once she left the school, the weakening of her brain became more apparent, but she seemed happy enough, hobbling about Ivy Lodge, holding imaginary classes and addressing imaginary assemblies of girls. She lived again in the heyday of her success when she had been adored by staff and pupils, and died quietly in her sleep a few months after she had left her school.

The same year Charles, who had now retired from the business, went completely blind in one eye, and could not read without discomfort. Vere or Hermione read the newspaper aloud to him every day. He preferred Hermione to read it, of course, and when Vere read it, would often pretend that he could not hear her.

Hermione was in good health, except that she suffered from rheumatism, which sometimes made her so lame that she had to walk with a stick. As they grew more feeble, Vere began to feel more responsible for them and turned her organising talents in their direction, arranging their days for them, making them rest or take their medicine at the proper hours. Charles resented her authoritative manner and developed a sort of mischievous obstinacy with her that reminded one of a little boy.

"We've spoilt her," he would say to Hermione, adding with a twinkle: "You should have let me make her eat that rice pudding."

His memory was beginning to fail, and when he wanted to annoy Vere he would deliberately exaggerate its failing, asking the same question over and over again.

The two of them delighted in evading her authority, and on the days when she went away to Women's Institute Conferences or other similar functions, they would go up to London together, feeling like a couple of children on holiday. Vere never allowed them to go to London without her when she was at home, considering that Hermione's lameness and Charles's bad sight made the busy streets and crossings particularly dangerous. The old couple, however, managed very well on these expeditions—Hermione leaning on Charles's arm for support, and pointing out to him any obstacle that his failing sight might not show him, and, though always glad to get back to Ivy Lodge, they thoroughly enjoyed the outings.

Charles liked a good musical comedy and Hermione enjoyed the shop-gazing for which her busy life had never left her time till now. Vere's manner to them was always cold and distant when she discovered the expedition afterwards.

Hermione felt very tender towards Vere, despite the irritation that her over-officious ways sometimes caused her. She felt that life had treated Vere badly. Her brusque manner had always hidden a secret hunger for love; and first the elder children in the schoolroom, then Mrs. Payne, then her lover, had flung her proffered affection back at her as a thing of no value. When she came to tell Hermione that the vicar had proposed to her but that she had refused him, Hermione glimpsed something wistfully appealing behind the curt manner in which she reported the incident.

"Darling," she replied, "I'm selfish enough to be terribly glad. I don't know *what* father and I would do without you."

She was rewarded by a tremulous, quickly veiled gratitude in Vere's blue eyes.

Chapter Thirty

PREPARATIONS for the golden wedding were in full swing. Hermione felt rather bewildered by it. It made her realise suddenly and for the first time that she was an old woman. Vere, of course, was organising the affair entirely, so that Charles and Hermione felt themselves to be merely one of her arrangements and an unimportant one at that.

"I shall be glad when it's all over," Charles had grumbled the night before.

But they could not help feeling excited, and awoke long before their usual hour.

Hermione got out of bed as soon as she awoke, and, slipping on her dressing-gown, went to the window. The sky was unclouded, and over the garden lay a haze that foretold heat. Workmen were already there putting up a marquee, and Vere, in a uniform-like blue cotton dress, was directing them. Her clear, crisp, authoritative voice cut sharply through the sleepy morning air. . . .

Hermione turned to the bed.

"They're putting up the marquee, Charles," she said.

Charles sat up. His bald head and flushed cheeks and twinkling eyes made him look like a mischievous baby.

"Vere there?" he said.

"Yes."

"Let's give them all the slip, eh? Get dressed and sneak off by the back door and go up to London and celebrate on our own? Shall we?"

She laughed delightedly. It was an impossible suggestion, yet it pleased her somehow that Charles had made it.

"We couldn't possibly, Charles."

"You'll get cold there, Hermione. Come back to bed."

"*Cold!* It's a glorious morning. . . . I feel I'd like to get up, but Vere said we were to have breakfast in bed."

"Oh, did she?" said Charles with spirit. "I'm going to get up, then, so you might as well get up too."

He went into the bathroom, and Hermione began to dress. The gentle warmth of the sun, the summer loveliness of the garden, filled her heart with a sort of yearning happiness.

One of the workmen in the garden was whistling, and the sound blended with the song of the birds and deepened the happiness at her heart to ecstasy.

She picked a rose from the Gloire de Dijon that framed the bedroom window, and put it in Charles's buttonhole when he was dressed, carefully arranging his handkerchief to show the correct inch above his pocket. He always came to her for the finishing touches of his toilet.

Vere was in the hall when they came downstairs. Her expression when she caught sight of them denoted patience strained very near the breaking point.

"Darlings, I *told* you to stay upstairs for breakfast. I was just going to send it."

"Well, I wanted to get up," said Charles, jauntily defiant.

Vere sighed. It was evident that he was in what she called an "awkward mood".

"Many happy returns of the day, darlings," she said as an afterthought, and gave each a cool, dispassionate kiss.

She went into the dining-room, rang for breakfast, and officiated in her usual capable fashion, pouring out their coffee just as they liked it, moving the curtains so as to keep the sun from Charles's face, cutting the crusts off his toast. Her attentions vaguely irritated him, though he would have felt aggrieved had she omitted them, and he asked her six times what train Alan was coming by. When he had strolled out into the garden by the French windows, Vere said to Hermione:

"Father seems in rather a difficult mood to-day."

"He's getting old, dear," replied Hermione soothingly.

Then she joined Charles in the garden, and, linking her arm in his, said: "You mustn't be naughty with Vere to-day, darling."

He chuckled and answered:

"I'll try not to be, but she puts one's back up, doesn't she?"

They went over to the lawn and watched the men putting up the marquee. Charles tried to think of some orders to give them, to show that he and not Vere was in charge of the arrangements, but could think of nothing.

They went to the seat beneath the cedar at the end of the lawn, and at once a crowd of Monica's children burst into the garden like a band of savages, waving sticks and shouting: "Many happy returns, granny and gran'pa, many happy returns. . . ."

Vere received them coldly.

"I particularly told your mother not to let you come bothering here this morning," she said. "I told her we'd be busy."

"Yes," shouted Jim, the eldest, triumphantly, "she said we weren't to come bothering here, but we're not going to bother, we're going to help!"

He and the elder ones ran to the marquee, eager to "help", getting in everyone's way, and considerably hampering the proceedings. The younger ones went with Charles to the orchard, scuffling around him like puppies, each anxious to be next him and hold his hand.

Hermione sat alone in the shadow of the cedar tree, watching the sun-misted garden. The family would all be there for luncheon. Alan was coming with his wife and the three-year-old daughter whose likeness to Gillian always brought a sudden catch to Hermione's heart. In the afternoon there was to be a garden party to which neighbours and friends were invited. For dinner there would be just her sons and daughters and Hermy, the only one of the grandchildren old enough to attend a dinner party.

A languorous dreaminess stole over her. . . . Her thoughts went back over her life, and she found it thrilling, mysterious, as if it had been the life of a stranger. She did not understand any of it. Why had she married Charles? What was she really like? What was Charles really like? Charles. . . . She had never seen him as a coherent picture. She had always been too near to him for that. He had been in turn hero, villain, father, child, playmate. . . .

She looked back again over the road of her life . . . some parts of it became clearer, some shifted into the shadow. Like a shining light in the middle of it was her love for Gervais Lynne—so short, so nebulous, so agonising, but so complete. Divorced as it had always been from her normal life, time had now dulled its torment and its ecstasy, till it was only a memory, something she had once dreamed of, something that had never been real as Gillian's death and John's unhappiness had been real.

Charles was coming back from the orchard. He was pretending to run, and the children were driving him with string tied to his arms for reins.

Vere hurried past Hermione, saying shortly: "Really, father is *silly*, overtiring himself like this before the day's begun. And in this heat."

She went over to the children and took the reins from them.

"You mustn't tire grandpa like this. . . . Sit down and rest, father."

Charles was, on the whole, not sorry to be rescued, and he came over to Hermione, smiling and wiping his forehead with his handkerchief.

"Fifty years," he said, sinking down on to the seat beside her; "it doesn't seem like fifty years, does it, old lady?"

She looked at him. For years she had not let herself think of Gillian, but now she deliberately faced the memory. . . . The expected wave of anger did not come. She had forgiven him. . . . More than that, she realised in a sudden flash of revelation that perhaps his love for the child had seen more clearly than hers.

She laid her hand on his. . . . He did not know that she was forgiving him for Gillian, but he raised her hand and pressed his lips upon her wedding ring, then dropped it, keeping it in his.

"Fifty years . . ." he said again.

Hermy had now appeared at the gate—a slight, bare-headed figure with hair that shone like spun gold in the sunlight. A young man was with her. She stood there for a minute, talking to him.

Even from where they were they could see that there was something lover-like in the young man's manner, that Hermy's eyes were bright, her cheeks flushed.

"Who's with her?" said Charles.

"Young Cornwall's boy," answered Hermione.

He chuckled. "We shall be having great-grandchildren before we know where we are, Hermione. . . . And as soon as Hermy marries, John and Cecilia will get married, of course."

The young man raised his hat and passed on. Hermy came into the garden and waved to Charles and Hermione. Charles rose and went to meet her, chiefly as a gesture of defiance to Vere.

Hermione sat gazing dreamily in front of her.

A sudden thrilling sense of the continuity of life had come to her. She and Charles would die—he had already passed his three-score years and ten—but life would go on. . . . Hermy would marry and have children, and when Hermy died her grandchildren would marry and have children. . . .

Charles came across to her over the sunlit lawn with Hermy clinging to his arm.

As the girl bent down to kiss her, it suddenly seemed to Hermione that she was not herself but Hermy being kissed by one of Hermy's children's children.

www.ingramcontent.com/pod-product-compliance
Ingram Content Group UK Ltd.
Pitfield, Milton Keynes, MK11 3LW, UK
UKHW030703020325
455687UK00006B/61